Time of
The Fourth Horseman

Time of
The Fourth Horseman

CHELSEA QUINN YARBRO

DOUBLEDAY & COMPANY, INC.
GARDEN CITY, NEW YORK 1976

All of the characters in this book
are fictitious, and any resemblance
to actual persons, living or dead,
is purely coincidental.

ISBN: 0-385-11076-6
Library of Congress Catalog Card Number 75–41677
Copyright © 1976 by Chelsea Quinn Yarbro
All Rights Reserved
Printed in the United States of America
First Edition

This is for my friend
Tom Scortia
for his
in-
as-
and per-
sistence

Time of
The Fourth Horseman

CHAPTER 1

From the first sight of the boy, something felt wrong. Natalie bent over him while Gil read off the results of his pulse, temperature, blood pressure, hemoglobin, respiration and the others as they were displayed on the vital signs unit.

"What is it, Nat?" Gil asked as he caught the quick frown between her sandy brows.

She waved him away, a distraction. Her concentration was riveted on the boy. How old was he? Perhaps seven, maybe as much as nine and small for his age. His skin was parched and his eyes had the glaze of fever. *Exposure* she had read on his admit workup. *Malnutrition.*

"You know, these kids are really sad," Gil observed as he studied the patient. "This one makes an even dozen for this floor."

"A dozen?" Natalie had been off work for a week and this chance remark sharpened her fear.

"Unhunn. Most of them were brought in while you were gone. They had a couple in the quarantine unit on the eighth floor while you were gone. County General is hardest hit, but they're always short of beds and they get the runaways up there. I heard they picked up over a dozen starvation cases last week."

"Starvation? Like this boy?" She schooled her voice to betray none of the alarm she felt. She did not trust herself to look at Gil.

"I guess it's all the same sort of thing. The Patrol finds them and the ambulance service picks them up." Gil had been riding in the ambulance more often than not, with the current shortage of paramedics. "Handy's been after the Supervisors to do something about it."

"Has it done any good?" she asked perfunctorily, knowing the hospitals were not high on the Supervisors' list of priorities.

The young, abandoned children were bright in Gil's mind. He had seen a lot of them, too many. "No. No good."

Natalie shifted her balance minutely, studying the display board for the clue she knew was there. All her instincts told her that she was close to the enemy she and the child were fighting together. Hoping to learn more, she said to Gil, "On the way in, did he say anything? Any complaints? Any unusual symptoms?"

"Just the usual."

"The usual. Be specific," she snapped.

Gil smiled, because he liked Natalie when she got mad. It was the only time he felt he had the advantage with her. "Yes, Sherlock, he did complain. He kept saying he was sore."

"Where? Throat? Chest? Kidneys? Hands? Head?"

Gil took a deep breath. "It sounded more like general muscle aches, the all-over kind. He'd been huddled up for three hours when we brought him in. He'd been under the big viaduct north of here, on Route 5. He was badly chilled, too."

"Headache?"

"Oh, I guess so. I didn't ask." Gil admitted to himself that he didn't want to ask. By the time they had brought that boy in, he had been working nineteen hours and was groggy. He still felt the fatigue as an undercurrent, even after getting a pick-me-up at the pharmacy.

"I mean at the back of his head, that kind of ache?"

"I don't know."

The last question was really unnecessary, and Natalie knew it. The answer had clicked as she watched the boy. He had polio.

And that was impossible.

She felt dazed as she spoke. "Have the standard tests run on him, will you?" She was forcing herself to proceed as if there were nothing out of the ordinary about the case, just another abandoned child in the midst of many. "Get me the results as soon as possible."

"We ran through the basics on the ambulance console. The print-out should be processed by now. Call Pathology."

She reached for the screen control, then hesitated.

Gil gave her a quizzical smile. "You onto something, Sherlock?"

She retreated into her most professional manner. "Oh, probably not, but it never hurts to check." She was afraid she lied badly, but Gil didn't notice. "I haven't seen what the lab's got out of the specimens yet, or the total arrival evaluation. I want to be on the safe side." As she spoke she wondered how the boy could have polio. Vaccination had wiped out polio over twenty years ago.

Laughing gently, Gil said, "If you're on your way to the lab, I think Mark's still there. If you need an excuse to see him."

"Found out." She accepted his teasing, eager to fall back on this excuse. "I never see him at home: we aren't on the same shifts."

"That bad?" Gil asked, the teasing gone from his voice.

"He keeps peculiar hours," Natalie said, wishing that she could change the subject.

"I can't sympathize, Nat," Gil burst out harshly. "You know what I think of Mark. He's a high-handed despot . . ."

"I know what you think. We won't discuss it."

Before their argument could break out in earnest, the boy on the table moaned and his hands moved fitfully on the sheet like curled leaves in a slow wind. His face was waxen now. He mumbled a few words, then was silent.

"What is it? What is it? Can't you tell me?" she whispered fiercely over the child. She searched his face intently, hoping to find confirmation or denial of his disease. She wanted to be wrong.

"You *are* spooked by this one, aren't you, Nat?"

A cold finger of fear slid down her spine. "Why, no, not really," she said, hoping to dismiss the whole question. "You know how mothers are. Philip was down with a cold last week and of course I read everything into it. I'm suffering from maternal hangover, I guess, because I can't identify this bug."

Gil nodded, not bothering to pursue the subject. Instead, he asked Natalie if he should buzz for the floor nurse.

"No reason not to," she said reluctantly. She hated giving up now, when she was getting close to the truth, when her hunches were so strong.

"And we can go on our break. We're over an hour late for it, as it is."

She gave a last look to the display of vital signs, her eyes still troubled. "I wonder if I should call Mark? He could push the lab results through now if they aren't ready yet."

Gil wrinkled a smile onto his face. "Come on, Mama. Call the good nurses and let them do their job. They'll put him in a nice fresh bed and look after him. I promise you. And let's you and me get some coffee. Come on, Doctor, be sensible."

Reluctantly she allowed herself to be pulled away. She knew that if she were more adamant, Gil would become suspicious and would try to find out what bothered her about the boy. She could not bring herself to tell him, not until she was sure.

"Coming?"

"I'm coming." She linked arms with Gil as he pressed the buzzer for the floor nurse. "Coffee and something sweet. One of those sticky goodies Chisholm makes. Or his cheesecake."

Gil grinned because Natalie expected him to grin. As he did he considered her, noticing that she was still flustered. She was upset by that boy; he could sense it from her stance and her choice of words. Her pale-green eyes had a veiled look, which always meant worry. Yet it might have been her son's illness, as she said, not this child's. And it might be Mark. It didn't have to be the boy on the bed.

As they waited for the nurse to arrive, Natalie turned back to the child. "Do we have a name on him yet?" she asked at last.

"We'll find out as soon as his information is processed. They'll get it from the medical records banks."

"No ID badge?"

"Nary a one. The parents take the badges away when they drop the kids, you know. They seem to think we can't trace them if the kids don't have their IDs. Poor kids. Inner City is starting up another halfway house for them. They've got over fifty on the waiting lists now. It's pretty bad."

Natalie almost spoke, then changed her mind.

"The battered ones are worse at County General, though. At least we don't have much of that to cope with here."

"Gil," said Natalie in another tone, "can we call the parents when we get back from break? I want to talk to them."

"That's City Patrol's job. Let them do it. Judging by the shape he's in, the parents aren't going to like that call. Let City Patrol handle it. They're used to it."

"Um."

Gil knew that Natalie was shutting him out. He shrugged and wished he could have found out what troubled her. He had to work with her, she ought to talk to him.

When the nurse arrived they exchanged a few words and politely thanked one another. It was an automatic ritual, the passing on of the medical flame, or the second stage of a relay race. The nurse gave Natalie a fixed, white smile as she took the boy over.

Then Gil hurried Natalie to the elevator and they dropped thirteen floors to the Staff Cafeteria, located near the boiler room in the second basement.

* * *

In the clean, unimaginative room there was none of the hospital smell which permeated the rest of the building. This room was a delicious counterpoint of coffee, meat and pastry with a subtle, pervasive scent of herbs.

Gil insisted on buying and brought coffee to the table in large white mugs.

Even by Natalie's tolerant standards the coffee was bitter. She sipped slowly, puckering her mouth.

"Yours as bad as mine?"

"I hope not," she said. "This is horrible. What's the matter with Chisholm? Is he off his feed?" She wrinkled her nose in distaste and turned her eyes to a faded poster proclaiming the tourist glories of Greece which some administrator had ordered years ago in a vain attempt to make the basement cafeteria look less like what it was.

Gil explained between gulps that Chisholm had applied for a leave of absence the week before.

"Where did he go?" The thought of Chisholm anywhere but the hospital kitchen was ludicrous. "And when is he coming back?"

"I don't know. I don't think anyone does. He just sort of left and hasn't been back." He paused, drinking the last of the dreadful coffee. "Odd, you know? This isn't like Chisholm at all."

"Well, whatever he's doing, I hope he finishes it in a hurry and gets back here. Soon." She punctuated this with a meaningful look at her mug. "Do you think the administration kidnapped him for their penthouse?" As always, the thought of the elegant dining room at the top of the hospital rankled her, because she was not allowed to use it.

"I wouldn't put it past them." Gil took this as an opportunity to ask, "Speaking of absences, how was yours? You haven't told me anything about it."

Natalie frowned. What did she have to say? She had waited in line after trying to find someone at the Housing Authority who could find a bigger apartment for the three of them. They felt stifled in their converted cellar. It was bad for Philip, it was bad for Mark, it was bad for her, living in those few cramped, low-ceilinged rooms. But there had been nothing available, not even for class-two priority listings. They were still in their cellar and likely to stay there.

"Oh," she said, "I did the usual things. Lazed about the place. Played mom with Philip. Went window shopping. Spent hours in hot baths. Vacation things. You know the routine: lovely, lovely sloth."

Gil realized that she was inventing most of it, but he went along with her. "I'm envious. I bet you never once thought of the rest of us, slaving away back here on floor eleven."

In point of fact she had not thought much about them, but she knew what was expected of her. "Every now and then you crossed my mind. When I was being particularly lazy." She didn't mind playing Gil's game. She was still depressed about the ten days she had wasted, ten days when she could have had some rest or gone out of town. Well, she told herself, it was too late to think about it now. Maybe next year.

"It's time to get back to the floor. Round two coming up." Gil rose, pushing his mug into the reclaim chute.

"Round two. It *is* a fight up there, isn't it?" She had always thought of it as a fight, and took strength when others thought of it that way, too.

"To the death," he said without smiling.

"Maybe the report will be in on that boy," Natalie said.

"You could ask Mark to hurry it for you," Gil suggested as he held the door for her.

They walked to the elevators in silence, avoiding each other's eyes.

*   *   *

"Here's the report on the boy, Dr. Lebbreau." As they stepped from the elevator the night nurse handed the printout to Natalie.

She took it saying, "Thanks, Parker," before she turned to Gil. "Well, here it is. Let's have a look."

Age: it read, *eight years, seven months. Height: one point two nine meters. Weight: twenty-one point three kilograms. Hair: red. Eyes: hazel. Distinguishing marks: mole on lower thigh above left knee, inner side, frontal. Strawberry birthmark on right hip. Medical history: standard treatment at birth (Inner City Hospital, 8–29–82) with pediatric follow-up at six-month intervals. Examination for fungus infection 11–16–83* . . . This was accompanied by a reference sheet detailing each examination. All prescriptions, injections, immunizations, therapies and treatments were in one column, and a record of their results were opposite. It was an ordinary record; it might have belonged to any one of a thousand kids in the area. How had this child managed to get polio?

At the top of the form it read: *Name: Alan Mathew Reimer.*

"What are you looking for, Nat?"

She shook her head, refusing to be pinned down. The chart was too general. "Oh, nothing." With a record like that, she had to be wrong—the boy could not have polio. He had been vaccinated for it, just like everyone else. Unless he had resisted the vaccination or the virus had mutated drastically. If it were mutation, there would be more than one case. She took a deep breath of the antiseptic air and played for time. Just the thought of a mutated disease scared hell out of her.

"Trouble?" Gil asked.

"I don't know. I'll have to have Mark check it out." If there were some new development with the virus she could easily have the right tests run on it. Mark would want to know about such a possibility, if the disease were changing. And if it were a simple case of resistance, a blood test would reveal that.

"Check *what* with Mark?" Gil was growing impatient. His face was set and the sound of his voice had a cutting edge.

"I'm thinking about mutation." She said it at last. "All right, I know it's a long shot, but if that's what we have, we're in big trouble. We'll all be under siege again, the way we were before we had vaccines. That's why I want this boy checked. If he's resistant, there's no harm done, but if he isn't, and he's infected . . . with anything . . . we'll have to get to work on him right away. The city'll be quarantined . . ." She turned to Gil. "Have a complete workup on him."

"But what for? What do you think he's got?"

"I don't know. Maybe a mutation . . ."

"A mutation of what? Come on, Nat." His voice was as close to anger as it ever was with her. He thought she was a foolish woman, but she didn't deserve what her husband was doing to her. He held his anger back.

"That's the truth. I know what I think he's got, but there's no way he can have that, so it must be something else. I want to know what that something is." There. Perhaps now he'd let her alone.

"If you think it's really that important, I'll have a series run for everything from septicemia to dandruff. Tally-ho the biological bloodhounds." He struck a pose, chuckling at himself.

"And Gil, if there are any more like this one, will you let me know about them?"

"You've got your hands full already. You know what administration says to extra case loads."

She said coolly, "I know what administration and our union say about extra hours, too. But we always seem to be doing them, don't we? You're almost eight hours overdue for your required rest, and I'm running an hour late myself. So what's one more case in the load?" She thrust her hands deep into the pockets of her smock.

He watched the tense look around her eyes, the paleness under her freckles, the tightness of her thin, square shoulders. There was something very beguiling about the way she stood now, defensive, unhappy.

"Gil . . . please."

"You want to know if we get another kid like this one. I'll be in the ambulance tomorrow and Friday. If I see anything there, I'll let you know about it. That's all I can promise."

She thanked him three times before she began her ward checks for the night.

* * *

At midnight she was off, and with a deep sense of relief she called at the labs hoping that Mark might have waited for her. But he had left the hospital sometime earlier. He hadn't left a message, so she assumed he was at home by now, and very probably asleep.

She wandered out to the overhead station and waited in the heavy night wind for a train to stop. Her thoughts were still troubled, and she hardly noticed the discomfort of the overcrowded car as she hung onto the commuter belt for her twenty-minute ride to her housing complex.

At least the light was on over the door. She sighed and let herself in hoping that Mark might still be awake.

Philip's junior bed was in the far corner of the tiny front room that was considered a living room by the Housing Authority. In it Philip lay sleeping quietly, one arm pummeled into his pillow. Just seeing him pleased her. With a smile she went to their walk-in kitchen.

There was some milk left in the coldbox, some tired squash and a bit of meat. She wasn't really hungry enough to eat any of it. She gazed abstractedly into the coldbox, wishing they had a real refrigerator, then stared at the ceiling before abandoning the kitchen for the bedroom.

The walls were a depressing shade of yellow-green, but Natalie did not notice this any more. She squeezed between the dresser and the bed as she pulled off her clothes, hanging them carefully on the two hangers clipped to her side of the dresser. Shivering, she slipped into the closet-sized bathroom, taking a quick, tepid shower before climbing into bed.

As she lay uncertain in the dark, waiting for the sleep she craved to come, Mark rolled toward her, murmuring. She went into his arms gratefully, savoring the sharp taste of his sweat as they came together.

* * *

By the time she woke he was dressed and ready to leave for the lab. His great tawny head looked out of place above the white collar of his lab coat. He was too leonine to be trapped in civilized clothes.

"Morning," she said to him from the bed, marveling again that this beautiful man had chosen her when he might have had almost any woman she knew. She still remembered the shocked look on Angela Darcy's face when they announced their engagement five years ago. Angela had said some unkind things at the time, but the years had proved her wrong. Mark was still with her; Natalie took strength from that. And if she was not always happy, she knew she could count on her marriage.

"Night. You should get some more sleep before you go back on duty."

She shook her head and changed the subject. "Is Philip up yet?"

"No. Go back to sleep. He won't be awake for another hour."

She stretched and studied him in the dim light. She loved his grace, the sinewy way he had of walking, taut like a cat. He was the product of another place, another time. Certainly he did not belong here among the cramped boxes bursting with pallid people. He was wild. He was feral.

"What are you looking at?" he demanded.

"You. Just you."

He dismissed this silliness with a shake of his head as he finished shaving. Then, as he was about to leave, he said, "There was a request for a recheck on a patient from your floor. Do you know anything about it?"

"Yes. That's *my* request. I wanted the boy checked out for possible vaccine failure." She studied the way the light fell across his shoulders, making a halo of his short, curly hair.

"What makes you think it's that?"

She was about to tell him she knew the boy had polio and wanted this confirmed, but she stopped herself before the words were out. If she were wrong, he would not forgive her for this error. Away from the hospital her fears sounded far-fetched and melodramatic, even to herself. "Oh, you know," she said, yawning to cover her hesitation. "He seemed to have a few more things wrong with him than he should have. A few symptoms out of place. I thought we'd better get a complete workup so we can find out what's going on with him. There are vaccine failures, you know," she added. "I wanted to be safe."

Mark sighed. "If you think it's all that necessary . . . I'll have Burnett run the check. Standard series with immunology factors, will that do it?" He looked suddenly grim. "And I'll bet you that this is a waste of time. And effort and facilities, for that matter."

"Thank you, Mark," she said quietly. "It will put my mind at rest. I appreciate it."

"I doubt it," he muttered. "So long as you don't make a practice of it." To take the sting from his words, he reached across the bed and ruffled her red hair with his large hands.

Ordinarily she would have purred contentedly at this treatment, but something in his manner robbed her of all the pleasure she might have felt from it. She was puzzled for a moment, feeling cheated. Then she smiled up at him. After all, he seemed to expect her smile, and it was suddenly very important to do what he expected of her. She felt the forcing in her face, but he did not seem to notice.

"I'll see you later?" he asked over his shoulder as he went to the door.

"Yes. Yes. Later." It was not said too hastily. But he looked keenly at her, very little friendliness in his face as he left.

There was the sound of the door closing and she was alone and awake, with the sudden knowledge of her fear. Again she tried to tell herself that she was unreasonable, that just because she had a hunch about a sick child, there was no point in letting her judgment become distorted. She consigned her fright to perdition and turned her head away from the small clerestory windows for her last hour of sleep.

But as she drifted into a dream she found she was still thinking of Mark. How had he known about the tests she wanted? He had left the hospital before the request was received in the labs. The night staff had told Gil that Mark was gone. Did someone call him at home? How had he found out? She was trying to sort this out when she fell asleep.

* * *

By the time she left Philip off at the Child Care Center, Natalie had managed to convince herself that her imagination had run away with her. It was with a clear conscience that she reported to work that afternoon.

"Top of the morning to you, Doctor. How was your night?" Gil teased as she joined him for their first rounds.

"Fair. Yours?"

"Fair." He stopped to adjust the saline drip on a geriatric patient. "She should really be down on four with the other geries," he observed as he worked, his whole face pulled forward in concentration. "That does it." He untangled himself from the various tubes feeding into and out of the old woman. "What were you saying, Nat?"

"*You* were saying that you had a fair night." She took one of the charts down from the wall and made her notations, checking off the medications which had been given and those the patient was yet to receive.

"That's right. Well, I couldn't get that Reimer kid off my mind. I know you spotted something I didn't. So last night I tried to figure it out. I must have spent three, four hours on it."

She hung the chart back on its wall clip. "And?"

"I couldn't for the life of me see what you saw."

"Gil"—she laughed, and it sounded almost natural—"you don't have to make me infallible. Remember the maternal instinct. I can find tetanus in a hangnail if I work hard enough at it."

Gil looked at her thoughtfully. "If that's what you want me to believe, I will. But you don't believe it, do you?" And with that, he walked on ahead of her to the next ward.

* * *

Somewhat later they were in the pediatric room where Alan Mathew Reimer had spent the night.

"Where's the boy?" Natalie inquired of the orderly after she and Gil had reviewed the bed charts.

"What boy?"

"Transferred," Gil said in a neutral tone as he read over the records. "It says here that he was transferred about three this morning. Here's the authorization." He handed the transfer to Natalie, wondering what had happened.

"Where did they take him?" she asked of the orderly.

But it was Gil who answered. "According to this, Inner City Pediatric." He scowled as he studied the sheet.

"What is it, Gil?"

"I've got a friend at Inner City on admit. He didn't mention anything about a transfer from here. He usually mentions the ones we send over. He calls them our rejects."

"Oh?" Natalie could feel uncertainty around her. Her senses were on the alert.

"Most of the time he kids me about them," he said slowly. "And Pediatric there . . . We've got everything they've got, and more. He was better off here."

"Maybe someone else did the admit," Natalie suggested to reassure herself.

"Maybe," Gil said carefully, realizing that Natalie might be right. He had not heard from Ed at Inner City.

"Or he hasn't seen the transfer yet." She could feel her fear closing around her like jaws.

"Or there might be some trouble with the parents," Gil said, satisfied with the idea. There was always trouble with the parents of an abandoned child.

*　*　*

It was two nights later that another child was brought in, picked up by the Patrol. This time it was a girl, about ten, thin, frightened and restless. Her delicate face was ashen.

Natalie did not hear about her until she was on her ten-thirty break. Gil had supplied the coffee, with the complaint that if Chisholm weren't back soon he'd be forced to go on strike against the cafeteria on the grounds that eating the dreadful food was cruel and unusual punishment. Even this heavy-handed try at humor made Natalie grateful.

"Say, Natalie," called Ian Parkenson from the door, "are you still collecting sick kids?"

"Sure, why not?" she answered. Ian was a good doctor and a kind man who knew more about the working of this hospital than any other three doctors combined. Natalie respected him, although she could never bring herself to like him, and often wondered why she didn't. He nodded to her across the room. "If you're interested, she's on the sixth floor. She was admitted a couple of hours ago. The Patrol picked her up near the main thruway. First report makes this exhaustion and a whacking good case of pleural bronchitis."

"The usual pattern for abandoned children, Ian?" Gil asked for form's sake, though he was not particularly interested.

Ian shrugged his big shoulders. "It's hard to say. She's been in the open for two or three days, by the look of her. Why don't you stop off on your way up to eleven and see for yourself. Manning has the case. He won't mind."

Natalie thought it over. "I'll see her," she said. "Thanks for telling me about her." The bitter taste in her mouth was not entirely due to the terrible coffee.

*   *   *

"Well, what do you think, Doctor?" Gil asked as they rode up from seeing the girl on the sixth floor.

Natalie shook her head slightly. She was staring straight ahead, unseeing. Her face was without expression.

"Okay, what is it, Nat?"

She didn't answer for a while, and when she did look up at Gil her eyes were flinty. "Gil, I want a blood specimen on that girl. Get it, will you? This time I'm going to do the lab series myself."

"What?" Gil stared at her. "That's crazy. The labs are closed. And you know you aren't authorized to . . ."

"I'll ask Mark to clear it for me," she said, knowing that she probably wouldn't.

Inwardly Gil sighed. He knew, as well as Natalie did, that Mark would not willingly give her a lab clearance. Mark had things just the way he wanted them, if the gossip around the wards was right. Gil knew that Mark would not let his wife into the labs; it would be too inconvenient.

But Natalie was saying, "I'll call the labs next break I get. Do you want to come with me, Gil?"

"If I'm free," he said, knowing that he wouldn't be. "But you're a glutton for punishment, Nat."

"Am I?" she asked, eyeing him sharply, her face suddenly intent.

"Well, just watch yourself," he said miserably. He heard his name on the paging system. Grateful for this intrusion, he said, "It sounds like an emergency. I'd better go."

"See you later," she said, and turned her attention to her patients.

* * *

A vial had been set aside for her at the nurses' station when she came off duty. There was no identification tag on it, no code. She slipped it secretively into her lab coat pocket while none of the nurses were looking. Even as she did it, she chided herself. *I'm not like this,* she thought. *This is foolishness.* Yet she knew that she was frightened, and that her fear would not go away, riding with her loud heartbeat in the elevator down to labs on the seventh floor.

As she entered the room adjoining the lab complex the clerk looked up. He was a faded, soft man with nervous hands and a pasty face. He recognized her, saying, "Dr. Lebbreau," as he tried to estimate the amount of influence she had with her husband. "Is there anything I can do to help you?" He remembered that Dr. Howland had said he was expecting a visitor. He had not said it was his own wife, but the clerk knew better than to keep Dr. Lebbreau waiting.

"Thanks. I can find my way around," she said in what she hoped was an easy voice.

"Dr. Howland is expecting you," said the clerk, spreading an unpleasant smile over his face. "Do you want me to announce you?"

Natalie felt her heart sink. She told herself that it was impossible, that it was nerves, that hearts could not possibly do what hers had done. She made an effort to smile. If Mark caught her now, she was lost anyway. "Never mind."

"But . . ." the clerk began, his hands moving nervously as he tried to make up his mind.

"I promise you I won't keep him if he's too busy," she said, hoping the words were arch enough. She had no intention of seeing Mark at all.

At last the clerk made up his mind. "Go on in," he said with an attempted wink. "I won't ruin your assignation for you."

Her sudden relief made her bones feel cold. She thanked the clerk as she went through the door into the labs.

* * *

The fourth station was open, set up for full analysis. Natalie glanced around one last time, then slid inside, pulling the door closed behind her. At this hour there were few people in the labs, and one closed door more or less would not attract attention.

Quelling her fear she punched on the light, letting the soft blue radiance shine around her. At one time she had found it beautiful, but now she did not notice it as she selected her supplies and set to work.

* * *

Fifty minutes later she had the answer, and her fear had returned manyfold. The girl Manning was assigned to had diphtheria—of that, Natalie was certain. The question was *how*. She had been immunized, like everyone else. She had no history of vaccine rejection. There was no evidence that the disease had mutated. How had she got it? Where had she got it? Did any more children have it?

But diphtheria had been wiped out, Natalie reminded herself. All the old diseases were gone, even most forms of cancer. The diagnostic computers had forgotten the diseases, refusing to recognize them . . .

"Oh, God," she whispered desperately as the implication hit her. If the diagnostic computers no longer recognized the diseases, there was no telling how many people were infected and did not know it. "I have to find Mark," Natalie whispered to herself. "He'll have to give up the Project," she said, trying to think how to convince him of what she had found. "This is more important than the Project."

She had the door ajar when she heard another door open. She stopped, wondering who it might be, determined to stay where she was until she could leave the lab unseen.

A woman's voice, light with laughter, said a few words, teasing, lilting words that Natalie could not hear.

The deep laugh that answered the first froze Natalie, for the voice was Mark's.

She stepped back into the station, pulling the door firmly. In a daze, she thought about what she had heard. She was mistaken, she had to be. It was just Mark's way, to put frightened women at ease with his casual, intimate words. That's all there was to it.

"Why do you think we came here?" he was saying, his rich voice vibrant in the quiet room. "It's absolutely safe. No one gets in here unless I clear them. I use my private entrance, and no one, not even that dumb clerk out front, knows I'm here. It's perfect."

"What about an emergency?" asked the soft voice provocatively.

"There's a lab right off the emergency room. They don't bother us. Relax. We're safe as houses. Safer."

The woman giggled and Natalie could hear the tap of her shoes as she crossed the room. There was a pause, and when she spoke again, her voice was softer, thicker. "You're good, Mark. Where do we go? Your office?"

"No. That's private." Natalie heard him thump leather. The examination table, she realized. "Here. Where else?"

"Oh, there," the woman said, surprised. "I never thought of that. It's big enough, I guess."

"Yes, it's big enough," he said with some asperity. "Look." There was a movement and the woman cried out delightedly, "Oh, *I* see. I can turn . . ."

"Like meat on a spit. And keep your voice down!"

"You've used this before, I bet. For 'research' like this?" She tittered at her own wit. Her shoes tapped again, then there was the sibilance as her clothes slid to the floor. "It's kind of cold."

"I'll warm you up. Come here. That's better," Mark said in a voice Natalie had never heard before. "Look at you. Look at what you do to me."

In the station Natalie heard the soft words, and then other sounds. She leaned her head on the door and did not know she wept.

* * *

She was still awake when Mark came home, but she resolutely feigned sleep. She felt his weight next to her and it seemed to pull her spirit down with the bed. She had relied on him so much. She remembered her joy when her pregnancy was confirmed, and his teasing words, "Well, you're good for something, aren't you?" There was no charm now, no affection in the phrase, and she wondered if there ever had been, or if it were her imagination only. He was so handsome, so coldly intelligent, she had been puzzled by his interest in her. "Plain women make the best wives; they're grateful," he had said at their reception, and laughed as he said it.

She could not turn to him now; not now or ever again. She tried to tell herself that the sick children meant more than her pride, that their welfare was worth anything she might endure at Mark's hands. But she said nothing, listening to him breathe as he slept, as the hours of the night went over.

* * *

"Morning," he said to her as she turned away from the light.

"Morning, Mark," she said dully.

"You were asleep when I got in last night. Tired?"

"Yes. We had our hands full on the floor. And you?" She knew he would lie to her. She expected it, but when it came, it was salt on a raw wound.

"You know this damn Project. If it isn't one thing, it's another. You know what sticklers the administration is on statistics. I got tied up at the lab, running experiments."

"Yes," she said. "I know." She watched him climb out of bed, his nude body beautiful as marble in the soft morning light. She closed her eyes so that she would not have to look at him. "We ran into a strange case last night," she said as conversationally as she could.

He stopped in the middle of pulling on his shorts. "Oh? What was it?"

"A new admit. It looked like diphtheria. I didn't think that was possible these days, but you might want to run a check on it. Maybe the strain's mutated."

"I haven't seen it, if it has," he said, making it plain that if he had not seen it, it had not happened. A crease of annoyance appeared between his fine brows. "What makes you think it's diphtheria? It's probably a bad case of bronchitis."

"That's what I thought, but the computer diagnosed it as unknown. An unknown viral infection. It would recognize bronchitis, wouldn't it?" She hoped she sounded cool and reasonable. "She's got the gray face and the cough."

His crease deepened to a frown. "I haven't heard of any mutation that could get through a vaccine. And this is just the one case, you say?"

"Yes." She opened her eyes and studied the ceiling. "That part has me puzzled, too. I thought the girl might be resistant to vaccines. I haven't found that with diphtheria before, but I suppose it could happen. It *is* possible, isn't it?"

Mark nodded, irritation fled. "That's it, then. I wouldn't let it worry me, if I were you. Not unless you see a lot of cases." He had pulled on his shorts and was stepping into his slacks. "You shouldn't let yourself get so involved, Natalie. You make errors in judgment if you do. It's a mistake to be so involved, believe me."

She nodded, not finding the words to answer him. When she did speak again, it was on something entirely different. "I thought I'd take Philip out to the Great Belt Park. I don't have to be at the hospital until two. It's a nice day for the Park, don't you think?"

"I guess so," he said as he reached for his smock. "Look, Natalie, I might be in late tonight."

"More work in the lab?" she asked, and heard no bitterness in the words.

"You know what the Project is like," he said by way of apology.

She felt her throat tighten as she said, "It doesn't matter, Mark," and knew that it was so.

* * *

The three hours she could spend with Philip felt too short. Often she wished for a whole day when she and her son could wander about the city without worrying about the time, about her duty schedule at the hospital. But three hours would let them see the Great Belt Park, the zoo there and the trees. She dressed for the raw winds and took the bus to the swath of green that girded the city, her son clinging to her hand.

While they were watching the birds by the Monkey Climbing Rock, Natalie noticed a woman on the adjoining bench, and felt the annoying sense that she was familiar. After a moment it came to her. "Mrs. Chisholm?" she said to the drab, muffin-shaped lady in the untidy coat.

The woman slewed about, confused.

"Mrs. Chisholm, over here. Here!" Natalie waved. "I'm Dr. Lebbreau, remember? Dr. Howland's wife. Natalie Lebbreau. This is my son, Philip."

Mrs. Chisholm's wrinkled face smiled lopsidedly. "I thought you were from the hospital," she said in an unaccountably shaky voice.

"Mrs. Chisholm, what's wrong? Don't you feel well?" Natalie started forward, her hand extended.

"Oh," said the older woman, rubbing ineffectually at her eyes. "I'm all right now, truly I am. It was simply seeing you, you know . . ."

"Me?" Natalie frowned, and thought she should not have spoken. She covered her mistake. "We're missing Chisholm, believe me. I hope he's back with us soon."

"Back?" She stared. "Oh, dear . . ." There were tears in the seams of her face. "I realize I shouldn't . . . I thought everybody knew . . . I'm not used to it yet . . . It's so soon . . ."

Natalie asked the question although she had already sensed the answer. "Not used to what? What has happened, Mrs. Chisholm?"

Mrs. Chisholm had pulled an old-fashioned handkerchief from her handbag and was swabbing her face with it. "He died. I can't get used to it. This is dreadful . . . forgive me, my dear . . . carrying on . . . I thought . . . Oh, dear."

"Chisholm is dead," Natalie said stupidly. "No one told me. I wouldn't have believed this, Mrs. Chisholm. If I'd known, I wouldn't . . ." She felt Philip tug at her arm.

"Yes. Edward died ten . . . was it ten? . . . ten days ago." She looked steadily at Natalie. "It seems longer, somehow."

"We were told that he was on a leave of absence," Natalie said, as much to herself as to Mrs. Chisholm.

"Mommy, don't," Philip said, pulling more firmly on her arm, alarmed. He realized that his mother was upset, and he was frightened. "Let's go, Mommy."

"It's all right, Philip." She lifted him into her arms. "Mommy has had some bad news, but it isn't about you." All the same, she pulled the child closer to her as she spoke.

"Is this your little boy?" asked Mrs. Chisholm, obviously relieved to have something else to talk about.

"Yes. This is Philip. He's three and a half. And he already knows how to read his name. Don't you, Philip." She hated herself for this, for showing off her child. She remembered how much her mother had done it to her, and how she had squirmed.

"I can read," Philip announced, eyes owl-wide.

"This is Mrs. Chisholm, Philip. She's a friend of Mommy's and Daddy's. I haven't seen her for a while."

"He's such a beautiful child. You're very fortunate, very fortunate. Edward and I never had any, you know. We couldn't afford them. My sister has two. She's very proud of them, of course. Edward and I used to enjoy seeing them. He was very fond of children."

Natalie sat with Mrs. Chisholm, talking about the weather, the condition of the city, the sad state of the local political squabbles, the new Limited Family tax plan, the rumors of famine in Mexico. There was no further mention of the chef.

Then, just as Natalie turned to go, Mrs. Chisholm leaned over and whispered, "They said it was his heart, you know, but it wasn't. It was something else. They didn't tell me, but I know it was something else. Edward's heart was as steady as a rock. I used to be a nurse. I know."

Cautiously, Natalie asked, "Do you have any idea what it might have been?"

"No. And that worries me. They wouldn't let me see him, not at any time after he took sick. They wouldn't even let me call him. They kept us apart. They said, at the hospital . . ."

"Westbank?" Natalie asked, wondering how Chisholm could have been in her hospital and she not know it.

"No, Strickland Memorial." Mrs. Chisholm frowned. "I don't know why they sent him there. They said that seeing me would upset him. But we were married thirty-eight years . . . I know he wanted to talk to me . . ." She dabbed at her eyes again, making a motion as if to fend off an attack.

"But what was wrong with him? Did they keep him in isolation?"

"Edward shouldn't have died alone."

She sounded so miserable, so frightened that Natalie was ready to discount her suspicions as the fancy of a lonely old woman. She put her hand on Mrs. Chisholm's shoulder, an awkward gesture of comfort. "I'm sure they did all they could to save him."

"They didn't, you know." She turned, looking evenly at Natalie. "They took him away. They told me he had been transferred to Central Intensive when I went to Strickland Memorial, but there was no record of him at Central Intensive."

The image of Alan Mathew Reimer rose before Natalie to haunt her. He, too, had been transferred without a trace.

"I'm sorry, Mrs. Chisholm. It must have been dreadful," she said, finding her fear returning.

After that, there was little to say. They parted company near the duck pond. Philip and Natalie walked back toward the housing complex. When Philip grew tired, Natalie lifted him, thinking how heavy he was becoming. As she walked, she tried to unravel the mystery she had found. Isobel Chisholm was not a woman to dramatize her grief, and if what she said was true, the Reimer boy's case was not an isolated incident, but a new practice.

"What's wrong, Mommy?" Philip demanded as they neared their building.

"Oh, nothing, Philip. Your mommy is a worrywart. Come on, I'll take you to the center and I have to get back to work."

"Why did that lady cry?" he asked.

Natalie looked down at her son, seeing how fragile he was. "She was frightened, Philip. And she was sad."

"Are you frightened?" His eyes, the same faded green as her own, were serious and intent. "Mommy?"

"Yes," she said. "I'm beginning to think I am."

CHAPTER 2

When she arrived at the hospital, the girl Natalie had tested for diphtheria had been transferred. After two phone calls, Natalie knew that there was no way she could locate the child. When she told Gil this, he raised an eyebrow.

"She had diphtheria," Natalie said in a steady low tone. "I ran some tests on the sample you left for me yesterday."

"What does Mark have to say about this?"

A fleeting pain passed over Natalie's face. "Mark didn't run the series. I did. He was busy."

Gil wondered at the bitterness in her voice. "Say, Nat, you're all right, aren't you? Is anything bothering you?"

"Of course something is bothering me. Two kids dead of diseases they can't possibly have. That's bothering me. And Chisholm's dead, did you know? I saw Isobel today and she's not satisfied that he had heart trouble. They transferred him, too, Gil. She doesn't know where he died. There's a lot that's bothering me, like what's going to happen if this thing grows . . ."

"Chisholm's dead?"

She quieted immediately. "I hadn't meant to mention Chisholm. You won't say anything, will you, Gil?"

"No, not if you don't want me to. But what happened?" He glanced over his shoulder toward the nurses' station, and was relieved to see that the two women there were paying no attention.

"I don't know. That's the terrible part."

"Hey," he chided her, "come on. It's not that bad. There's just a big misunderstanding, that's all."

She laughed sharply. "A misunderstanding. Of course." She moved away from him. "Let's start rounds, Gil."

This was not what he had anticipated, but he accepted it. Doctors had certain privileges that paramedics had to respect. He let it go, thinking that she might open up later while they were on their break.

But Natalie was busy when their coffee break came, as if she did not want to go to the cafeteria so soon after Chisholm's death. "There's two more kids down on the eighth floor. I want to check them out while I have the chance," she said when he asked her to join him.

"And flirt with Mark while you're at it?" he teased, and was surprised at her vehement "No!"

"Sorry, Nat. I didn't mean anything by that."

"I'm on edge," she muttered. "Just leave me alone for a while, Gil, please. Please."

"If you say so. But you might tell me what this is all about."

She did not answer. She walked down the hall to the elevator and took it to the eighth floor.

* * *

The two girls turned out to be battered children. Natalie watched with pity as Ian Parkenson prepared the younger of the two for surgery. Both legs of the older girl were bruised, open wounds draining on her left shin. But the younger had been so badly beaten that broken shards of her tibias poked through her skin smeared with marrow.

Ian cursed softly as he worked, his square carpenter's hands moving delicately to assess the damage.

"Parents," he said as he finished the younger girl and turned his head away. "But what can you expect? Six kids living in three rooms. The wonder is that there aren't more of them."

"How do you mean, Ian?" Natalie asked, keeping out of the way of his paramedic and surgical nurse.

"You know about frustration and overcrowding as well as I do, Natalie. We see the results of it every day. Psychiatric is as full as it can hold of people who can't take the pressure any longer. Beatings, sexual assault, all the terrible violence we clean up after. It's a product of the way we live. Take those kids. You know how lucky they are to get to a hospital? Any hospital? There are at least one hundred cases like this which go unreported and unattended for every one we see. And quite likely there are more. It's worse than rape." He turned his attention to the older girl, to a large bruise swelling on the back of her neck. "This isn't good."

Without being asked, Natalie began to monitor the display board for Ian.

"The old way was kinder, Natalie," he said as he worked. "Even if you lost them in childhood, at least you didn't kill them with your own hands."

"Oh, Ian, you don't believe that," she murmured, making a note on the printout. "Temperature anomaly on the skin. You've got some nerve trouble there, it looks like."

"No," he said, lowering the girl back onto the table and pressing her lids closed over unequally dilated pupils. "We aren't going to save her. She's been hemorrhaging too long."

"Isn't there anything you can do?" Even as she asked it she knew from the display that there was little or nothing that would save the child. And if they kept her alive, it would be as a vegetable. There was brain damage, and the printout showed it was spreading.

"She'll live a few more hours yet. The sister may make it, but there's no way we're going to keep that right leg. I think we can save the left, but not the right. Maxim or Angela will amputate as soon as there's an OR free on twelve or fourteen."

"Ian, I'm sorry . . ."

"So am I, Natalie." He signaled for his paramedic and retired to a chair next to the emergency unit. "God, I'm tired."

"Ian," Natalie began when the gurney had been removed, "did you know that Edward Chisholm is dead?"

"Chisholm? No, I didn't. I'm sorry to hear it. I knew he was having trouble of some kind. It was his heart, wasn't it? I understood it was heart trouble." He rubbed at his eyes as if trying to banish his fatigue.

"His wife didn't think it was heart trouble."

"Wives. They never agree with doctors."

"She was a nurse once, Ian. She knows what heart trouble looks like."

"Christ." He glared at his paramedic who was standing nearby, moving nervously. "What is it?"

"There won't be OR space until four, Doctor."

Ian grabbed at his face, pulling the skin forward. He looked more like an out-of-work clown than a surgeon. "Call those bastards on nine and ask them if we can use an orthopedics emergency unit. It's got enough equipment for an amputation. Get Maxim on it."

"Yes, sir," the paramedic said before she sprinted away.

"About Isobel Chisholm," Natalie persisted as Ian stared after the paramedic. "What if she's right?" She discovered she had been pleating her lab coat, and she smoothed the wrinkles carefully.

"If Isobel Chisholm thinks that there was some irregularity in her husband's death, she knows enough to report it to the medical authorities. If not, she should not go around exciting young and inexperienced doctors who don't know enough to keep their own council. How's Mark's famous Project doing? He told me he and the Statistical Department are getting some results at last."

"We don't talk about it much. We don't see each other very often." She took the rebuff as well as she could. "Would it make a difference if I'd been here longer, Ian?"

"Sure it would. You'd know when to interfere and when to get involved. And it would help if you hadn't been in trouble with administration before. You should have stayed out of that battered-child case."

She turned on him then. "You can say that, after those two girls? You can honestly tell me that I should have let those kids go back to their father? You saw them when they were admitted. Remember the fracture on the boy's skull? Remember pulling all those lead splinters out of it?" She stared at him, waiting for an answer.

"Peter Justin made the only decision he could. And it put you in a very bad position, Natalie. Look," he said, his words more kindly than they had been, "I know how you feel. But we can't afford to stick our necks out on every case. We have to be careful. There are times when we know we can make a difference, and those are the times we should take a stand. When the question is obviously crucial. But in cases like that one, when Justin had to decide on the matter of word . . . You didn't have a chance. Justin doesn't have the authority to take the matter to court without more than your testimony against that of the children's parents."

"But they had been beaten with electric cords. You said so yourself." Natalie felt this was not happening, that Ian could not be saying this to her. He had always taken the part of the unprotected child, and now he was telling her she should not have tried to save the three Swanson children.

"Sure. And it was true. They had been beaten with electric cords and lead-weighted thongs. You had no proof that the parents had done it. Even if the kids wouldn't talk, they knew who had beaten them. And we were right, Natalie. You know we were right."

"Yes," she said somberly. "We were right. They were dead within six months of their release."

"But we can't prove that the parents did it," Ian said patiently.

"Who else, then? The milkman?" She spat the words at him, very angry now. "Don't kid yourself, Ian."

"I may be," he said, pulling himself out of his chair. "But if I were you, unless I caught someone in the act, I wouldn't bring any kind of complaint against anyone for a while. The administration doesn't like embarrassments like the Swanson case. Take my advice, Natalie, and keep a low profile. Otherwise you're going to land in big trouble."

She studied his lined, sensitive face, knowing that his advice was meant to help her, and that she should listen to him. "Come on, Natalie," he said, "there's lots of years yet. Get in here a little more solidly, and then you can take on the administration, maybe even make a change in the Battered Child laws. That's important, and you'd be good at it. But you're not up to that fight yet. Remember that."

"I'll remember," she said truthfully. "Thanks, Ian. I don't agree with you, but thanks."

* * *

As she got into the elevator, Natalie noticed the other woman waiting for the car. This made her hesitate. She badly wanted the chance to be alone with her thoughts. The other woman was plainly upset, and would probably start to talk to her as soon as the doors closed. Natalie studied her as she pressed the "hold" button. She was an angular woman without being thin, her graying hair was in disorder, and when she spoke, it was in jerky, breathless phrases. Natalie made up her mind and entered the elevator, and as she had expected, the strange woman began to speak to her as soon as the doors were shut.

"Are you a doctor? You look too young. But it says *doctor*. Your name badge says *doctor*."

"I am," Natalie said as the elevator moved.

There was a moment of silence, and then the other woman made up her mind. "You tell me, then: what kind of place is this? Can't any of you keep track of anything here?"

"The hospital is very efficient," Natalie said, somewhat defensively. "What's the matter?"

"It's my boy. Why can't you tell me where he is? Anybody should be able to tell me. But they don't. They say he's transferred. They're giving him intensive care, but not here. Somewhere else. On another floor. But I've been all the places they've told me to go, and he isn't here. They won't let me see him or talk to him."

Fear washed over Natalie more strongly than ever. She made an effort to soothe the woman. "When did you bring him to the hospital?"

"Last night, early. He was real sick. He had this rash on him, real bad, big sores, almost like something'd been biting him. He's never had one like this before. When I brought him in they said it was an allergy. They said they'd keep him for observation and run tests on him." Her voice rose. "Some observation, when they can't even find him."

"Mrs. . . ."

"Verrcy. Laura Verrcy. My boy is David. His father is Hugh."

"Mrs. Verrcy, if you'll give the desk your name and address and a number where you can be reached and your phone service hours, I'll try to find out what I can about this. It's certainly not usual for the hospital to withhold information from parents about their children," she said, thinking grimly that it was becoming usual. "Do you happen to remember the name of the doctor who examined your son? Or what floor they sent him to? It could help me trace him if you remember."

The angry, frightened eyes regarded her with unveiled suspicion. "What can you do the others can't?"

"I can ask a few questions. It's worth a try, isn't it?"

"I don't know. They tried to make out that his being sick was our fault. Maybe they want to blame us for his being sick. Maybe that's what you're planning to do."

"Mrs. Verrcy, please. I know what you've gone through with this staff. But, truly, I think I can help you if you'll let me." Natalie hoped that this was a simple matter of administrative foul-up and not another child lost.

"The doctor's name was Braemoore."

Jim Braemoore. That wasn't good, Natalie knew. He was one of the most firmly established of the staff doctors and adhered to hospital policy as if it were dogma.

"He's going to be okay, isn't he?" Laura Verrcy asked as she saw Natalie's face. "That isn't bad, is it? Doctor Braemoore is okay, isn't he?"

"Jim Braemoore is one of the most respected doctors on the pediatric staff," she answered, comforting herself with the thought that this was true. "But he's off duty right now. You don't have to worry about your son David if Jim Braemoore is taking care of him. Ask anyone on the staff about him, and they'll say the same thing." She hated herself for closing ranks this way, supporting a toady like Braemoore so that this confused woman would not ask the wrong question.

The elevator stopped. "Well, I get off here," said Mrs. Verrcy.

"Look," Natalie said impulsively, "I'll check up on your boy. Don't worry about him. I'll let you know what I find out. Just be sure to leave your name and address at the desk. Tell them that it's for Doctor Lebbreau."

"Dr. Lebbreau," she repeated. "I will. If you think . . ." The door closed on the rest of what she was going to say.

Natalie rode up to her floor with troubled thoughts.

* * *

"What's the matter with you?" Gil demanded with none of the easy banter he generally used with Natalie when she was upset. Their rounds had been tense and now he was getting angry.

She motioned him away from the patient they were checking. "I've been finding out things, Gil, and they scare me. I know it sounds crazy, but there is something really wrong around here."

"Not *that* again." Even his eyes were scornful.

"I found out about a kid who had smallpox."

"Aw, Nat, come on. You're overdoing it. Nobody gets smallpox any more, and you know it."

"Listen to me, Gil," she pleaded as her eyes narrowed and she looked cautiously down the hall. "There's something wrong here. And I'll go on saying it until someone listens to me. Someone has to listen."

"You said it yourself, Nat: it's crazy." He put his hands on her shoulders, but she shrugged them away. "Maybe it is," she said softly. "Will you give me a chance to prove it, one way or the other?"

He stared at her. "How?"

"I'll tell you that when I'm through."

For a moment he felt like getting angry and telling Natalie to get back to her job and forget her ridiculous theories. But he knew her well enough to know that she would not let the thing rest until she had resolved it. "All right. Take your time with it. But don't blame me if you get caught. Or fired."

Her expression was enigmatic. "Thanks, Gil. You're a prince."

* * *

It was after midnight when Natalie went back to Mark's test-tube domain on the seventh floor. The rooms were deserted and even the officious clerk had gone for the night. Her passkey had worked, to her surprise and relief. Still, she moved on tiptoe, seeking the coldroom where all the vaccines were kept. She hoped that this would be quick, that she would find she was mistaken after all and would have to bear with Gil's teasing. It would be so much easier to face Gil's ridicule than what would happen to them all if she was right. For a moment she hesitated, wanting to turn back. But she had come too far.

She turned on her flashlight and removed the throat attachment that had directed the beam to pencil fineness, then played the full force of the light over the orderly shelves where the neatly labeled bottles stood in military precision. It took very little time to find what she sought, and she took all she would need with her to the lab station. Setting her flashlight aside, she set up the scanners and began to work.

The tests took her much longer than she had anticipated: almost four hours.

When she was through she put the bottles back, and, walking as if in a daze, she left the labs quietly and went to the surgeon's lounge for some sleep, if she could sleep. Her head ached, and her neck, but that was not what haunted her.

Please, she thought as she stretched out on the couch . . . please, don't dream, don't dream.

* * *

"Natalie," said Mark's voice, and for a moment she thought she was at home and it was time to get up. But the way he said those familiar words and the pain behind her eyes reminded her where she was, and why.

"Natalie, get up." There was no friendliness in him at all. She opened her eyes and looked up at her husband. Mark's face was ominously dark. He extended his hands to her. Her flashlight lay in them.

"Oh," she said. "That was clumsy of me. I wasn't thinking clearly."

"Yes." He waited. "I saw what you'd done. And now, Natalie, you will tell me why." The fury in his eyes belied his soft tone.

"I had to find out, that's all. I can't stand to have patients dying for no reason. And I found out more than I bargained for." She looked up at him fearlessly. He had no threat in him now. "I know about you, Mark. I know what you're doing."

He was not listening. "What were you trying to prove?"

"It was the children," she said, rubbing at the kink in her neck and wishing that she did not have to argue while she was so tired. "I saw children with diseases they could not—or *should* not have. I had to find out how they got them. Don't you see that?"

"Oh, I see, all right."

She rose stiffly. "No, you don't. That's the trouble. All you ever see is that damned lab of yours. The statistics and the dabs of blood and tissue. You don't have to see diphtheria and smallpox up close on human beings. You deal in pathology." She ran her hand over her wrinkled lab coat. "One third of your vaccines are totally useless."

"Of course," he scoffed. "What do you think my Project is all about?"

For a moment she was aghast. Then she stared at him as if she had never seen him before, never touched him. "You don't know what you're doing. You can't understand the enormity of it."

He laughed as he knotted his hands into fists. "I don't know what I'm doing?" he mocked her.

"You couldn't. Mark, all those people . . . all those dead people . . ."

At that he swung toward her. " 'All those people,' you say. All is the operative word, Natalie. *All*. There are too damn many of them. And it is getting worse and worse. Each year the quality of life is poorer, the crowding is denser, the education more shoddy, transportation more dangerous, food less nourishing, sanitation less trustworthy. Of course I know what I'm doing. It's not as if this isn't being monitored and controlled. We're a test area, because you and I know that a thing like this can get out of hand if it isn't watched. And I'm for it, Natalie, because it's fair. You would be, too, if you thought about it a little." His hands opened and he spoke more softly. "Gil told us about your hunches. You're very bright, Natalie, but you're very blind."

"You're wrong," she whispered, moving away from him. "You are wrong."

"Listen, you said it yourself. There are too many people. Don't you realize we can't take care of the ones we've got, let alone the ones who haven't been born yet?" He reached his hand out to her, his face lined with concern. "Look at the problem sensibly, and you'll see that something has to be done before we're all lost. You'll see this is the only way. Ian understands. Jim understands. Even Gil does. They know the danger we face, and they all agree that this is the most humanitarian way to deal with the problem. No élitism, no judgment beyond the judgment nature makes. Even the killing of the vaccines is done by computer. No one makes a decision about it."

Suddenly Natalie remembered what Ian Parkenson had said as he worked over the two battered sisters. She knew then that he would support something this desperate, this crazy. "But they're doctors," she said to herself, forgetting she spoke aloud.

"Yes," he agreed, his voice at its most persuasive. "They are doctors," and they're anxious to make a better life for all of us. You can . . ."

"Plague is a better life? Because that's what you're getting from this Project of yours, a plague."

Mark's eyes grew bright, but he controlled his temper. "Think about it, Natalie. If we had fewer people, think of what it would mean in terms of space and food and work and life . . . living, Natalie. We aren't living now."

"There are other ways." She felt defiance rising up in her, and with it, doubt. What if he was right? What if this were the only answer?

He snorted. "Birth control, you mean? When people talk about limiting families, they mean someone else's family, and you know it. You've seen it. How many women come in here on their fourth or fifth and tell us that they're special, their case is different, they should have children because they are brighter or more capable or richer than other people. But they're wrong. We tried it, oh so patiently, so politely, to tell them that they cannot make exceptions of themselves, and it didn't work."

"That's no excuse for what you're doing," she said doggedly, wishing that he would leave her alone so that she could think.

"Excuse, hell. It's reality, girl. Believe me, if we don't change fast, good old Mother Nature is going to cook up her own plague and get rid of us as a general pest." He started to pace up and down the room. Natalie remembered the many times his feral grace had fascinated her, the power of him, his control. It still fascinated her, his lithe movement. But his power she now saw as ruthlessness.

"Can't you see," he was saying, "there's nothing really wrong with what we're doing. We're the ones who've been wrong all the time. We're supposed to let the weak ones die. Natalie, the dead vaccine batches are computer controlled. Nobody knows which batches are good and which aren't. Chance picks the victims, don't you see? The only reason you find this hard to accept is that we've got used to having life so far out of balance that this unnatural immunity seems normal. But it isn't." He stopped pacing and leaned toward her. "Think about it."

"If people knew. Mark . . ."

"People don't know," he said flatly. The menace in him was much stronger. "They don't know and there's no reason for them to know."

"No reason? When it's their lives?"

"Don't pull those big eyes on me; save them for Gil. It might work on him. There is no reason for people to know about our Project . . ."

"Project?"

"Certainly. What did you think the Project has been all this time? We're a test area, this county. If the program works here, then similar projects will be started in other parts of the country. You don't think we'd take on a full-scale Project without doing test areas first, do you?"

She stepped toward him, trying not to touch him as she said, "I am not afraid . . . You're doing something terribly wrong and you have to be stopped."

"*You're* going to stop us?"

She bridled. "The government will. The courts will."

"Who the hell do you think authorized this in the first place, the American Medical Practitioners?"

"They wouldn't." In the quieter part of her mind, Natalie wondered if anyone could overhear them. This was the surgeon's lounge. Anyone might come in. Anyone might be listening. And what then?

"Don't hope for a timely rescue. Ian's outside." He pushed her shoulder and she sat down, startled. "You're a problem, Natalie. You found out about something that was none of your business."

She tried to rise and was forced to sit again. "What do you mean, none of my business? This is very much my business. Look at my patients' admit records. Your Project is absolutely my business."

"Will you get off this emotional binge and listen?" he asked as if he were speaking to a ten-year-old. "You've found out about the Project. And you are not going to say a word to anyone. Because if you do, I guarantee that you will be shut up. Officially. You will be fired. And there won't be a city or a county hospital in the whole state that will hire you, now or ever. You'd be lucky to get a job cleaning bedpans. Do you understand that?" He waited, studying her face.

"Yes. I understand."

"Now. You are going back to work. You are going to keep on working. You are also going to keep your mouth shut. Remember, we're going to need doctors badly, Natalie. You can't afford to give up."

She said, as if far away, "What about the people who already know? How do you know you'll be able to trust them when their kids are dying?"

Mark shook his head slowly. "What would they say?" He strode to the end of the room, his hand on the door. "No one knows which batches are which or where they go once they are prepared. There's no way we could trace them, even if we wanted to."

"Somebody is going to find out." She stood up and walked down the room toward this man who was her husband. "Even if I don't talk, Mark, someone will. You can't hide polio and smallpox and diphtheria and all the rest. It's bound to come out, and what then? Who will you blame?"

"We'll worry about that when it happens." He turned to her with real affection and respect in his face. "I didn't think you could fight, Natalie. I'm very proud of you, even though you're wrong."

She choked back angry tears. "I can't live with you any more, Mark." She tried to look away from him, but could not.

"Fine."

"And neither can Philip."

"All right."

They stood together silently.

"May I leave now?" she asked in a moment.

He shrugged. "Why not?"

On the other side of the door Ian Parkenson faced her, his deep eyes sad. "I'm sorry for this, Natalie. I wanted to be the one to talk to you. Mark doesn't understand what we go through. He doesn't know what we face."

"Do you know, or have you forgotten, Ian? You're kidding yourself, if you think this plan will work."

Ian took her by the shoulder, regret in his face. "I know better than you do what we're up against. That's why I'm for this. If you want to talk about it when you've had a chance to think it over, I'm willing to listen. Let me know."

She pushed past him. "That's very generous of you, Doctor. I might take you up on it after I talk with Justin or Wexford." She knew that Ian would not like to be compared with the two most bureaucratic of the hospital administrators.

"Natalie . . ." he began.

But she was already out of earshot.

* * *

She stopped at the first phone and dialed the desk. "This is Dr. Lebbreau. I want to talk to Peter Justin in administration. His office is in Statistics on the sixteenth floor."

"Dr. Lebbreau?" asked the operator. "Just a moment, Doctor. We have a message for you."

"Oh?" Natalie was not willing to be put off. "Who from?"

"From a Mrs. diMaggio. I think it . . ."

"It's from my son's school." A sharp pain lodged itself in her throat as she waited. She told herself that it was psychosomatic, but that did not make it go away. "What does the message say?"

"I'll read it to you, if you like. Just a moment." There was a pause and Natalie heard the rustling of paper. "Here it is. 'Dr. Lebbreau: we have sent Philip home with a bad cough. Will you please advise us when you are ready to return him to school? Miss Sczieker will stay with him until you can get home.' It's signed Florence diMaggio. Will you wait to talk to Dr. Justin, Dr. Lebbreau?"

Natalie's hands had gone numb. She fumbled with the receiver with unfeeling fingers. "No. No. I'll talk to Dr. Justin later."

* * *

It took her forty minutes to get home, and all the while she was in turmoil, outraged. Over and over she told herself that Philip had only a cold, that Mark would not let this happen to their child. But the selection for vaccines was random, and no one knew which batches were good and which were not. She wished there was someone she could talk to, someone who would understand and help her fight back, someone who would share her horror.

"It's only a cold," she said aloud, blushing when the other passengers stared at her.

By the time she left the bus she was calmer. Her temper was under control and she had realized that she could not buck the whole administration. One thing at a time, she told herself, and the most important thing was her son.

Before she opened her door, she took a deep breath and steadied herself against the frame. At last she knew she would not panic, no matter what she saw. She went into the little apartment.

"Mommy!" Philip wailed as he saw her.

"Dr. Lebbreau," said the stout young woman on the sofa. She rose with surprising grace, extending her hand. Her hair was the color of highly polished cherrywood.

"Yes, Philip," Natalie said as she took the proffered hand. "Mommy's home." She turned to the other woman. "You're Miss Sczieker, aren't you?"

"Yes, I am. How do you do, Dr. Lebbreau?"

Natalie made some answer, anxious to see her son.

"I'll be leaving now, Doctor, unless you want me to stay?"

"No, thank you," Natalie said, wishing now that she could confide in this polite, plump woman. It would be so much easier to endure her fear if she could confide in someone.

But Miss Sczieker was already at the door, a light jacket over her arm. "He's a fine boy, Dr. Lebbreau. You must be very proud of him. Well, if there's nothing else I can do, I'll say good-bye."

Natalie stood uncertainly in the center of the room after the door had closed. Then she walked the few feet to Philip's bed, each step feeling like miles. "Now, Philip, what's this about a cold?"

From his mound of covers he said, "I don't feel good, Mommy. Make me better."

"I'll have to look you over first, and then we'll fix you up perfectly. And soon you'll be well and you can come with me to a new house." She wondered where she was to find housing for them, now that her marriage was over, then forced that concern from her mind. "You'll like a new house, won't you?"

The boy laughed, which quickly dissolved in a thin, wheezing cough. Natalie tried not to be too alarmed. This could be a recurrence of croup, she told herself. For about a year, Philip had had bouts of croup, and this could be more of the same. She reminded herself, as she reminded other parents, that children go through some pretty terrific colds which don't amount to much later on. But she didn't believe it.

"Mommy, I feel funny," he whined, putting his hand into Natalie's. His fingers were cold, the palm hot and dry.

Despite her stern mental orders to herself, Natalie's voice broke as she said, "Philip, will you sit there just a moment. Mommy's going to turn on the light and have a real doctor look at you. All right?"

She felt her son nod.

And in the light she saw that his face was waxen and gray, that his movements were fever-restless, and she saw what she had feared from the start. "Oh, Philip . . ." It was too late. If she had known two, three days ago, if she had not learned what was happening to her county.

Philip looked at his mother uncomprehendingly. "Mommy, what's the matter?" he asked, then started to cough again. "Mommy?"

"It's nothing, Philip. Mommy's tired, that's all," she lied, taking Philip nearer the window and rocking him gently. Yes, his face was gray, and his eyes were becoming affected. Only three years old and now this was happening to him. He was dying of diphtheria. It was such a stupid waste. "You lie back and get some rest. Everything is going to be fine."

As she phoned the hospital she felt desolate. There was no hope for Philip, and there was no hope for her now. It was too late.

"It's going to be fine," she said to Philip as she went back to him. She had told the admit desk that he had croup, not diphtheria. Maybe if she went along with them, they'd let her see her son before he died. Perhaps if she really worked at it, found a way around the red tape, she might be able to save him, even yet. There was a slim, slim chance. She put her hand to her eyes. They would not give her permission, not after what she had been through with Mark this morning. They would treat Philip the way they had treated the other children and he would be dead shortly. Nothing short of heroic measures would save him, and she would not be allowed the heroic measures.

"Don't worry, Mommy," Philip said once as Natalie rocked him through the afternoon. "Daddy'll fix everything."

For one dreadful moment Natalie thought she might laugh. "Yes," she said when she could trust herself to speak. "Daddy certainly will fix everything. He's a great fixer." She looked down into Philip's pinched face, seeing Mark and diphtheria there. "A great fixer."

And when the ambulance left later with Philip, Natalie went back to the hospital alone.

CHAPTER 3

"Never mind," Dr. Smith snapped at the intern. "He's dead." Angrily he jerked the feeder lines from the support module, bitter exhaustion showing in his face. Another dead kid.

"But what happened?" asked the intern. He was both hurt by the death of the child and frustrated by how little had been authorized to save the boy.

Dr. Smith finished closing down the monitor display before he answered. At last he said, "That child was admitted with minor bronchial inflammation, possible croup." He looked down at the ashen face, the tension fading from the features as the little body surrendered. "Fever developed long before he got here and his chest was badly congested. We performed a tracheotomy." He fingered the disconnected tube that dangled from the boy's thin neck. "We did not get permission to use the intensive care units on five, which might have helped. So we did the best we could with precautionary support. About ten minutes ago the monitor picked up trouble and now we have cardiac arrest. That's what happened. That's the official record."

The intern shook his head, feeling helpless. "But don't you know what did it? This wasn't croup. The computer diagnosed unknown viral infection. You'd think they'd let us have space downstairs." He knew that units in Intensive Care were hard to come by, and that they were particularly difficult for their floor, the sixth floor, which was General Medicine, the catch-all for the hospital. "Unknown viral infection. Don't you have any idea what killed this kid?"

"No, I don't." With that, Dr. Smith stepped out of the room and rang for the removal units.

As he walked away from his intern he was scowling. No, he didn't know what had killed the boy, but he knew that the child should not have died, not in his hospital. He had not known what had killed the other fourteen children he had seen. Fourteen dead in less than a week. He had run every sample he could think of through the diagnostic computer and he had got the same answer every time: virus, unknown.

"Dr. Smith, Dr. Smith," the paging system called idiotically. "Dr. Smith to floor sixteen. Dr. Smith to Statistics on floor sixteen."

"Damn," he said. He did not want to deal with Justin and his crowd. He knew the epidemiologist well enough to dislike the cool statistical mind that lay behind the politic smile and large gray-green eyes. Halfway down the hall he picked up an emergency phone long enough to say, "This is Harry Smith. Tell Justin I'm on my way."

* * *

Peter Justin had his smile on automatic when Harry walked in. He waited until Harry had chosen a seat, then flung a stack of diagnostic printouts on the desk.

Harry Smith's eyes flickered between the charts and Dr. Justin's face, settling on the latter. "Yes?"

"Would you kindly explain these? You and Dr. Lebbreau have been busy."

"Dr. Lebbreau?" He didn't know any Dr. Lebbreau, which was not surprising at this hospital, which employed seven hundred thirty-odd doctors and almost two thousand on staff: paramedics, nurses, interns, lab personnel and the tremendous bureaucracy of the administration. Harry considered denying his part in the investigation and letting Lebbreau, whoever he was, take the blame. But he did want some answers. He laced his fingers together over his knees. "Just checking," he said.

"Do you seriously call this checking? There are fourteen different post morts in full series here. I think you have some explaining to do."

"Do you?" Harry asked, smiling genially. "In the last week I have lost fifteen patients under the age of ten. All were admitted for unknown viral infections. They all died. I want to know why, and since your department doesn't seem to be doing anything about it . . ." Harry felt his voice rise; he forced himself to take a deep breath. "I thought someone ought to check it out."

Peter Justin's elegant brows drew together, his wide lips pursed. "Yes, I see. Fourteen on your service, did you say?"

"Fifteen, as of twenty minutes ago," Harry corrected.

"Fifteen. And you indicate here," he tapped the printouts, "that all these were in roughly one week's time. That's quite a large number for so short a period. All children, too, apparently."

"All under ten," Harry said, a sardonic smile touching his mouth.

Peter Justin drummed his slender fingers on the high gloss of his masonite desk. "That is a significant increase."

That was Justin. Give him death or a disease and he would try to fit it onto a graph and make statistical comparisons. Harry forced himself to keep these thoughts private.

"Fifteen. And Dr. Lebbreau reports something around a dozen." Peter Justin muttered. "Yours were mostly bronchial? Very unusual." He looked up, the smooth smile returning to his face. "Yes. I am glad you brought this to my attention, Smith. Ordinarily your actions would warrant a board review, but under the circumstances . . ."

Under the circumstances, thought Harry, you don't want to get caught in a neglect suit. The smile he directed at Justin was thinly veiled rage.

"Yes. You must let me know if you get another one. Any viral admits, particularly bronchial, in the next two weeks, provided the patient is within the proper age bracket, should be reported to this office. I really must thank you for calling this to my attention. I don't know how I could have overlooked it."

Harry had a retort to this, but left it unsaid. He was very tired and was due back on the floor in less than six hours. So he rose, saying, "Anytime. It looked suspicious and I thought it should be checked."

Justin nodded. "You were right. Although you should have contacted me before you went ahead with this check. We don't like this sort of unauthorized research."

Harry raised his brows. "We do have a certain responsibility to our patients. And if you find out what the unknown virus is, you'll let me know, won't you?"

"Certainly, certainly," Justin said blithely. "A thing like this takes some tracking. I'll get the labs on it right away. It might be a while but we'll get results. You know what a stickler Howland is. Good afternoon, Dr. Smith."

"Good afternoon, Dr. Justin." He closed the door with a bang.

* * *

Number sixteen was waiting for him when he came on night duty. This time the child was very young, no more than three or four, and

the only son of another doctor. Harry was surprised when he saw
that the father was Mark Howland, Chief Pathologist. How ironic
that Howland's kid should get the unknown virus.

"He's the son of *two* doctors," the intern corrected him. "Dr.
Howland and Natalie Lebbreau are married."

"Lebbreau?" he repeated, remembering the name from his inter-
view with Peter Justin. "What floor is she on?"

"Eleven, I think. General/Pediatric service. The kid's name is
Philip Howland. Age three years, seven months. He's underweight
and his eyes need correction. He was hospitalized last year with a
broken wrist."

Broken wrist? Was that his parents' doing? There were more and
more of them being brought in: children beaten, starved, maimed,
burned, tortured. Harry had seen too much of it and it sickened him.

"The wrist was broken at his day-care center. He fell from a ladder," the intern said, as if reading his thoughts.

"Thanks. What's been ordered so far?"

"The usual. IV, oxygen unit, standard monitor hookup and support systems."

"Good," Harry said absently. "I don't suppose we can get an intensive care unit from five?" He didn't expect an answer. He was already checking over the boy, touching, listening, probing for some
clue of the disease that was wasting him and had killed fifteen others.
He looked in the throat. "I could swear the kid has diphtheria, and
pretty advanced."

"Diphtheria?" the intern asked.

"Yeah. Look at the throat. It's classic. What tests have you run?"

"Standard series."

"I wonder if his father has seen them. Post the results in Dr. Justin's office." There was grim satisfaction in being able to upset the
urbane Peter Justin and his staff of number keepers.

"How long has his breathing been augmented? Has the breath
therapist been to see him yet?"

"Not yet. There's an emergency on eight, in quarantine. But he's
had a breathing unit for roughly two hours . . ." The intern frowned
at his information as he read it. "Two hours? He isn't going to make
it, is he?"

"No," Harry said shortly. "Not now. Not in this condition. Not
without intensive care." He stepped back from the fragile child on

the bed. "I think you'd better notify his parents. Get them over here if you can."

The intern was only too glad to have this chance to escape. He did not want to see the child die, not after the fight to save him.

Left alone with Philip Howland, Harry found himself helpless. There was only so much he could do now, only so much he was authorized to do, then the case would be decided by the administration. Harry wanted more equipment, more medication, an intensive care unit and all the help that brought. But he could not get it. Not now.

During the next ninety minutes Harry watched the boy's condition deteriorate. Breathing became shallow, his pulse light and erratic. As his circulation worsened, the tiny nails took on a bluish cast, the sunken face turned gray. Harry watched the monitor display, his face impassive, as the readout went inexorably on, a Greek chorus foretelling a necessary end.

At 11:37 Philip Howland was dead. He had died alone.

* * *

Harry sat in the darkest corner of the surgeon's lounge, wondering why he had become a doctor. It felt . . . *good* to save lives. And when he had specialized in pediatric surgery, lengthening his schooling by eight years, it had all seemed worthwhile. When had he lost his faith? He rubbed his forehead with clammy palms.

"Emile Harrison Smith?" asked a troubled voice.

Harry looked up, startled. It was rare to hear his full name, especially in the surgeon's lounge. For a moment he was confused.

The woman in front of him was angular and slight, her too-square shoulders made even more unattractive by her hospital whites. Her light-red hair might have been pretty, but it was caught at the back of her neck in a bun, emphasizing her jaw. Skimpy brows grew straight over pale-green eyes. She had been crying.

"Dr. Smith," she repeated in a surprisingly appealing voice, "I am Natalie Lebbreau."

Harry's face stiffened as he recognized her. "I see."

"I came as soon as I could." She looked away from him. Her hands were jammed deep into her pockets. "Not soon enough, though. You see, no one told me where he was until around noon. I didn't know . . ."

"I'm sorry," he said, not knowing if he believed her.

At first she said nothing, just stared toward the window where bright spring flowers nodded in the wind. She made a shudder like a sigh, then turned toward him. "Well, thank you. For what you did for Philip, I mean. I had hoped we'd be through with the two we have up on eleven, but . . . they were stronger than Philip. They lasted longer."

Harry studied her, wishing she would let go of her tense control, let herself mourn. Then he asked, "What two on eleven?"

"Sick children like Philip. They have diphtheria, too."

"Diphtheria?" He frowned. It was true that the disease looked like diphtheria, that the symptoms were classic, but the computer had said "unknown virus," and it could not mistake something so garden-variety common as diphtheria. Then he understood. She couldn't handle the shock of losing her child yet. And she had been working with sick children herself. With growing compassion he began to sense the guilt she would be feeling now, the conflict she must have undergone while she worked with other children, learning that her son was dead.

"They're all coming back again," she said wearily as she watched Harry. "All the old diseases. They will be back and we will have to fight them all over again. It's hard, so hard."

Fight them all over again? "How do you mean that, Dr. Lebbreau?" He knew he sounded like an ass, but that didn't matter. He did not want to think that this woman was giving way to the strain of her work.

"I've treated children with polio, with diphtheria, and there's even been an admit with smallpox. I saw him."

"Smallpox?"

Yes, yes, nodded the flowers in the window. Oh, yes. Natalie covered her eyes with trembling hands. "Oh, hell," she whispered.

Harry reached out to comfort her, but as he touched her shoulder she pulled away. She was in worse shape than he had thought, but not as bad as he had feared she might be. "I'm truly sorry. You look so unhappy. I figured you might want to let it out."

Her expression was one of complete disbelief. Then her eyes brightened and her face sank into sadness. "Oh. I see. You mean about Philip." She shook her head. "No, I can't, not now. If I started mourning for him now, I'd never stop." She looked around nervously, as if frightened. "There are all those others to mourn for."

So she was back to the others. Harry thought momentarily of notifying the Chief Resident on her floor, but then, perhaps because he did not trust the hospital administration, decided against it. "Let me call your husband," he suggested gently, thinking she would want to be with him now.

"No!" She was even more startled than he at this vehemence. "I mean," she went on in some confusion, "it isn't necessary. No. I am sure he knows by now. He had to know. He knew Philip was sick, and he knew why. He knows about . . . the diseases. He knows."

Harry tried to remember Dr. Howland: he was the one in charge of the labs, a tall young man with that tawny handsomeness that does not age well. He could be very charming—at least, that was what the nurses said. But Harry remembered now that he had always thought Mark Howland's eyes were colder than Peter Justin's.

I'm doing this badly, I'm all wrong, Natalie thought, wishing she did not think of Harry Smith as the enemy, particularly now, when she wanted, needed an ally, someone who would understand, who would see the horror that had begun and fight to stop it. But she had no words for the open-faced blond man who looked at her now with critical reservation.

"Is there . . ." He paused as he chose his words. "Is there anyone I should notify? School? Relatives?"

She shook her head again. "No. No, thank you. I'll do that. Just file the death report for the county." She glanced anxiously at the door again. "I really have to get back. I'm supposed to be on rounds right now. They'll wonder . . . I'll get checked on if I'm gone too long."

"Then, maybe I'll see you later." To his own ears the words were stilted, but Natalie Lebbreau gave him the semblance of a smile. "Oh, yes. Thank you, Dr. Smith."

Just as she went out the door she said impulsively, "It was diphtheria. We'll be seeing a lot of it soon."

*   *   *

Harry walked slowly back to his on-duty station, his hazel eyes clouded in thought. Obviously Natalie Lebbreau was in shock; emotionally she wasn't ready to handle her son's death. Her husband was certainly no help to her. For that reason she was inventing things, making up plagues to take her mind off her own loss, to make her son's death bearable.

"She can't be right," he said aloud.

For if she was, they were headed for disaster.

* * *

The seventeenth child did not appear for two days and Harry was beginning to hope that they had treated the last of the mysteriously sick children. He had almost decided that they had seen a random virus that was as short-lived as it was virulent.

The late-night city patrol changed that. They brought in two children, a boy and a girl found sleeping under a freeway interchange. They had been abandoned the day before and were cold, hungry, frightened . . . and sick.

"What's your name?" Harry asked the girl. She was the older of the two, about nine. She was sitting on her unit bed, scrawny arms dangling from the capacious hospital gown. Her dark eyes were defiant and her young face was set into an expressionless mask. She had locked herself away from him.

"Stephanie," she said, as if it were a swear word. "Where have you taken Brian? I want to see him."

"He's in another unit, just like yours."

The bright eyes showed scorn. "Why? Why'd you put him there?"

Harry suddenly felt the desolation Stephanie must know. She had been left along a roadside with her brother, her parents gone to another city, another state. This was what it meant to be abandoned. And now they were in the hands of strangers who had separated brother and sister. He reached over and thumbed a concealed toggle. "There, Stephanie. Now, do you see this knob?" He pointed to the large red knob that controlled the phone screen.

"Yeah?" she said with grave suspicion.

"Good. When I'm through checking you over, all you have to do is turn the knob to this position . . ." He moved aside so that she could see more clearly. ". . . and then you tell the lady on the screen who you want to talk to. You and Brian can have a long, long talk."

"Why can't I see him?"

"But you can. That's what the screen is for."

The girl gave a derisive snort. "I mean in person, mister. I don't trust these things. You could be faking it."

That bothered Harry. "I'm afraid you can't see him in person for a while. I'm sorry, Stephanie, but we have to do it that way. It's the rule." He wished fervently that just this once it wasn't the rule.

Stephanie lapsed back into sullen silence. It continued through the examination in spite of Harry's attempts to get her talking again. The only sound she made was one of pain when Harry tried to touch the keloid welts on her back.

"I'm sorry you're hurt," Harry told her before he left the unit.

*   *   *

"There's a message from the labs, Dr. Smith," said the pert nurse's assistant as Harry headed for the elevator.

"A message?" Harry wondered why his request for a symptom check on his patients was delayed, for that was all the message could mean.

"From Dr. Howland himself." Calculating eyes watched his face as he read.

From the desk of Dr. Mark Howland, said the memo. Request for symptom check on transferred juvenile patients denied. Insufficient reason provided to this laboratory to make such a check. All further requests will be denied unless Dr. Smith can demonstrate the critical need for such comparative checks. Our lab has better things to do than test sore throats and runny noses. This statement reflects official hospital policy.

"Damn!" Harry crumpled the memo into a ball and hurled it across the alcove into a wastebasket. "What an arrogant son of a bitch." Even if the death of his son had upset him, Harry was sure that it should have made Mark Howland more receptive to such requests, not less.

"Is there any reply?" the assistant asked, enjoying Harry's temper.

Harry realized that the assistant must have read the memo. He turned to her. "No answer. I know when I'm being told to shove it."

*   *   *

"Well!" Jim Braemoore beamed happily at Harry. "We haven't seen you down here in quite a while." He gestured expansively at the cafeteria. Braemoore was chief on the thirteenth floor, where most of the patients were terminal cancer. He usually ate in the administration dining room on the seventeenth floor, not here in the first basement. "Hasn't been the same down here since Chisholm died, of course. A fine chef, that man. Told me once that he had his personal spice racks back there in the kitchen. He grew herbs by the parking lot, too. Quite illegal, but the food was much better."

Harry made an absent reply. He found he didn't trust Braemoore's effusive outpourings. It was too bad about Chisholm, yes. It was too bad about everybody. He studied his cup of coffee, recalling the time, over five years ago, when the artificial grounds replaced the real thing all over the hospital. Chisholm had made the stuff tolerable, so the outrage was limited. Now, no one seemed to notice that their coffee tasted like ink. He supposed that in a year or so the doctors who were complaining about the bad food served since Chisholm's death would no longer be aware that their meals were pap. A year from now . . . He didn't want to think about a year from now.

"You look glum," observed Jim Braemoore. "Working too hard, I can tell. Just don't take the job so much to heart. Ruin you if you do, Harry. Tell you what"—he sat down, easing his bulk into the uncomfortable chair beside Harry—"we're mechanics. Much easier if you think about it that way. Otherwise, thinking about what doctors do, it'll drive you nuts."

"Mechanics?" he repeated numbly. Was that the secret? How had he missed it all these years?

"You and Natalie. Get all involved, go about in a lather, say foolish things, get into trouble with the administration. No good. Wear yourselves out that way. Can't do it, Harry. Can't do it at all."

"Natalie? Lebbreau?"

Jim looked up, startled. "So you were listening, after all. Wouldn't have thought so. Natalie Lebbreau is the one I meant. Pity about her marriage, but then, I suppose it was inevitable. Too bad about the child, too. Natalie Lebbreau's a good girl, fine doctor. Intense, very intense. Plain girls often are, don't you think?" He offered the sugar bowl to Harry. "Energy?"

It didn't pour like real sugar, but what the hell. It was sweet and it probably did give energy. At least it disguised the taste of the coffee.

"Take me, now," Jim Braemoore went on, his sausagelike hands spread over his broad chest. "Know my limits. Don't take the office home with me, don't bother much about the leftover CAs and other terminals. Better off letting them go. Why save 'em for more agony, that's the question. No reason for it at all. Put money on the ones who can get well. Ought to be doing the same thing yourself, Harry." He took a bite out of a droopy slice of pastry. The icing clung like snow to his mustache. "Can't be a good doctor the way you're going. Hear you've been handling the kids with bronchial trouble. No use fighting for 'em, Harry. Saw a few cases of it myself last week. Can't save 'em. No earthly use trying. Set 'em up, make 'em comfortable and get on with the strong ones. Do some good that way. Otherwise . . ." He shrugged his massive shoulders.

"Triage?" Harry asked, thinking that he could not be hearing this, that it was all a mistake.

"That's a thought severe on us, Harry," Braemoore said, his words muffled by the pastry.

"What are you saying to me, Jim? Are you telling me it isn't my job to save lives?"

"Didn't say that—not at all," Jim Braemoore protested. "Nothing of the sort. Did say that you shouldn't bother about terminals. Let 'em be. Put your time on the ones that can survive. Don't call it triage, though. Most people don't like the sound of it. But those toddlers with that virus, now, they aren't worth the effort."

"Are you sure it is a virus?" Even as he asked, Harry knew that, for some reason he could not understand, he no longer believed that they were treating an unknown virus. Jim was being almost too much the jolly old GP. There was something wrong when a doctor of Jim Braemoore's standing tried to throw a resident like Harry off the track. And that was what he was doing.

"Of course it's an unknown virus. Couldn't be anything else. Got to expect it in a city like this."

"And what do the diagnostic samples say? Or doesn't Mark Howland do yours, either?"

Jim looked flustered, his normally pink face turning red as he answered. "Type unknown. Damn it all, you should know. You're the one who's been ordering tests. Howland's been a little high-handed, but he's right. The lab's too valuable to do routine. Don't mind telling you that Justin is pretty unhappy about you. Not that it isn't his job to keep track of things, but you're pushing him. He's a busy man," he added hastily. "Hard to tell about Peter sometimes. Noticed how he likes having the records straight. Damned strange fellow when he's crossed."

"Am I being taken off the case?" Harry asked, as calmly as he could. He studied the residue in the bottom of his cup. Some people used to tell the future with coffee grounds, he remembered. But with fake coffee, there would be a fake future.

"Taken off?" Jim Braemoore said, horrified. "What for? You know the field. Just a little advice, that's all. Help you keep your perspective. This overconcern, preoccupation—that can happen to anybody.

Happened to me once, oh, long time ago. Took quite a while to set myself straight again. What I wanted to do was let you see how it is, help you to understand." He pushed back from the table. "Sorry to leave you so soon, but must scrub for a CA. You'd think people would remember to get their immunizations, wouldn't you?" He sighed a ponderous sigh. "Mastectomy. Pity. One inoculation every five years and there's nothing to worry about. But they forget, and then we have them up on thirteen." He broke off, beaming at Harry. "Delighted to have seen you, Smith. Don't have nearly enough time to talk these days. Just remember—one child, even half a dozen—doesn't make that much difference. Not worth the bother, Harry." With that as a parting remark, he strode to the door and bellied through it.

* * *

"Brian shows three broken ribs and an improperly healed fracture of the left wrist, as well as bruises and blisters on the ankles," the new intern reported. She was long, lanky and the color of caramel apples. "We found nylon fibers in the infected areas."

"Okay. So they kept him tied up. What else?"

"Bruises on the side of the face, recent. Burn scars on the left and right forearm. He is suffering from exposure and psychological shock, but will probably pull through."

"And Stephanie?" Harry found it more and more difficult to keep the detached professional attitude that was required of him. Yet he dared not show greater interest in this woman, obviously a plant from Justin or Braemoore. Or both. He wanted to chide himself for paranoia, to reassure himself that he was borrowing trouble; he found he could not do it. He sensed he was being watched and he looked up at the woman, challenging her eyes.

"The girl," the intern went on, smiling blindingly at him, "is in somewhat better condition, at least outwardly. She does have a fever complaint and general stiffness in the body. Her head is particularly sore and she is moderately disoriented."

The first sensation of alarm began to nag at Harry. "She probably tried to keep her brother warm and has had more exposure," he suggested, covering his dread, which was turning into a cold fist in his guts. What if Natalie Lebbreau were right? She claimed she had had a patient with polio, and these symptoms, the aches, fever, muscle stiffness . . .

"I've taken photos of her back for the police records. Ian Parkenson had a look at her earlier. He said that the scars were probably caused by lashings with an old-fashioned electric cord. So many are. Electric cords are easy to come by."

"I see," said Harry. "Why did you call Dr. Parkenson in on the case? Is there anything wrong with the way I've handled it?"

"Dr. Justin sent him over. He said that he was checking up on virus admits in pediatric cases. I understand that was your idea, Dr. Smith," she went on. "But as you see, neither of these children have serious bronchial inflammation."

Justin is checking on me, Harry realized. What for? Was Justin just gathering figures for his blessed charts, or was this more sinister? He told himself to stop it, to put his mind on his patient. Aloud, he said, "He must be watching pediatric admits pretty carefully, then."

"Oh, yes," said the intern. Then she giggled.

Harry scowled at her. "What was your name again, Doctor?"

"Gloria Powell," she said, straightening her name badge over one unrealistically firm breast. She pointed. "See? Powell."

"Thanks," he said dryly. "I want to see the boy first and then the girl. Get Parkenson's report for me, will you?"

"Certainly, Dr. Smith." All business, Gloria Powell led the way to the pediatric units.

*　*　*

Brian lay on his side, restless. He had reached that stage of fatigue when normal sleep is impossible. As Harry stepped through the door, Brian succeeded in twitching his blanket off the bed. He gave a low whine and wriggled onto his side.

"Hello, Brian," Harry began, forcing himself to smile.

"Go 'way." He squinted up at Harry. "I don't like you."

Harry bent to pick up the blanket, noticing that Gloria had leaned over him, obviously too near. He stepped back as he stood up, knocking her off balance. "Here, Brian. You'll want this later on." He held out the blanket.

The boy took it, wadded it and held it.

"Look," Harry began again, "so long as I'm here, why not let me check you over?"

" 'Nother doctor already did."

"Yes, I know," Harry said, becoming impatient. "But I am *your* doctor and I would like to examine you. It won't take long, Brian."

"Where's Stephie? They said I could see her." The boy twisted in his sheet, then sat up. "She said we'd be okay, just us together. We'd

be fine. What have you done with her?" His face turned red as he
started to cry.

Gloria Powell looked disgusted and started to tap on her chart
board.

Harry had to admit that the puckered, scarlet face buttoned with a
runny nose was not very appealing. He also knew he was clumsy
with children. Reluctantly he sat on the side of the bed and put his
arm around the wailing Brian.

"It's okay, Brian. Really. Don't worry about your sister. I saw her
earlier and she was just as anxious about you as you are about her."
He remembered he had shown her how to use the phone screen and
wondered why she hadn't. "She probably thinks you're sleeping now
and doesn't want to wake you up. And she's right, you know. If you
have some sleep you'll feel much better. I can give you some hot
chocolate that will help you sleep. You'll feel better, and the sooner
you feel better, the sooner you can go home . . ." He stopped.
Abandoned children did not go home. "The sooner you can leave
here," he amended.

"I want Stephie!" Brian yelled.

"Doctor, really." Gloria shook her head impatiently, her pretty
mouth set in a disapproving line.

"Why hasn't this child been sedated?" Harry demanded, feeling
the tension in Brian's slender shoulder. "In this condition he could
develop complications from simple lack of sleep."

Gloria was nicely confused, but the confusion did not reach to her
eyes. Whatever she was sent to do, she was doing it. "I didn't think
we gave sedatives to children. I didn't order any for him."

"Well, what's stopping you from doing it now?" And what stopped
Ian Parkenson from doing it when he had examined Brian? "Never
mind. I'll handle it when we leave." He turned his attention back to
the child, whose sobs had become short, jerky sighs. "Come on,
Brian, a few more minutes and then you can sleep. When you wake
up I'll take you to Stephie, myself." He glanced at Gloria and saw
distress imposed on her lovely features.

"What is it?" he asked her sharply.

"Not here, Doctor," she replied, and let herself out of the unit.

*   *   *

Shortly afterward he joined her in the hall. "Will you explain
about this? What is the matter with his sister?"

"Come with me," she said, quite professional once more.

But Harry didn't move. "Not until you tell me why."

She gave him a cool stare. "I am about to show you why, Doctor. If you'll come with me." Without a backward glance she led the way to Stephanie's unit.

"I think it's dreadful about those children," she said severely.

"Yes," Harry nodded, pleasantly surprised to hear her so sympathetic. "It's criminal the way the parents are allowed to abandon them."

Gloria opened startled eyes at him. "I meant that they were allowed to have them."

In Stephanie's unit the girl lay under a breathing-assist console. The machine squatted over her body like a large, profane bird. The gauge registered LIGHT RESPIRATION. The vital signs monitor read NEAR CRITICAL.

"I see," Harry said, fear coming into him. "When did this happen?"

"About an hour ago," Gloria said. She had come no farther into the unit than was absolutely necessary. "One of the orderlies noticed the irregularity on the monitor and rang for an assist. She's pretty serious. She might die."

Harry bit back a retort. "Is it too much to hope that there's a record of what's been done for her and her progress?"

"Oh, yes, here." She traced through the slips on the case board and finally handed him one, retreating to the doorway immediately.

"Thanks." He read, stopping suddenly. "This authorizes transfer."

"Hum? Yes it does." She nodded.

"There's no indication where she's going. Which hospital is taking her, do you know?"

She looked at her copy of the report. "No, there's no mention here." She frowned, then brightened. "They're probably short of beds and don't know which facility they'll be using yet. It'll be filled in later. Check it with administration in the morning."

"What's wrong with keeping her right here? It isn't good to transfer patients in her condition," Harry persisted. "This child should not be moved."

"Dr. Parkenson signed the authorization," she stated, her mouth narrowing.

"I know. I saw the report." It frightened him, but he did not say so. "I'll check this with Ian. He can't have seen her since they brought the assist in. He'll see that she mustn't be moved. He'll change the order."

Gloria Powell stared at him, her bosom upthrust, then she turned and walked away. No intern would do that, but she did.

Harry watched her go, anger growing in him. "Tell Justin. Tell Parkenson. Tell Braemoore. Tell Wexford. I don't give a damn who you tell if it will save this child."

He studied the monitor as his anger cooled. After five minutes he knew that Stephanie was number seventeen.

* * *

The voice on the phone was tired, still husky from sleep. "Yes? Dr. Howland here."

"Dr. Howland, is Dr. Lebbreau available?"

"No," growled the voice.

Harry gritted his teeth and went on. "Can you tell me when you expect her?"

"I don't." The line went dead.

Alone in the visitor's lounge Harry stood, stupidly clinging to the receiver. What could have become of her? Where had she gone? He could put out a hospital alert—and rejected the idea as soon as he thought of it. There was a risk if Justin and his cronies found out. He tried her floor with no success. No one on the eleventh floor had seen her for hours.

On an off chance he tried the cafeteria and was startled to find her there sitting in the far corner, alone. He picked up two cups of coffee and went to her.

"Like another one?" he asked her when he reached her. He made a tentative smile, the offering of a truce.

"Oh. Thank you."

Putting down the cups he said, "Mind if I join you? You look kind of lonely all by yourself." Since there were only three other men in a room designed for two hundred, this could be said of any of them. She gestured to the opposite chair. "Please."

"I've been hoping to run into you. After the other day I owe you an apology."

"Why?" Eyes listless, hands shaking slightly, she looked squarely at him. "You didn't believe me the other day, so it doesn't matter."

"But I believe you now," he said, pulling his chair closer. He leaned forward, speaking quietly, "I have a patient right now, a girl, nine years old, abandoned with her brother. She has polio."

Natalie's face sharpened. "When was she admitted?"

"City Patrol brought her in yesterday. The initial diagnosis for her was exposure."

"Where is she now? Can we run some tests on her? Unofficially?"

Harry sighed, defeated. "No. The labs can't be bothered with sore throats and runny noses. And Parkenson authorized transfer for her. She's on breathing assist and she's being transferred."

Although her voice was no louder, it had taken on intensity. "Do you know where they're sending her? Can we get someone on that end? Do you think we can follow her, at least her records?"

"There was no destination on the authorization card."

Now her faded-green eyes were nerve-bright. "It's going to get worse. It's going to get bad so fast. Dave Lillijanthal got a tetanus. A real one. They can't claim that's a mutant virus."

Harry stared at her. "How old is the patient?"

"An adult. Late twenties. They've got him in a decompression chamber."

"What's going on? Tetanus. Do you know what's happening?"

"Mark knows," she said, not allowing her voice to change.

"Then, why the hell . . ." He made an effort and tried again. "Why don't they tell people, warn them? Why aren't you doing something about it?"

For the first time she looked ashamed. "Because I can't. They'd say I'm an hysterical woman who can't adjust to the loss of her own child. And then they'd fire me because I'm obviously not responsible for myself."

"Come off it," he said annoyed.

"I have it on excellent authority that that is exactly what would happen to me. I know they mean it. And I haven't got the courage to quit."

The room was very quiet. One of the other men left the cafeteria.

"Believe me, they'll do what they say. And that would mean I'd have to stop practicing. I can't do that, not now!" In her outburst she leaned forward. "They're going to need every doctor they can get."

"What's happening, Natalie? What's really going on?"

For an answer she shook her head. "Not here. If we talk much longer we'll be noticed, and then you'll be in trouble, too." She glanced at the clock. "It's one-twenty. Do you have to be on the floor just now?"

"Not now. I'm on call at two-thirty."

She closed her eyes in thought. "Can you leave the hospital for a few minutes? Get away from here so we can talk?"

"Yes," he said uncertainly. "I suppose I can, sure."

"Good. I don't think we should leave together. They'd be sure to notice that." She stared down at her untouched coffee. "That was kind," she said.

*　*　*

The park across from the hospital was darkly secluded and unsafe after dark. The City Patrol ignored it, leaving it to the juvenile gangs and other violent persons who waited there for the unwary or desperate. Harry waited at the entrance, sensing eyes on him, and wishing that Natalie would hurry.

When she joined him a few moments later, Natalie surprised Harry by walking into the park, veering off to the path which bordered the neat artificial lake. She moved quickly until they were out of sight of the hospital and the traffic on the arterial. The night was cool for spring, and the flowers covered the grimy city air with a sweetness that was as elusive as it was delicious.

"I've been thinking," Harry began as they came to the lake.

"You mean, now you aren't sure about the girl, and you think maybe I am a little crackers, is that it? Because I wouldn't talk to you where Justin or Braemoore or Mark might hear about it. Maybe you're right." She hurried toward a bench. "We can talk here, if you still want to."

"You're really frightened, aren't you?"

For a moment Natalie thought she would scream. A stricken look crossed her face before she answered. "Yes, oh, yes. This is going to be bad." She sat down, ducked her head as she fumbled with a scarf.

"How bad?" Harry asked, reserving judgment.

"What they've done . . . God, what they've done." She looked at him. "You won't believe me, but I'll tell you anyway. I have to tell someone."

"Go ahead."

". . . I ran some tests down in Mark's lab before Philip . . . got sick. I was testing out my patients. I thought they had the old diseases, not this unknown virus the computers were finding. It was like a textbook, the case I saw. It was classic. I thought it might be vaccine failure, so I tested the vaccines later. It happens, you know. They do fail sometimes." She stared out at the lake. "The vaccines . . . about one third of them are useless. They've been destroyed in random batches. One third of all vaccines. For everything—diphtheria, tetanus, cancer, all of them." She pushed a stray hair off her brow. "The program started about five years ago, from what I've learned. We're a test area. God knows if there are others. If it works here, they'll try it elsewhere. It's a clandestine government thing. Mark's . . ." She swallowed. "Mark is in charge of it."

"In charge of this? How *can* he be?" Harry wondered if this were her bitterness speaking. Her husband had betrayed her, and she thought of him as betraying everyone. Harry clung to the hope that this was so.

"He thinks it's a great idea. Fair—there's no way to know who gets what, and only one third of the vaccines are nonviable. There's a two-thirds chance that we're fully protected." The sarcasm in her voice gave way to despair. "I can't do anything. Not anything. Christ!"

They were silent for several minutes. "How many have you treated so far?" Harry asked.

"Children? Thirty-seven. Not so many since they transferred my paramedic to County General. They're trying to keep me off the cases now." Gil hadn't been gone long, but she found herself thinking of him in the distant past, like her marriage.

"I've had seventeen cases in three weeks." It was a confession.

In a faraway voice she said, "I wish I knew how many cases there are now. Really."

"Justin would know."

"Justin would lie."

"What if we tell Parkenson? Or Wexford?"

"They know all about it."

Again silence. Even the lake was still.

"Ian told me it's better than battered children, that this is the natural way. It's not as if we're really killing anyone. He said we're being crowded out of existence. And this is *fair*. They all think it's fair."

Harry said nothing as he studied his shoes.

Natalie went on after a moment. "I watched Ian take care of some kids about a month ago. One lost a leg and the other was too far gone—both tibias splintered, a shoulder dislocated. Deep shock. The parents might be fined, I hear. If Ian will testify."

"Then you agree with them?" Harry was incredulous. If she felt this way, why had she told him about the vaccines. What did she want of him.

"I don't agree with it. I think it's immoral, unethical . . ." She stopped, then went on again. "I dread what it's going to do to us. But sometimes I wonder, Harry . . . what are we saving them for?"

CHAPTER 4

Peter Justin was trimming his nails. Anyone who knew him would recognize this as nervousness. He brushed the clippings into the wastechute with a fussy gesture. When he looked up again, a stocky blond man was leaning over his desk.

"I want some information," Harry said. "I want it now and I want it to be correct."

"What about?" Justin asked, playing for time and advantage. He was aware of Harry's anger, for it filled the room like a smell. "Why are you here, Harry?"

"You know why I'm here," he exploded.

Justin made a second attempt at urbanity. "If it's about Dr. Lebbreau . . . or the children we've transferred . . ."

"Can it! How many kids have been through this hospital and what did they die of? The real figures, Justin. And no more unknown virus crap."

Justin sighed and wiped imaginary dust off his desk. "I don't need the printout. In the last two months, three hundred thirty-two with diphtheria, fifty-six with smallpox, twenty-nine with polio, three with tetanus, eighteen with TB, one hundred sixty-nine with meningitis, twenty-two with leukemia. There are a few others; perhaps a dozen with measles. But you must remember we have almost three thousand beds here, Harry. This amount isn't significant . . ."

"In total or fatalities?" Harry demanded, his brows drawn down over his eyes.

"Fatalities. The figures for adults aren't that high—I think the total is somewhere around four hundred in all." He looked pleadingly at Harry. "Something had to be done. You know what conditions are. There was no other way, Harry."

"Sweet Jesus, that's over a thousand. This hospital alone, over one thousand people dead."

"County General is running slightly higher. Inner City is lower on diphtheria. But they're higher on violent crimes, so it's about the same."

"They're higher on abuse, too," Harry snapped. He had done his internship there and had seen the way the young, the old and the weak were treated. His first patient had been a five-year-old with the burn from a steam iron on his back. There had been others after that, women assaulted, old men beaten, children abused. He came to hate the cruel invention of the people there.

Peter Justin looked away uneasily. "It isn't going well. There are too many. It's too early for so many. The projected curves aren't this steep. It's not what we expected. I think the next time they try this, they'd better cut down the percentage to one fourth rather than a third." He adjusted his handsome face carefully. "But we mustn't be too concerned."

"Why?" Harry demanded, horrified. "It's not according to the projected curves? Panic isn't allowed for? How shocking!" He gave a sardonic bark that was intended as a laugh. Justin shifted uncomfortably in his chair. "All figured out in advance, is it, Peter? Like the Tolerable Losses tables at the Pentagon? So many hundred thousand per million population?" He rounded on Justin, his clenched hands shaking. "I hope you bloody fools get your asses burned for this."

Justin favored him with the travesty of a smile. "Of course we anticipated certain variables. The figures are high, yes, but it *is* like a war, don't you see? Only an irresponsible leader would not allow for certain losses. Battles are won that way, and we are fighting a terrible battle. We must do something or the weight of people will pull us all down."

"You don't know what you've started, do you? You haven't been down on the floors in a long time, Peter. You don't know what it's like down there. Howland doesn't know, either. He's too busy with his microscopes and screwing to know. I just hope you live long enough to see what your damn charts have done!" He slammed out the door.

He was heading for the central admissions desk on the first floor.

* * *

The pale-haired woman at the desk balked at his order. "But Doctor, I can't give out that information without authorization from one of the administrators. Those are regulations. You know what that means."

"The regulations have just been changed." He leaned over her partition. "I want the admit records for the last twenty-four hours. Especially pediatrics. Young kids with mutant or unknown virus diseases and those suffering from exposure. And I want this information now."

"Doctor Smith," she said reasonably, "you haven't got the required signatures of authorization . . ."

"This is the last time I repeat." His smile was singularly unpleasant. "Then I am coming into your office. I will take your records, every one. Then I will go down to the second basement to the storage computer with a large magnet in my case. May I have those records, please?"

The woman was visibly frightened as she went into her office. When she came back with the printout sheets she shoved them at Harry. "Here. Take them."

"Thank you."

"I'll lose my job if Dr. Justin ever finds out," she accused him.

Harry gave her a fierce wink. "No way, lady. You're going to be here a long time. Maybe till you die."

With this assurance he went down the hall.

* * *

"Dr. Lebbreau, paging Dr. Lebbreau. Report to floor six, please. Dr. Lebbreau to floor six."

Natalie turned as she heard the call. Her patient smiled. "A call for you, Nat." She was into middle age, divorced, and had been in the hospital since the holidays, recovering from three deep knife wounds, the result of an attack by a teen-age gang. She knew that the prognosis was good and that this was largely due to Natalie's persistent determination to save her. Her paralysis would be partial instead of total, as first feared.

The page was repeated.

"It might be important. You'd better go, Nat," Mrs. Dwyer said kindly.

"Yes," she said reluctantly, fearing that Justin had found out she had talked to Harry Smith. "I'd better go. If you don't mind, I'll send Carol Mendosa in to finish up. She's on the floor now and you've had her before."

"No rush, Nat. I'll be here yet awhile."

* * *

By the time she stepped from the elevator on floor six, Natalie had developed a protective scowl. She tried to build her defenses, in case she had to deal with Justin or Wexford or even Mark. There was too much at stake—she knew she had to remain calm.

"Good. I'm glad you were fast." It was Harry who stepped up to her. He thought she looked better, stronger, not as frightened as before.

Already some of the worry had faded from her face. This was not the confrontation she had anticipated. When she spoke there was vibrancy in her words. "What is it? What do we have to do? How much time do we have?"

He hesitated, then took her arms as they started down the hall. "I've been talking to Justin and I've got some figures out of him. You were right. He admits that much."

"Justin?" Her fine, straight brows drew together once more. "You've seen Justin?" Why had they not been fired?

"Yes, I've seen him." He guided her into an empty sunroom, pushing the door closed behind them and locking it. "It's much worse than you guessed, and that was bad enough. There have been roughly eleven hundred fatalities in the last two months at this hospital alone. County General is running higher, Inner City a bit lower."

She was badly shocked. "Eleven hundred." She sat slowly, blindly. "Eleven hundred. I thought it wasn't much above five hundred. In just two months?"

"Natalie, it's getting started. That damned crew of idiots has really made a mare's nest this time." He did not wait for her to speak. "We've got to make some changes, and quickly. There's too big a risk, no matter what Peter Justin's Tolerable Losses allow. All the computers have to be reprogramed to recognize 'extinct' diseases. That's where a lot of the trouble is coming from, the diagnosis end. The computers don't recognize diphtheria and smallpox and common cancer because they were wiped out years ago, so they come up as unknown virus and our hands are tied. Damn it, some of these patients are in the wards, and God only knows how many others on the wards are vulnerable. We've got to get doctors who are willing to take on the fight. We need help. We need a lot of help." His eyes were bleak as he thought of what they were up against.

"Yes," she nodded, breathing more quickly. "We'll need help. Now."

"Is there anyone else on floor eleven with you?"

She thought briefly, ignoring the tap on the door. "Dave Lillijanthal. He'd be willing, I think, if he understood. Gil, my old paramedic, might if he were still here. He was transferred, I don't know where. Sometimes I think he caught something . . ." She pushed the thought away. "I think maybe we can get Stan Kooznetz up on eight; he's already working with contagious diseases. He'd be a lot of help. Even though he's young he's a good doctor. So is Lisa Skye. She's in the stroke unit on nine. She hasn't got a lot of stamina, though. Carol Mendosa. She's on eleven, too. She's tough and she doesn't let go."

Harry heard these names and felt better. "I can get Patman and Divanello in pediatrics here on six. If we work hard we might be ready when this thing really strikes. It's about to break wide open."

She sat up suddenly. "What about *us?* We might not be immune ourselves."

Harry whistled softly. "Good lady. I hadn't thought of that. But you're right. Of course. We'll have to reinoculate. It won't be good if we all start coming down with bugs. I wish we could get someone out of the labs to take care of that angle."

"We have to get a pathologist. We'll need someone to identify any mutant or unknown strain that really does crop up," she said, the task becoming more overwhelming each time she thought about it.

"Mutant strains. I hope we won't get them. There's no way we can fight a new variety, not now."

"But there's a good chance we'll have to." She slid further into the chair. "We'll have to have a lab somewhere."

"And if not, we'll take our chances along with everyone else."

"*More* than everyone else," she said. "We'll be working closer to the diseases. We'll have greater exposure." She looked at him, thinking that if there was enough time, if they were far enough ahead of the real outbreak, they might—just might—scrape through. Please don't let the diseases mutate, she thought. If there was a mutation, then they would lose their fight. But it was a possibility she knew she had to face. "How long do you think it will be before new diseases appear? It might be a good idea to do some random tests as the patients come in, just in case."

He narrowed his eyes at the window. "If we can get the administration to put a quarantine into effect, and have the City Patrol enforce it, we might be able to keep the disease in pockets. And we can start up a regular house-call system. Otherwise, there isn't enough bed space for what we'll be handling."

"Oh God, beds."

"One more factor for Justin's charts," Harry said. "We'll have to have a meeting with the administration as soon as our plans are fixed. They've got to make a move soon, and we'll have to convince them. And the government can go screw itself."

Suddenly Natalie turned to him, her body tense and her face anxious. "But, Harry, what if the administration won't help us? What if they kick us out?"

"They can't afford to do that. But they might not accept our plan," he conceded.

"Harry, they could turn us out."

He said, "Of course not. They need us too much. They wouldn't dare." How much he wished he could believe that.

* * *

There was no one at the nurses' station as Natalie filed her midshift report. She felt tired and there was a dull ache in her middle. She had told herself she could not afford an ulcer, and did her best to shut out the gnawing sensation. How much she wanted to forget, to go back to a time when there were no dead children and no trouble. She rubbed her eyes, forcing her attention to the report.

"Natalie?" said the soft voice behind her.

She turned and the little color she had drained from her face. "Mark," she said.

"You've been busy," he said, showing her a spectacular smile. "You're in with Harry Smith, aren't you? That takes real guts. I understand you are all in trouble with the administration."

"Not so far, not that I know of," she said cautiously, not trusting him. She put down her report and waited.

"It's going to happen," he told her. "You're interfering, and we can't afford that. Still, you're quite a girl, aren't you? You know this is a government trial project, and you're willing to buck it. I admire that." He came a few steps closer, but she moved away.

"What's this all about? Are you trying to intimidate me?"

"You're going to get fired, Natalie. I thought I should warn you. We had a meeting up on sixteen tonight and Wexford handed down his sentence. You'll be fired, and you will not be rehired in any hospital in this state. That's the decision."

She leaned against the wall. So it was happening. "Stupid, stupid bastards," she said.

"Not so stupid as you think," Mark said, keeping his distance. "You're a smart girl, Natalie. You know what this means: you're blacklisted. And you don't really want that, do you? You're not that kind of doctor, Natalie. You're not willing to give up your practice for this kind of principle. I know you. Medicine is the most important thing in your life."

"You're blackmailing me."

"You're not going to let this happen to you," he persisted, a confident smile in his eyes. "And you know that the only way you can stay on here is to go along with the policy and do your best for the few victims we see."

She turned on him. "Few? Eleven hundred is a few? That's how many are dead, Mark, if you care. What kind of figures does it take to make you realize what's happening?" She felt herself shaking and willed it to stop. "You're crazy. You're all really crazy."

For a moment Mark said nothing, then, "You want to survive this thing? Well, *do* you?"

"Of course I do," she spat.

He smiled with hooded eyes. "There's only one way to be sure, and that's if I take care of your vaccinations. I'll check them out first. Then you'll know you're safe, and you'll be able to treat every patient without fear. Let me tell them upstairs that you're giving up this holy war of yours, that you've seen reason, and you won't have anything to worry about. You'll be safe."

She told herself that she was not hearing him correctly. "You said the system was fair, no one knows who gets what. And you call this fair? Do you? How many other people have you helped this way? How fair is it really, Mark? Tell me."

Mark's fists clumped at his sides. "Okay, Natalie, I've tried to be reasonable. But you aren't willing to go along with me. You're a ruddy fool. But I warn you, stay out of it, get away from Harry Smith, or as of tomorrow you are out. And there's no coming back."

She took the full force of his threat and did not falter. "You aren't even human," she flung at him. "Fire me, if that'll make you feel better. I don't want to deal with you again."

"This is your last chance."

"Liar," she said.

He lifted up his hand to strike. She faced him. "Go ahead."

He spun on his heel and was gone.

Half an hour later, when her tears were spent and she was herself again, she called Harry. "We have to work fast. We have to be ready now."

"Why?" he asked, alarmed. So she told him about Mark.

* * *

It was afternoon when they met again, outside the emergency room on the first floor. Harry had deep lines in his face and the subtle gray wash of fatigue colored him.

"You look awful," Natalie said.

"I might say the same of you," he rejoined caustically. Then he relented. "Sorry. I've been up about thirty-four hours now, and it shows. What have you got?"

"I talked with some people. Carol Mendosa is with us. Lisa Skye wants to but isn't sure she can. Dave Lillijanthal will do everything possible, including storming the higher-ups, if necessary. He has some pull with the administration, and he'll use it if we give him the word." She pulled some notes from her pocket. "Stan Kooznetz is a yes with reservations. He thinks we're overreacting. I couldn't get near the labs, so there's no help for a pathologist. We'll have to find someone later I guess . . ."

"Don't worry about it now. I talked to Patman," he said, glancing over his shoulder at the stretcher being pulled from an ambulance. Burns were Latham's specialty. He turned back to Natalie. "He can't do it. He's got that bad ulcer, and knows he couldn't take the strain. He'd be a liability. But he'll scrounge for us, if we need stuff. He's good at that."

"And Divanello? Is she willing?"

"She is," Harry said. "She's over forty, and she's got a little heart trouble. She'll make sure she's got the stuff to take care of it, so we won't have to deal with it. She's determined to make sure we wipe out this problem. She's seen a lot of kids die recently, too."

"Why didn't she do anything?" Natalie asked, surprised that Amanda Divanello would let such illnesses go by unnoticed.

"Because she went to Justin and he told her that the labs were checking out new viruses. He said he wanted to see her reports on everything that bothered her because that would help him get his material organized for a full report."

"Oh, great." Natalie leaned on the wall and pinched the bridge of her nose. "I wonder how many others got that treatment? It never gets easy, does it?" she asked. "What a run-around."

"Maybe there's more of us than we thought. But I want to find out who they are: we can use their help."

The paging system broke out stridently calling for Dr. Hangstrom and Dr. Lescu. Natalie felt the apprehension she always did when psychiatric reinforcements were called in. "I wish Radick Lescu were with us. I have the feeling we could use him."

"You mean to keep the kinks out of the system?" He smiled, but he knew she was right. Already he felt the strain telling on him. It would get worse.

She sensed his thoughts. "We're all going to be under a lot of stress."

"We'll make it," he said with a confidence he had no faith in. "We have to."

She nodded. There was trouble close to them, closing in. "I only hope we get the chance," she said. There was a wistful note in her voice which Harry tried to ignore.

* * *

The notice had been up for over an hour when Harry saw it at noon the next day:

The following doctors are relieved of service in this hospital. Dismissal for cause. Those named below are requested to leave these premises before midnight, this date 4–13–91.

Alexes Castor, floor 8
  infectious diseases
Amanda Divanello, floor 15
  obstetrics/pediatric surgery
Kirsten Grant, floor 9
  orthopedics
Dominic Hertzog, floor 13
  radiology
Stanley Kooznetz, floor 6
  general medicine
Natalie Lebbreau, floor 11
  general medicine
Radick Lescu, floor 4
  psychiatry
David Hans Lillijanthal, floor 14
  anesthesiology

Edward Eugene Lincoln, floor 1
  emergency room
Carol Mendosa, floor 11
  general medicine
Roger Nicholas, floor 5
  intensive care
Maria Pantopolos, floor 10
  exotic diseases
Eric Patman, floor 7
  immunology
Lisa Skye, floor 12
  surgery
Emile Harrison Smith, floor 6
  general medicine
James Varnay, floor 1
  emergency room

Howard T. Webbster, floor 2
  outpatient service

Under the authorization stamp were the scrawled signatures of Peter Justin and Miles Wexford. The administration had made a clean sweep of the dissident doctors. They were out.

*   *   *

"What kind of nonsense is this?" Harry demanded, slapping a torn copy of the dismissal notice on Jim Braemoore's desk. His face was flushed as he spoke, and there was taut anger in his voice.

"Don't blame me," the other said, making a dismissal with his large, soft hands. "Told you what would happen if you kept on, Harry. Didn't want it to happen, myself, but there wasn't a lot I could do when you insisted on this course. Ruined yourself, m'boy. Thought for a while there you might see sense, but obviously not. Pity."

"What are you talking about: sense? I want to see Wexford!" Harry picked up the notice and stormed toward the door.

"He doesn't want to see you, Harry. Not that this is what he wanted, either. He tried to smooth things over, make allowances for you, for all of you, but you're beyond that now." Jim smiled sympathetically. "Can't say I wouldn't have done the same thing myself, years ago. I admire your stand, Harry. Good to know there're doctors like you and the others left. It's going to be hard to get along without you. But there's no choice, is there? You're a rare breed. Thought you'd vanished. But we can't afford you, you see. You can't stay on."

Harry looked puzzled, still breathing hard. "Jim, don't you know what they're doing? A couple of months, there's going to be hell to pay. Doesn't that bother you at all?"

"Thinning down the herd a bit, that's all. Culling the weak ones. We'll have a moderate epidemic, relieve the pressure a bit, give the government an idea of what they can expect elsewhere. We need this, Harry. Hate to say it, but it's true. Got to be done sooner or later. You see that, don't you?"

With all the control at his command, Harry began, as if to a foolish child, "Jim, one third of all vaccines are useless. One third. They have been for about five years now. This isn't just a bad run of flu, Jim, this is major. We aren't talking about just one disease—not just a smallpox epidemic or a cholera epidemic or a meningitis epidemic. This is a pandemic, Jim. It has something for everyone. For God's sake, call whoever is in charge of this before it's too late."

"There's enough vaccines stockpiled," Jim Braemoore said reassuringly. "We can stop it if it gets out of hand. It won't be like a pandemic at all. You're letting yourself be railroaded, if that's what you're afraid of."

"Damn right I'm afraid. Think, Jim . . ."

"Harry, this is a well-controlled experiment. You'll see. It can't turn out the way you think. Precautions have been taken. It's quite safe."

"Bullshit!"

Jim spread out his hand to Harry. "Tell you what: you get your kit and go along home. I'll have a word with Wexford in the morning. You'll be back on the job in no time, everything straightened out. That's the ticket."

"There isn't time . . ."

Jim reached over and buzzed his door opener. "Glad you came to see me, Harry. Knew we could sort things out if you did. Just wait until the worst blows over. Wexford'll take you back. Shouldn't be more than two, three months. Make it the end of summer. Don't let this bother you. It isn't like you. You're a sensible man. You use those months for a vacation."

"Vacation? With all this . . ."

"See, there you go again. Can't do that, Harry. Take a rest, let yourself unwind." Pointing to the door, he said, "Glad we had this chat. Knew you'd understand once conditions were explained to you. Not natural you wouldn't."

"But, Jim, you don't realize . . ." Harry was desperate now. His hands closed on the edge of Braemoore's desk, his knuckles white.

"Hate to kick you out, Harry, but there's a meeting in administration. Must run." He was out the side door before Harry had a chance to speak. He stood in the empty door and felt his courage fail.

* * *

"What do we do now?" Natalie asked half an hour later as she sat in the desolation of her tiny office.

"We call for help," Harry said, his face grim.

Stan Kooznetz turned from the window, worry making his long face even longer. "Where do we get help, Harry? We can't very well ask Congress."

Harry shook his head, looking from Stan to Natalie to Eric to Lisa. There were so few of them, and they were out in the cold.

"I called Inner City," Natalie said. "They fired eight doctors over there. They wouldn't say who." She was very tired, and her feet hurt. "I could use ten hours' sleep," she remarked to no one in particular.

"Not Congress," Harry said suddenly. "We call West Coast Control in L.A. They're in control of the medical system from here to Denver. They'll have to do something about this."

Lisa Skye laughed cynically. "What makes you think so, Harry?"

"Look" he went on as he saw the doubt in the other faces. "If one or two of us said something, they wouldn't pay any attention. But damn it, there are seventeen names on that list. And eight over at Inner City. Has anybody checked Strickland or County General?"

"They aren't giving out that information," Natalie said in a parody of the secretary's voice.

"Then you can bet some of them are fired, too. That means we have real ammunition. Amanda is a recognized expert in pediatrics. That gives us clout. We can talk to Radick and ask him to add his evaluation in an official complaint. Once L.A. starts investigating, it's all over. They'll have to put a stop to this thing."

Does he really believe that, Natalie asked herself as she watched Harry. She knew that they would not be allowed to contact anyone. If the situation was this far out of hand, there would be no chance to stop it now. "I don't like to bring up unpleasant things, but we've been ordered to house arrest as of an hour ago," she reminded him. "Do you imagine we'll be allowed to contact L.A.?"

"She's right," Lisa said. "We won't get the chance."

"Then we'll make the chance. What's the matter with you people?" he demanded. His face was reddening and he could feel his pulse race. "You're giving up, is that it?"

"Retreating," Lisa amended. "We don't have a lot of choice, anyway. We might as well give up."

"And where would we go, assuming they let us out of our apartments?" Stan paced the floor. "We aren't going to be allowed anywhere near a hospital, and we've got to operate from somewhere. But you know what the housing situation is like. There isn't a snowball's chance in hell that we could find a place big enough and private enough . . ."

Suddenly Natalie looked up. "The Van Dreyter house!" she said, her face brightening. "We can take over the Van Dreyter house."

"Oh, sure," Stan agreed caustically. "They'll hand over the biggest landmark in the city without a murmur."

"You're tilting at windmills," Lisa agreed.

"Let her talk," Harry said sharply. He sensed Natalie's change of mind, and her awakening strength.

She set her jaw and went on. "In a couple of weeks it won't matter what the city says. The house is sitting there, all thirty-six rooms of it. It's furnished, it's got all the utilities. We can take it over and use it like one of those old-fashioned co-ops. We could live there and work there. The house is central. Everyone knows about it. Word of mouth would do the rest."

Lisa started to laugh, then sobered. "Okay. Call me Sancho. What makes you think it'll work?"

Natalie gathered up the remainder of her things. "Because it *has* to."

*   *   *

Harry felt the bus lurch as it went over the potholes. He tightened his grip on Natalie's shoulder.

"You sure you don't mind?" Natalie asked for the sixteenth time. "I could ask Carol if she'd mind if I stayed with her."

"Jack Mendosa would love that, wouldn't he?" Harry said cordially. "And with all that room they have: three rooms and a closet. A great bargain. One more should fit in somewhere. Maybe you could sleep in the bathtub."

"All right," she muttered. "But this will be awkward." She stared past him out the window. Behind them the hospital was almost lost to sight, its seventeen white stories grimy with the foul air.

"Only until we move into the Van Dreyter house."

She touched her valise. "How much room do you have?"

He grinned. "I'm lucky. I'm in one of the old apartment blocks. I've got four rooms, a kitchen and a bath. There's lots of space. My brother and his wife used to share it with me, but they've moved to Phoenix, and the Housing Authority hasn't evicted me yet. The rooms are good-sized, with nine-foot ceilings. You'll like it, Natalie. You can have all the privacy you want."

"House arrest," she said bitterly. "On top of everything else."

"It won't last."

The bus shuddered as it paused. The doors creaked open as passengers jostled each other and a few struggled out onto the pavement.

"One more stop," Harry promised her. "We get off at the next one."

A woman across the way began to cough, a thin, persistent noise that came through the susurrus of conversation.

"God, Harry," Natalie said as the coughing grew worse. "There's so little time."

CHAPTER 5

A mechanical voice informed Harry that his call could not be completed as dialed and advised him to try again when the lines were open. He slammed the receiver back into the cradle, swearing.

"No luck?" Natalie asked, knowing the answer.

"I can't get through," he said, coming back into the living room. The frustration he felt showed on his face. "I'll try to get Denning again. He should be willing to listen if I can reach him." Harry did not entirely trust Hall Denning, knowing that newsmen were a chancy lot, but he could think of no other possibilities.

"They won't let you. We're not going to talk to anyone until it's too late." She sat down, her head in her hands. "Besides, Denning is local. We need national attention on this. We might not be the only test area, you know. There might be others."

Harry paused before sinking into the old chair opposite her. "Yes." He studied the floor, a complicated parquetry of pine and oak that was once the pride of its first owners. Now some of the wood was gray with wear, some of the pieces missing altogether, the pattern patched with linoleum or old carpet.

"You tried to call the others?" she said when the silence between them had lengthened.

He nodded. "I can't get through. They need official authorization. I haven't got it."

"Do you think we could sneak out?"

"There're guards out there, remember?" he snapped, then relented. "I don't know, Natalie. Maybe we could. But where would we go?" He wished she had an answer for that, but knew that she was as isolated as he.

"Did you hear the news this morning?" Natalie asked, changing the subject. Her hands were tightly laced together in her lap, and the tension increased as she waited for an answer.

"No."

"They reported an outbreak of flu—a new variety, they said. They advised listeners to see their doctors if they became ill, and gave the usual warnings about avoiding public contact. You know the routine."

"Yes."

She stared out the window into the warm spring day where a gentle wind slid between the crowded buildings and tickled the river into ripples. Summer would be hot this year, and that would make it worse.

"What do you think about Senator Hammond? She might force the issue for us." Harry said this hopefully.

"I tried to call her local office and they wouldn't connect me. Besides, she's in Washington right now. Congress is in session. I doubt we'll see her back on this coast for a couple of months yet." Natalie felt the deep fatigue of helplessness settle over her. For the last three days she had told herself that surely the hospital administration would call off the experiment by now, that they would realize what they had done and would attempt to reverse the pandemic. But she knew that this had not happened when she heard the news on the radio. By the time anyone could be convinced to help, it would be too late. It was too late now.

Harry rose from his chair, his hands swinging together and meeting in a blow. If he felt pain from this, he did not notice it. "We're overlooking something. There's got to be a way. I can't simply sit here while the whole city dies."

"And you think it's easy for me?" Natalie demanded, stung.

"Well, you sure haven't come up with any working alternative." Quite suddenly he turned into the hall again and picked up the phone, dialing angrily. "Yes," he said in a moment, "this is Dr. Smith. I would like to speak with Robert Craley . . ." He paused, and his expression grew thunderous. "No, no authorization." In the next instant he had slammed the phone down. "No help from the Justice Department, either." He walked slowly back into the living room, turning to Natalie again. "I'm sorry I snapped at you."

"I know," she said, turning away. She studied the pattern of light and shadow on the wall behind her. "Even if we could get them to listen, no one would believe us. The hospital would offer some glib explanation and point out that we've been dismissed, making sure that they dropped a hint that we were guilty of something awful, and that would destroy what little credibility we have."

"People aren't that dumb," Harry insisted, pacing the room. "If we could reach them, we can make them believe us."

"The way you believed me when I first told you about it?" She waited while he thought this over. "Are you going to hand out broadsides in Stockton? Well? How are you going to get the attention you need, Harry?" Her own sarcasm hurt her and she got up, saying, "I can't take much more of this, Harry. We've got to do something. You're right about that."

"I went to school with Bob Craley . . . he might listen to me," Harry said. "His office won't connect me, but maybe I could call him at home."

Natalie was about to object, then only sighed and left the room.

* * *

This time the news was calming: the city hospitals were taking care of all the flu patients in special wards, and for the time being were keeping them in total quarantine. The hospital administrators felt that this way the risk was minimized.

Harry watched the smooth face of the announcer as it flickered on the screen. "No one can visit," he said, disgusted. "For their own protection, of course."

Natalie pulled her hands together. "It won't be much longer. They're going to have to admit there is more than a flu epidemic going on."

"But what good will that do? You've read the listener-response reports: almost everyone in the city thinks that the hospitals are doing a great job in keeping the public safe. They're all certain that the emergency will soon be over. You know that's not true, and so do I, but we're nothing compared to the rest of them out there. Crap." He flung himself across the room. "Deutch is on duty outside. I asked him if I could go out for some food. I said we were running low."

"And?" Natalie asked, knowing what had happened.

"He asked for a list and told me he'd pick up what we need tomorrow."

"I said I wanted to get some underwear. Same answer." She thought for a moment. "Not that we could do much good even if we could get out. They're not going to let us see the others or treat anyone. And if we open our mouths they'll toss us in jail."

Harry kicked at the floor, dislodging another worn parquet square. He bent over and shoved the wood back into place. "Never mind," he said as he straightened up, and it was hard to tell if he meant the damage to the floor or the ruin that was waiting with the plague. "What's for lunch?"

"Eggs," she said. "Not real ones. Just the standard substitutes. There aren't any real ones available until the first of the month. I signed up for a dozen. Deutch put my name in."

Harry thought fleetingly of that. It was like everything else. There was not enough to go around. There was never enough. Not enough real food, not enough space, not enough time, not enough contact, not enough of life. His gloom descended once more.

Over lunch their thoughts turned, and Natalie looked away from her sulphur-colored omelet toward the grimy windows. "I miss the smell of spring. I used to take Philip out to the Great Belt Park, and this time of year it could be lovely." Sunshine was reflecting off the white plastic counters and metal sink, making the small room shine.

"The smell is different this year."

They fell silent and tried to eat the omelets.

After a while he began to hum, thinking of the bright flowers he missed, then filling in the words familiar to him since childhood:

> Ring around the rosie
> Pocket full of posie
> Ashes, ashes, all fall down.

"Shut up!" she yelled at him.

"Humh? What for?"

"Don't you know what that is?"

"What's wrong with a nursery rhyme?" He thought perhaps it reminded her too much of her dead son. "I didn't mean to hurt you. I should have remembered." He rose and came around behind her.

She pushed his hand away from her shoulder. "It's the plague rhyme. It's about the Black Death."

Her voice was flat, all anger gone from it. "I'm sorry *I* snapped at *you*." She was saying that too often, but it was true: she said wounding, hurtful things to him to save herself from her own vulnerability.

Harry made an effort to change the subject once more. "I wonder if they'll call us back?"

If there were anyone to call them back. He had heard that the administration at the hospital had been laying off staff members. Harry had heard the names and knew that they were getting rid of the fighters, the mavericks who could not be trusted to go along with this carefully planned disaster.

But Natalie was talking. "It's like being on a sinking ship with hundreds of other people and two leaky lifeboats, isn't it? The odds aren't good. Do you think we'll make it?"

"Don't talk that way." He went to pull the blinds down.

"Knowing people . . ." she said as if she had not heard him, ". . . they'll trample each other to death or hack the lifeboats to pieces."

"Natalie, stop it." He was about to reach for her when there was a tap at the window. His flat was four floors aboveground and the window was difficult to reach. The tap was repeated.

Cautiously he looked out.

"What is it?" Natalie asked from the table, almost afraid to be interested.

"I don't know. I thought I heard—there it is again." He looked more carefully, edging the window open.

Twelve feet beyond the window on the narrow building maintenance landing, perched a ten-year-old girl. One hand was filled with gravel, the other hand had two fingers stuck into her nose. "You the doctor?" she whispered.

"Both of us," Harry answered, surprise growing slowly in him.

"Can you come quick? Just two floors down. My sister is sick."

Harry frowned. "What about your mother? Can't she get a doctor for you?"

"They left," the girl said simply. "Mom and Pop both. The hospital doesn't answer when I call—the line is busy all the time. I tried earlier, and it didn't work."

"Do your mother and father work?" asked Natalie, who had joined Harry at the window.

"Nope. Left. For good. Ces'lie's real sick. Can you come?" She thought something over. "You can't go out the door. Cops are watching it. I tried there first. But if you crawl along the ledge there . . ." She pointed to the narrow ledge under the window, which would provide little more than a handsbreadth to stand on.

"I don't think . . ." Harry began.

"*I* can," Natalie interrupted. "You'd never make it, Harry. Not along that. Get my bag for me, will you?"

He would have protested but the girl put in, "Yeah, she's right. You're too big."

As Harry raised startled eyebrows, Natalie giggled and said, "There, you see? That settles that."

He looked down at her in exasperation. He said, "Okay. I'll get the bag. But be careful."

"I will," she promised.

When he came back from the bedroom she had buttoned on her white hospital oversmock that she had been wearing the first time he saw her. The slacks she wore were old, but the knee patches did not bother her. She smiled when she saw him. "While I'm gone you're going to have to do something to make Deutch think we're both in here. Unless this is very serious, I'll be back within the hour. If the child is really sick, I'll find a way to get her over to Lisa Skye. She lives over that big day-care center and should be able to get this child to the hospital."

"Yes," he said to her, and it meant a reaffirmation to both of them.

"Now, wait until I get out the window." She climbed onto the ledge. "I'll have to secure my foothold before you give me the bag." She lowered herself gingerly.

Suddenly he was filled with concern for her. "You don't have to go," he told her abruptly.

Her washed-out green eyes softened. "Someone has to," she said. And then she was inching along the ledge toward the girl who crouched, waiting for her.

Harry sat at the table for some time afterward, while his lunch grew warm and his coffee got cold. They had been sought out, he realized, and if one child could come to them, so would others. He had not thought of that before, that there would be people who would want them, need them enough to come to them.

He spread out his hands, a silent whistle escaping between his teeth. There was a way, he thought, if the people on the outside were willing to help. If that child could reach them, she could reach the others, without their guards knowing. There was still a chance. He rose from the table, and after reluctantly washing the remains of his lunch down the sink, he went for a pad of paper. Now he had work to do.

* * *

"How'd it go?" Harry said anxiously as he helped Natalie climb in the window. "You were gone a long time. I was worried."

"Tell you in a minute," she said as she put her feet on the floor and took a deep, relieved breath. "Let me sit a minute."

He pulled out a chair for her, suddenly enjoying this old-fashioned courtesy. "Coffee?" he asked when she was seated. "I made some fresh a little while ago."

"Please." She waited while he handed her a mug, then she said, "Let me tell you about the kids. First off, they don't appear to be seriously ill. I'd say the main trouble is malnutrition. Not very serious yet, but enough to make them very vulnerable to infections. That has me worried. I took some cultures," she gestured to her pockets. "Not that I can find out much without a lab. I've got an old microscope with me, but without the proper facilities I'm kind of stuck."

"We'll work out something," Harry assured her.

"I hope so. Well, there are other kids in that building who've been deserted. Alison told me about them."

"Alison?"

"The kid who came to the window. Her name is Alison Procter. She's a very resourceful girl, Harry. I wish there were a way we could use her."

"There *is* a way," Harry said, smiling. He poured himself another cup of coffee and beckoned. "Come on. I'll show you."

Frowning, Natalie rose and followed him into the living room. "What's that?" she asked when she saw the stacks of paper spread about the floor.

"It's my plan. Look," he said, pulling her toward the old couch. "See? This is a map of the area."

"Yes."

"The red marks are hospitals. The blue marks are where the various doctors like us live. The Van Dreyter house is here. That kid Alison?" Natalie nodded. "She can't be the only one looking for a doctor. There's a chance we can use her and some of her friends to reach the others. If we can do that, then it doesn't matter if there are guards on the doors."

Natalie narrowed her eyes. "It might work."

"Might? Hell, it's bound to work. Look, City Patrol can't keep us locked up like this much longer. The disease outbreaks are going to start getting to them pretty soon. When that happens, we've got to be organized. We've got to be ready to set ourselves up in the Van Dreyter house at the first opportunity. And in the meantime, Alison can start bringing people to us. She must know who's sick, who needs a doctor."

"She did mention some other kids in other buildings," Natalie conceded.

"Then we aren't trapped, after all. So long as we keep the communications open with the others, we'll be ready just as soon as we have to be. Don't you see, Nat? We don't have to stand by and watch. We can do something."

"What about labs? We're going to need lab space, Harry."

"There are a couple of independent labs in the city. We can use them."

"Are they any good? Are they up-to-date?" She tapped the specimen packs in her pocket again. "These should be processed right away."

"I know. We'll think of a way."

She put down the coffee. "I called the hospital to see if Mark would do a special run on them. No luck." She did not want to discuss the cruel words they had exchanged, or the threats Mark had made if she persisted in what he had called her folly.

"It doesn't matter. I called Dr. Dagstern this afternoon and he's promised his facilities to us if we need them."

"Dagstern? I don't know him," Natalie said, trying to recall those few physicians still in private practice.

"He's a chiropractor." When he saw the skepticism in her face, he hurried on. "Look, the man has a small lab and a lot of space. You know he's got to be careful, because he could be sued for treating pathological conditions without medical consultation. We can take those samples there tonight, if you don't mind climbing back out the window."

She smiled. "If this keeps up, I'll get good at it." She drank the last of the coffee. "Well, if I'm going back out tonight, I'm going to want a rest first. Call me in a couple of hours, will you?"

"All right," he said. Then, as she started from the room, he added, "if you can find any large jars or bottles and can bring them back, will you do it?"

"Why?"

"I'm going to start boiling water and storing it. Once the city's sanitation goes, the tap water won't be safe."

She nodded. "You're right. Okay. If I find any containers we can use, I'll bring them back."

"I'll call you at seven," Harry told her as she left the room. Then he went back to his maps and his charts. The idea had to work, he told himself. It had to work or they were truly lost.

* * *

The sign was weathered but very neat, planted firmly in the middle of the lawn in front of a commonplace prefab house. DR. ERNEST J. DAGSTERN, it read, CHIROPRACTOR. Natalie studied the sign before going up the walk and ringing the bell.

In a moment the door was opened by a short, muscular man in his early thirties. "Good evening," he said. "I'm afraid you're after my usual hours, but if it's an emergency . . ."

"Dr. Dagstern?" Natalie interrupted.

"Yes?" His tone changed. "You're Dr. Lebbreau? The one Dr. Smith said would call?"

"Yes. I'm Natalie Lebbreau. I understand you have a lab . . ."

He stood aside and motioned her into the foyer, which was taken over by a receptionist's desk. "Come in, Doctor. Yes, I have a small lab here. I'll take you to it. If there is anything I can do to help you . . . ?"

"Oh, I don't think so," she began, then changed her mind. "You might give me some coffee or tea."

"I'm afraid I don't have anything but herbal teas, but you're welcome to that. Here." He opened a door. "Go on in and set yourself up. The equipment is old-fashioned, but I promise you I can do almost all the basics here. If you can't find anything, just ask for it."

Natalie thanked him, then took the specimen packs from her pocket. The room was small, neat and immaculate, and she looked for her slides so that she could begin work.

She was interrupted just once, when Ernest Dagstern brought her a cup of tea with the words, "I thought you could use this blend, Dr. Lebbreau. It's supposed to help concentration."

"Thank you," she murmured as she put the first of the slides under the microscope.

* * *

"So at least there are no major infections to speak of," Natalie told Harry late that night as they sat once more in his living room. "But that's trivial, really."

"What's the matter, then?" Harry asked. In the time they had been sharing his apartment, he had learned to read her face, and he knew that she was deeply troubled. "Tell me, Natalie."

"I talked to Alison," she said, letting a sigh escape her. "I tried to convince her, Harry, I truly did. But she is afraid to. She says the other kids won't understand."

"Understand what? What other kids?" Harry took one of her hands between his and was shocked to discover how cold she was.

"I don't know. She refused to tell me. Anyway, it doesn't matter. The underground is a good idea, but it isn't going to have a chance to work."

"But it *has* to," Harry said, desperation coming over him once more. "If we can't get it organized and going, we might as well lie down and die right now. Are you sure you told that kid . . . Alison . . . what we're facing? Did you make her see what we have to do?"

Natalie withdrew her hand. "Yes, Harry. I tried everything I could think of, and there was no budging her. We'll have to think of something else. But not now. I'm too tired."

But Harry wasn't ready to give up. "We could ask Dagstern. He must have some professional contacts we can use. He could enlist his patients . . ."

"Sure," she said with tired sarcasm.

"All right, then," he said, his voice suddenly loud. "What do we do? Just wait around and die?"

"Harry, I'm tired. I have to get some sleep." She got unsteadily to her feet. "Maybe all we can do is die. I don't know." She wandered to the door. "I'll see you in the morning."

Harry didn't answer.

* * *

"All right, all right, I'm coming!" Harry called as he felt himself jarred awake by the pounding on the door. He pulled a robe on and stumbled for the door, part of his mind puzzling vaguely at this summons. Who could want him?

He met Natalie in the hall. Her eyes were frightened. "Is it the police? Are they going to arrest us?"

"I don't know." He waved her away and went to the door. He hesitated for a moment before pulling the door open. "Yes? What is it?"

Their morning City Patrol guard stood there, his hand raised for further pounding. "Doc?"

"Good morning, Deutch. What's the meaning of this disturbance?" Harry felt his confidence give way, but knew enough not to betray himself. "It's very early."

"I know, Doc. But I had to see you. It's important. You've gotta help me."

"Why?" Harry glanced over his shoulder and saw Natalie come nearer.

"It's Jeanie, Doc. She's sick. They say they can't take her at Westbank, and Inner City is out of room. You've gotta come and look at her. It's probably just the new flu, like the doctors said, but I can't help it, I'm scared. I've never seen her this sick before."

Harry felt the old manner come back almost automatically. "Don't get upset, Deutch. I'm sure we can do something for her." He turned toward Natalie. "You heard?"

"Yes." She came to the door then, saying to Deutch, "You mentioned you've already called Westbank and Inner City. Can you give a little more information about that?"

"Well, there's a waiting list to get in. But," he added in a confidential rush, "I know some people have gone there who haven't come back. I don't know what's happened to them. My cousin, he went in with a sore throat and a little cough; we haven't heard anything from him since then. I know Jeanie's sick, but they won't take her now, and to tell you the truth, I'd be scared to take her even if there was room."

"I see," Harry said slowly. "Where is your wife?"

"At home. Over on Stockton Parkway. It isn't far." Suddenly he hesitated. "I know you did something bad, or they wouldn't want to have you guarded like this. But it wasn't anything real bad, was it? I mean, you didn't kill anyone, did you? . . ."

"Not the way you mean," Harry assured him. Then he turned to Natalie. "I think I'm going. We may still have a chance, Nat."

Natalie fingered the neck of her flannel gown. "But we can't do it alone, Harry. We still need help."

Harry nodded. "I know how." Again he moved his attention to Deutch. "If I'm going to help your wife, there are a few things you're going to have to do for me."

"What are they?" Deutch asked, suspicious.

"When we were put under house arrest, there were several other doctors who were also confined to their homes. I'm going to give you their names and addresses. I'll need to contact them in case your wife needs more care than we can give in your home. If you can arrange for us to have a conference, perhaps after we examine your wife, we can better determine what should be done for her."

Deutch frowned, and there was fright in his eyes. "I don't know, Doc. I'm not supposed to do this, you know. If I let you see the others, then it could be my job."

Natalie moved closer to the door. "Look, Deutch, you're worried, of course, and it's only right that you should be," she said, making a motion to Harry to be silent. "But you know what it's like when you go to a hospital—there are all the labs and machines to do a lot of things we may have to do without assistance. That's one of the reasons we need to see our colleagues, so that we can really take care of your wife. It's important that we be sure we do everything for her."

"Yeah . . ." Deutch said uncertainly.

Once more Harry took over. "Dr. Lebbreau's right, Deutch. We ought to have the others in. Sure, this might be simple flu, but if it's not, we don't want to make any mistakes, or overlook any possibilities. Vaguely Harry felt this was unethical, scaring Deutch this way, but it was his only chance. He decided that for the moment he would ignore his conscience. This had to be done, and it was just possible that he would need that conference with the others, in case Deutch's Jeanie really was ill.

"I've got to think about it," Deutch said miserably. "It's a big risk."

"Yes," Harry agreed. "And we'll be taking a risk, too, leaving quarters. They could really lock us up if we get caught."

Natalie plucked at the back of Harry's robe. "Come on, Harry. We need some coffee," she said, and reached to close the door. Almost as an afterthought, she looked up at Deutch. "Come back in half an hour, Deutch. If you still need us." Then, taking the edge of the door, she closed it firmly.

Harry watched her as the silence became oppressive. "Well?" he asked at last.

"It might work. I don't know." She leaned against the door, forcing Deutch from her thoughts.

"If it does?"

"Then you can take care of his wife and I'll go to the others. I won't be as noticeable as you are. There are more women on the streets during the day than men. And no one will be looking for us, anyway. They won't expect us to be out." She clenched her hands together, her washed-out eyes suddenly very intent. "It's the only chance, Harry. It's our last chance. It has to work."

Harry nodded, reserving his judgment. Now the risks seemed very large. "Let's have breakfast. No use just waiting around for Deutch to make up his mind." He put out his hand to her. "We'll make it," he said to her.

Natalie thought that perhaps Deutch would be too scared, that he would change his mind at the last minute and go to the authorities. "Do you really think so?" She avoided his hand as she went toward the kitchen, her face wan in the clear morning light.

* * *

"Okay," Deutch said when he knocked on the door over an hour later. "I talked to Jeanie. She's not getting any better. The Visiting Nurse was over and gave her some medicine, but it isn't helping. I've gotta do something. You've gotta help her."

Harry wished he knew what the Visiting Nurse had given her, but he would have to wait to find out. He did not want to alarm Deutch further. He knew that once he stepped out the door, he would be committed. He tugged at his inconspicuous tan pullovers, then reached for the simple zipper valise which contained most of his tools and his working smock. "I'm ready," he said, putting a reassuring hand on Deutch's arm.

"What about *her?*" Deutch said, scowling.

"Dr. Lebbreau is going to leave a little later. She has some minor chores to do here first." He did not mention that those chores were to make sure the apartment wasn't spied on or broken into while they were gone.

Deutch looked acutely embarrassed. "God, I hope we don't get caught. I mean, they could lock us all up if we . . ."

"We're not going to get caught," Harry said more forcefully. "No one is going to keep an eye on us as long as they think you're here." And as long as Natalie took care of her safeguards.

"Yeah," Deutch said, but without much conviction. "If Jeanie weren't so sick . . ." He let the words trail off. "Dexter takes over at four. You'll have to be back by then. He'll check up on you."

"We'll be back by then," Harry assured him, growing anxious now that Deutch might change his mind at the last minute.

"Well, you'll have to." Deutch still lingered by the door, a few last reservations holding him back.

"Come on, Deutch," Harry said, making the words gentle. "Jeanie isn't getting better while we stand here talking." He strode past the guard into the hall. "Let's go."

Deutch made up his mind then. He nodded curtly and led the way out of the building into the soft April morning.

*   *   *

It was perhaps twenty minutes later when Natalie left the building. She had run a last check on her various safeguards and was confident that they would protect the apartment from anything less than full forceable entry. For her trip through the city she had dressed as nondescriptly as Harry, and had deliberately made herself even plainer than she was, choosing ill-fitting clothes in an unbecoming shade of mustard-yellow. Her hair was skinned back against her head and gathered into an unruly knot at the nape of her neck, which made her ears stick out, and she had painted her mouth a bright, ugly red that turned her complexion pasty under the freckles.

She waited a long time for a bus, much longer than she should have. When one finally arrived, she remarked on the lateness to the driver.

"It's the flu," he said, plainly harassed and fatigued. "We're working on a reduced staff, lady. If you don't like it, walk."

She murmured something conciliatory, then made her way to a seat, alarmed at how few passengers were riding with her. The reason was soon obvious. During the short ride to the apartment block where Carol Mendosa lived, Natalie kept a sharp lookout for signs of trouble, and she found them everywhere. Stores, a few banks, one or two offices, she saw, had signs in the window:

CLOSED TEMPORARILY ON ACCOUNT OF ILLNESS

She knew that this was worse than it appeared. For every person staying home there were two at work, not quite sick enough to miss that one day's pay, or that important appointment, or a chance to cash in on the competition's misfortunes. And that meant the diseases were spreading, and spreading rapidly.

By the time she left the bus, she had a story all prepared to give Carol's guard. So it was with the proper deference that she walked up to the man, saying, "Pardon me, officer," in a still, meek voice.

"Yes?" The man was older than Deutch, and, Natalie realized immediately, tougher.

"I'm Dr. Mendosa's therapy assistant from Westbank?" She made it a question. "I don't know if you were called . . . I have to talk to Dr. Mendosa."

"Sorry."

"But you don't understand . . . Oh, dear, I knew I should have made sure you'd been phoned . . ." She gave him a bewildered smile, hating herself as she did. "But Mr. Clifford said that someone . . . Dr. Justin's assistant . . ." She paused, hoping the names would sink in, then went on, still as if talking more to herself than the guard. "It's such a bother, you'd think that Dr. Justin would make sure . . . And it *is* so important . . ."

"Dr. Justin sent you?" The officer cut into her monologue.

Natalie looked up, feigning confusion. "Dr. Justin? Dear me, no. His assistant, Mr. Clifford, told me that they need some information about a particular patient of Dr. Mendosa's, you see." She hoped he would not wonder why the hospital had not simply phoned Dr. Mendosa with the question.

"Maybe I'll call this Dr. Justin," the guard said, giving her the most of his overbearing presence.

"Oh, *would* you? It makes things so much easier, of course. I'm afraid to interrupt him myself, but I'm sure Mr. Clifford would . . ." She was sure that Mr. Clifford would have her arrested immediately if he knew what she was up to.

The guard smiled indulgently. "I guess you can go in. But don't stay too long. This isn't really within regulations."

"Oh, I know," Natalie said, letting one hand flutter nervously near her face. "When I think of all those doctors dismissed, and then this flu epidemic, well, I certainly wouldn't want their consciences. I mean, when so many people in the city are sick, they're at home doing nothing."

The guard chuckled indulgently at her indignation and opened the door. "You tell Dr. Mendosa that."

Natalie simpered at him and closed the door.

In a moment Carol Mendosa came in, puzzlement on her face quickly turning to surprise when she saw Natalie. "What on earth? How did you get here?" She dragged Natalie away from the hall. "What is it?" she asked when they were into the tiny living room. "You look furious."

"I hate silly, stupid women," Natalie whispered, her teeth tight. Carol waited for an explanation. "You know Mrs. Grossnecker?" Natalie asked, thinking of the fifty-year-old maiden librarian who watch-dogged the admissions records on the third floor of Westbank Hospital, a woman whose affected coyness must have been intolerable in her youth, and years ago had hardened into a travesty of girlishness.

"I know her. Ghastly old bitch."

Natalie nodded. "I've been being her for your guard." She sank into Carol's sofa. "I'm a therapist here consulting you about a patient on Dick Clifford's request, if you want to know the cover. The guard might ask you."

Carol nodded, her large dark eyes molten. "What are you doing out?" she asked, tension making her voice thick.

"We're getting our underground going, just the way we planned," Natalie said, trying to be nonchalant and failing. "The wife of one of our guards is sick. Harry's off seeing her now."

"And?" She rose, her dark cloud of hair obscuring her face, but Natalie could see the force there. "And I'm out trying to reach our bunch. You're the first. Now listen to me. There's a chiropractor named Dagstern who'll let us use his lab, so we can do some basic pathology. And Lisa's got a cousin who runs a medical supply place. After you get out . . ."

"How am I supposed to do that, Nat? It's a minor point, but . . ."

"Don't be sarcastic, Carol," Natalie said, feeling dangerously tired now that she was safe again. "I got out through the kitchen window."

"Mine's a four-story drop. No good."

"What about a laundry chute? These buildings have them, don't they?"

"Sure, but no one ever uses them." Carol tugged open a small closet and shoved some boxes out of the way, revealing a smaller door. "This is it. I guess it goes to the basement laundries."

"Can you fit in?" Natalie asked, rising. "It doesn't look very big."

"Oh, I can fit in it, all right. But how do I get back up, assuming I can get out at all?"

"Use a rope," Natalie said, feeling decisive now. "Tie one end to the clothes bar there, and let the other end dangle down the chute. That's simple enough." She inspected the closet, saying little. "Is there an outside entrance to the laundry, do you know?"

Carol's brows drew together. "I don't know . . . Wait a minute. Yes there is. I remember now. It opens on the inner court."

"Will that be a problem?"

Carol laughed. "Not around here. God, I want to get to work." She turned away from the closet abruptly. "What's it like out there?"

"Bad." Natalie sat still now, thinking of what she had seen. "It's getting worse fast, too." Her fear returned, then she forced it down. "Do you have any coffee? I don't have a lot of time and I have to see the others."

Carol ducked into her small kitchen. "Tell me about this chiropractor," she called as she put water into the pot.

"Dagstern," Natalie said, wandering closer to the kitchen. "Harry found him. If you can get over there Thursday night . . ."

"Day after tomorrow?" Carol asked, surprised. "That soon."

"We've got to get working now. The situation's bad already, and it's going to get worse fast. We'll meet at Dagstern's. We'll work out something. It won't be like Westbank, none of this neat business, like having Orthopedics, Paraplegics, Therapy and Stroke units all on the ninth floor, and Quarantine on eight. We'll have to make do with what's available."

"What about the Van Dreyter house? Do you think we're going to use that?" She came out of the kitchen, wiping her hands on a towel. "It'll take a couple of minutes, Nat."

"Good." She glanced uneasily at the door. "What about your guard: Is he likely to give you trouble? Does he check up on you unexpectedly?"

"Sometimes," she admitted, and her face darkened.

"Can you tell him you're down with a mild case of the flu and make him believe it?" There was real anxiety in Natalie's face now. "We're going to need every advantage we can find. If the authorities, or whoever's in charge of this mess, ever find out what we're trying to do, they'll stop us flat. We have to have these three days or we're sunk."

Carol nodded. "I'll tell him I think I have a touch of it, and that I don't want to be disturbed because I might be contagious." She rubbed her hands on her white slacks. "I can make him believe me, if I have to."

"Is it hard on you, Carol? Having the guards?"

A shadow crossed Carol's face, part of the things she never talked about. "Not the way you mean. I sent my father to my brother in

San Diego last week. I'm alone here." The words were carefully chosen, and she looked away as she spoke. "I'm going to check the coffee." She was gone, to reappear in a little while with a china cup filled with coffee. "You'd better appreciate this: it's real."

"The china or the coffee?" Natalie teased, and drank, wishing that she knew where Carol bought her food.

At that, another alarm sounded in her mind. Food. She looked up. "Carol. What kind of supplies do you have here? I mean, food supplies?"

"Oh, about enough to last me a week, why?"

"Because we're going to have to think about food. There isn't going to be more food coming into the city for a while, and we'd better be ready for that."

Carol looked up, worry beginning to show on her face. "Christ," she murmured, "I hadn't thought of that. I should have."

"Never mind," Natalie said, relief making her calm. Now that she had thought of the problem, she knew that she could handle it. "I'll take care of what I can now, and when we meet later on, we'll work out the long-term problems. I'm glad you reminded me of it." She drank down the last of the coffee, then handed the cup to Carol. "There's still a chance, Carol. We can still make a difference."

"How much of one?" Carol put the cup in the kitchen. "I'll be there Thursday night, Nat. What time?"

"Eight-thirty? Make it eight-thirty. Dagstern is listed and the office is right on the 44C route, so you won't have to transfer." Natalie stopped at the door. "Oh, the buses are not running very much on schedule. Better allow some extra time." She put on the irritating smile she had worn for the guard as she opened the door. "Thank you so much, Dr. Mendosa," she said, raising her voice to an irritating note. "I know Mr. Clifford will appreciate this."

Carol went along with her. "I'm glad I could be of help. The next time you have trouble, let me know, and there won't be this sort of emergency."

Natalie closed the door and gave the guard a simper. "Thank you so much, officer. It *must* be difficult for you, having this duty. I can't tell you how pleased I am to have had this talk with Dr. Mendosa. She's so helpful . . . you wouldn't think, would you, that she's been dismissed . . . Oh, dear. I know I shouldn't have said that." She started down the hall, saying as she went, "It's so difficult having those doctors gone just now, what with the flu epidemic. When you consider what we have to do . . ."

*   *   *

It was easier getting to Lisa Skye, who worked at a children's center where her daughter went after school. A few words to the principal and Natalie had fifteen uninterrupted minutes with Lisa, and came away feeling more satisfied, more confident than she had after her talk with Carol. She knew that Lisa would have no trouble getting to the meeting, because the principal had assured Natalie that the accusations against Lisa were ridiculous.

Dave's apartment was unguarded, and Natalie was surprised to learn that he had bribed his guard several days before and had made a few exploratory trips through his district of the city already. He motioned her to a chair on his old-fashioned balcony as he told her.

Natalie looked at him narrowly. "Didn't you have any trouble at all? Bribing guards can be tricky."

"They don't mind what I do as long as I stay away from the rest of you," he said with a sudden grin. "Lovell didn't care so long as I was in when he was relieved. It's less work for him, really, having me gone. He can use the place with his girlfriend some afternoons, so he isn't hard to bribe. And he stays bought. But the night guard, Park, he's another matter. One of those superscrupulous Koreans. So I might have some trouble getting out for a night meeting, but I'll be there. Maybe I can talk Lovell into trading duties with Park. I'll tell him he can have the place for the night. Park's usually griping about working nights. I think that's why he's so hard on me."

"But Dave," Natalie said, fighting down a qualm, "once you were out, you could have called one of us, or stopped to see us . . ."

"Sure, and have your guards report it? I'm not that kind of a fool. I've been checking up on the diseases, and it's not good. But what would calling you do? I'm more use working than being in jail."

"Well, of course," Natalie said uncertainly. To her left, a pot of old geraniums struggled in the warmth. "It's going to get worse with the summer," she said, thinking of the city's chronic summer water shortages and the oppressive heat which began in June. "June isn't that far off."

"What?"

She looked up, startled. "Never mind," she said as she collected her thoughts. "I've got too much on my mind, I guess."

"Thursday night, then," Dave said, giving her a wide smile. "I'm glad we're not still stuck at Westbank. It must be a madhouse there, with all these diseases breaking out. I hear they're sticking to the flu story. They aren't going to do that much longer, I'd bet."

"Why do you think so?" Natalie asked, watching Dave carefully. She had always liked Dave Lillijanthal, as much for his easy charm as for his unruffled competence as a doctor, but she had never seen him away from the hospital, and now, seeing him here, listening to the nonchalant words, she felt some of her liking diminish.

"They'll call this off before then," he said. "You worry too much, Nat. Oh, this underground thing is a great idea. It'll make sure there's a backup when the hospitals get overcrowded. But you know as well as I do that the government isn't dumb enough to keep this up for long. They'll see it doesn't work, and they'll call it off. And then we'll be called to testify, and after that we can write our own ticket anywhere we want."

She wanted to ask him if that was why he wanted to be with them. But she kept the words back. "I hope you're right," was all she dared to say.

"Of course I'm right. About Thursday night. I'll be there."

Natalie gathered up her bag and jacket. "I've got to get to Jim Varnay and Radick Lescu yet," she murmured. "And then I have some shopping to do."

"You've seen all the others?"

"No," she admitted, and wondered if she should tell him. "But some of them are helping me." At the door she turned to him. "I wish you'd called us. We wouldn't have lost so much time."

He took her chin between his finger and thumb. "Poor Natalie. Always carrying the world around on your shoulders." He gave her a peck on the cheek and closed the door.

* * *

"You look exhausted," Radick Lescu told her when at last Natalie reached his small house. It was a tiny building, sandwiched in between two giant apartment houses and only allowed to exist because of an edict of the fire department.

"I am tired," she admitted, and was grateful for the understanding in his eyes. Radick had always been a puzzle to her, for he was atypical for the psychiatrists she knew, an elegant man, cultured, genuinely interested in people, but occasionally she had caught him off guard and had seen naked pain in his face.

"How is it going, then?" he asked politely and settled back to listen. As Natalie told him, she admitted that Radick Lescu was very good at listening.

When she was finished, he nodded. "It sounds good. But I agree with you about Lillijanthal—he will bear watching. He does not handle stress well, you know. That's one of the reasons he cannot allow himself to think this situation serious." He saw her face and went on, mild amusement lightening his voice. "I know you didn't say that much about Dave, but you didn't have to. It's my job to hear the things that people *don't* say."

Relieved, Natalie returned his smile. "I didn't want to say that, but I'm just as glad you picked it up. Thanks, Radick."

He waved a dismissing hand, but said in another tone, "If you don't mind, I'm going to call my sister. She and her family can use this house for the summer. Oh, I'm not kidding myself. I know they'll be as vulnerable here as they are in their apartment. But here they can have some little privacy." He picked up the phone.

"It might be bugged," she warned him, hating the thought of any misfortune coming to Radick.

"Of course it's bugged, my dear," he said, smiling, a kindness in his eyes. "But I will be careful." In a moment he spoke. "Marya, this is Radick. I'm sorry I couldn't make it over the other evening . . . Yes, I'm fine, thank you . . . I was wondering if you might have an hour or so free? I'm getting very housebound, and I would appreciate your company . . . I'm sure the guards will let you in . . . All right. I'll expect you, then. Thank you, love." He turned to Natalie as he hung up. "She will be here soon. Would you like to stay and meet her? I think you'd enjoy one another."

The warmth in his face surprised Natalie, and she felt a sudden desire to stay. It would be easy to cast off her fears for a while and have the pleasure of an afternoon with Radick and his sister. "I can't, Radick. I'm truly sorry. If I didn't have other things to do, I'd love to."

He accepted this but asked, "What do you have to do now, Natalie? Where are you going?"

Bleakness washed over her. "Food shopping," she said.

CHAPTER 6

"Where have you been?" Harry demanded as Natalie slipped in the door. "It's five to four, for Chrissake. Deutch goes off duty at four. You're late."

"Take this," she said, shoving a heavy box at him.

"What's this?" He looked from the box to her, and bewilderment began to replace the anger in his face.

"I've got another one in the hall, and there's one more in the basement by the emergency generator." Her breath came in jerks and her hands were shaky with strain. "I can't carry them any longer. It's too hard."

Harry lifted the box, and was startled by its weight. "What's in here, anvils?"

"Dried food. Fifty pounds' worth. It should last us about a month." She pulled off her jacket and walked into the living room.

Torn between the boxes and Natalie, Harry hesitated, then lugged the food into the kitchen. He went for the other box in the hall, hoping that Deutch had not seen it, or that his replacement had not. When both boxes were safely in the kitchen, he joined Natalie in the living room. "What's this all about?" he demanded.

"Oh, Harry, I should have thought of this before. We should have realized. It's food, Harry. We never talked about it, I can't think why. But when I saw Carol she gave me some coffee, real coffee, and I remembered."

"But where'd you get that stuff?"

Natalie gave him a tired smile. "At sporting goods stores. I bought it all on credit. I don't have very much money. Mark'll be furious when he finds out." Her attempt at a laugh failed badly. "I said I was taking some kids camping. I went to five different stores, so they wouldn't get suspicious."

Harry sat down beside her. "You mean you carried that stuff back here by yourself?"

"No. I got a shopping cart—you know, the old-fashioned kind that they used to attach to the side of bicycles." She yawned. "What's wrong with Deutch's wife, anything bad?"

Harry rubbed his hands together, very somber now. "Yes. I'm afraid so." He looked blankly across the room, seeing the young woman who had been pretty not too long ago. She had been so trusting, and he hated to admit that he could not help her. His face showed something of this, for Natalie turned to him.

"What is it, Harry? What's wrong?"

Harry found it hard to answer. "She's got polio. Very bad, I think. I told Deutch to call through to Justin and tell him there was something wrong. Maybe Justin will do something." He felt desolate. He knew that all he told Deutch would very likely be useless. The woman was too sick, and it was only a matter of hours until she would need breathing assist. Without that assist she would die.

"God." Very slowly Natalie got up. "I'm sorry, Harry." She looked at the floor. "We'll have to get more food tomorrow, you know. There's a lot to be done." When this did not get a reaction, she went on. "We're going to see a lot more of this before we're through. Our meeting is set up for Thursday night at Dagstern's. Eight-thirty."

"I hear you."

Natalie's body ached, her face felt rigid and she knew that she was near senseless tears. She knelt beside Harry and held him close. "You can't give up now, Harry. Not you. You fought the whole administration at Westbank. You can't stop now. There's too much to do, Harry. There's too little time. It's important that you do it, because I can't do it alone." She felt him relax a little. "We need sleep, Harry. When you're rested, you'll be able to think clearly again." She hoped that she, too, would think clearly.

For a moment he returned her embrace, then he pushed her away from him. "Yeah. I need sleep. So do you, Natalie. I'll see you in the morning. God, I wish we had some of Carol's coffee."

"Maybe she'll bring some with her," Natalie suggested. Now that she thought about it, real coffee might help. Harry was right. She'd call Carol in the morning. Not call Carol. The lines were bugged.

Harry shook her shoulder gently. "Go to bed before you fall asleep. You almost fell over."

She looked muzzily up at him. "Right."

* * *

Alison's face was set firmly, and her young mouth compressed into a line. "I can't," she said stonily. Her eyes dared Natalie to argue.

"But it's important, Alison," Natalie explained patiently as they sat in the litter of Alison's apartment. "I told you, a lot of people are going to be sick, and we need your help."

"No way," Alison shook her head. "Tristam wouldn't like it."

"Tristam? Who's Tristam?" Natalie thought there had been fright in the girl's voice when she said the name.

"No one." She got to her feet. "I gotta go." Then she faltered. "I know you helped Ces'lie, and all. She'd be a lot worse off if you didn't help her. But you know how it is."

Natalie rose, too, thinking that she did wish she knew how it was. "If you change your mind, you can find me at the Van Dreyter house. Next week."

"You aren't going back to the hospital?" Alison asked, her eyes narrowing.

"No." She waited to see what effect this news might have.

Alison nodded once. "Okay. I'll pass it on."

Pass it on to whom? Natalie wondered as she left the apartment.

* * *

"That's a nasty cough you have," Natalie said to the owner of the third sporting goods store she visited.

"I know. It's this damn flu. Everyone has it, I guess. My clerk's off with it, or I might have gone home. What else are you looking for?" he asked politely as he stacked up the two boxes of dehydrated food.

"Do you have an outdoor stove and fuel?" There would not always be power available, she knew, and a camp stove would help. "And a couple of battery lanterns. And maybe some spare batteries, if you have them."

"How many kids you taking on this trip?" the owner asked, breaking off to clear his throat.

"It's a day-care center trip. There are about fifty kids and we're going for six weeks. I thought I'd better make sure there's enough food for them all." She observed him narrowly, seeing the leaden cast to his skin. "Have you seen a doctor about that cough?"

"Don't have time with the help off. I promised my wife that if it didn't get better I'd go over to County General and have them check me out next week." He pulled a few boxes off his shelf. "Will these lanterns be okay? They aren't the brightest, but they last the longest, and they don't go out in water."

"It sounds fine." She pretended to consider her problem with the fictitious day-care center. "Do you think I'm forgetting something? . . . Oh," she said, as if just thinking of it, "bandages. You know how kids are. Some of them are bound to get hurt."

Chuckling indulgently, the owner added three large boxes of bandages to her purchases. "I wish we could afford to take that kind of vacation. Back when I was in day-care centers, we didn't take trips like this. Oh, no. We were lucky to have half a warehouse to ourselves, and that's a fact. Still, I don't suppose it can hurt them to get off from the city once in a while. And the parents probably love it." He cast a calculating eye over the boxes. "Is that it, then, ma'am?"

It was certainly all she felt safe to buy. "Yes, I think so. Will you put it all in a big box for me, so I can carry it in one load?"

"It'll be pretty heavy," he said as he began to pack the items.

"I don't have far to go," she lied, thankful for the wire carrier she had. One more sporting goods store and she should have all she needed for six months. She thought briefly of Harry, who was not only contacting the rest of the doctors that day, but who had volunteered to bring home enough bottled water to keep them going for several months.

"Sure wish I was going with you." The owner shook his head. "Got your credit card, please?" He held out his hand.

Natalie gave him cash, the last cash she had. "Here. We're all buying in for supplies," she said glibly. The last time she had tried to use her card the purchase scan had indicated she was over her credit limit.

He took the money, remarking, "On big purchases most people use credit cards. But I suppose cash is better."

When he offered to carry the box for her, she refused, and said again, "You really should see a doctor about that cough." But it might be hopeless. She felt his hand hot and dry in hers when she shook it, and knew that his temperature was well above normal. "Why not take the afternoon off? Business is light."

He shrugged philosophically. "Maybe if I don't have too many more customers I'll knock off at three." He waved to her as she staggered out of the store, the box held tightly against her.

*　*　*

Ernest Dagstern smiled at Harry. "What's in the truck?" he asked, pointing to the delivery van idling in the driveway.

"Water," Harry said. "Can I get that thing in? I don't want the truck noticed."

"Why?" Dagstern looked puzzled even as he went to unlock the garage.

"Because I stole it." He grinned at Dagstern's consternation. "I did. We need bottled water, and that van is full of it. Nothing but big five-gallon jars of it. It's exactly what we need. So I took the truck. It was at a service station. When I showed up, the service station owner asked if I was the replacement driver. I said I was. Nothing easier."

By this time Ernest Dagstern had raised the garage door. "I hope you know what you're doing," he said with a shake of his head.

"We'll find out tomorrow night. The meeting is set for eight-thirty."

* * *

Natalie sat on the couch, rubbing her feet and watching the evening news. "The National Business Bureau," intoned the figure on the screen, "has released figures for the first quarter of the year, which indicate that buying has shifted . . ."

"Anything interesting?" Harry asked as he strolled into the room.

"The usual. Nationally there's nothing about the 'flu' or the experiment the government is running on its citizens. Locally there's still the usual warnings about the flu, and a few figures on absenteeism, which I very much doubt reflect the truth."

"Likely not." He sat opposite her and flicked the screen off. "How was your day?" he asked.

"I've got a total of three hundred pounds of dehydrated food. Also three portable fire extinguishers, nine battery-powered lamps, two camp stoves, sixteen boxes of various kinds of bandages, and five basic first-aid kits. Oh, and seventeen envelopes of vegetable seeds."

"Impressive." He paused, then told her about stealing the water truck. At the end of it she was almost weak with laughter. "Oh, Harry, that's wonderful. A whole truck, and no one stopped you."

"Another thing, Amanda was in, and I got to talk to her. She's going over to her sister's business and raid it."

"What for?" A frown threatened in her face.

"Her sister owns a supply house for hotels. That means all the bedding we can use. And with the kind of inventory Laetitia has . . ."

"Is Amanda's sister named Laetitia?" Natalie's frown was gone, and there was light in her eyes again.

"Laetitia Clothilda, Amanda tells me." Harry felt himself smile, too. "Anyway, because of the revolving inventory, what we take won't be noticed, and we can get them cleaned by the company, if we have to. It's going to make our job a lot easier."

Natalie sat up. "You're kidding," she said. "We can really get bedding and laundry service?" For a moment tears stood in her eyes, but she pinched them away impatiently. "Harry, we might make it."

"We might." He leaned toward the table and picked up the day's mail. "Is this all?"

"That's it." She turned over a couple of envelopes. "None of them are from out of town, did you notice that? I should have heard from Alec Corbaine a couple of days ago. I sent him some information for his latest book, and he always acknowledges within a month."

"Maybe he's late."

"And maybe they aren't bringing in mail from the outside any more." She stretched, and felt the muscles knot.

Harry opened his mail and stared at the pages, not really seeing them. "You know, I've got a cousin in Canada who usually writes me the first of each month. I haven't heard from him. Until you mentioned it, I hadn't noticed. Maybe we are sealed off . . ."

"It's one way to handle it," Natalie said with savage satisfaction. "No information in, no information out. That way, who's to know what's really going on here? I mean, if there were too many letters coming out, and to the wrong people, there might be some worry, or an investigation." She pounded her fist into her palm. "They're thorough."

Harry sat back to read his letters, and thought that Natalie could be wrong. But he didn't believe it. When he put the mail aside, he said, "Did you get to talk to Alison?"

"Yes, for all the good it did." Natalie put her chin in her hand. "I don't know, Harry, but I think she's afraid of someone. She mentioned a Tristam, but she wouldn't talk about him."

"Do you have any idea who he might be?"

"None at all. But he might be the one who scares her. I don't think we should try to force her, Harry. She might change her mind later if we just leave her alone. But I don't think she's going to change her position."

"Okay." He got up. "Have you eaten?"

"No. Have you?"

"With Ernest. Were you planning to eat?"

"Not really."

Harry went and stood over her. "You can't do this to yourself, Natalie. You've got to be in good shape. You can't lose your strength now."

Natalie made a complicated gesture, then looked at Harry in annoyance. "You know, Harry," she said with an edge in her voice, "I wish you weren't always right."

He held out his hand and pulled her off the sofa.

* * *

The front of Ernest Dagstern's house was dark, but in the back lights burned brightly. "I thought this might attract less attention, as it is after my office hours," Ernest explained when Harry and Natalie arrived. "The others will see the sign."

"It's a good idea," Harry said, and followed Ernest to his living quarters at the back of the house.

"Dr. Divanello called earlier to say that she would not be on time. She mentioned that there was an errand she had to run for her sister, and said you would understand." He cocked an eyebrow. "I gather that message was for the benefit of whoever might be listening."

"Yes," Harry admitted, and hoped that the listeners would not be as acute as Ernest Dagstern.

"I've taken the liberty of ordering more lab equipment. I thought you might want it." He opened the door to his small laboratory, revealing several more boxes of supplies. "From what you've told me, Dr. Smith, we are in for some very difficult times."

"What do you think is happening?" Harry asked, wondering how much he had accidentally revealed.

Ernest Dagstern had learned quite a lot. His words were crisp and his summation accurate and rational. "Am I right?" he asked when he was through.

"You're right," Harry said, his respect for the man growing. "But I didn't say that much, did I?"

"Well, no. I have my regular patients, too, and I do my own lab work on them, you know. I know what they have, Harry." Both of them knew that Ernest had joined them. "And I am not the only chiropractor who knows. But we didn't know what to do without your help. That's not the sort of thing we treat, although I've done some work with polio victims after the fact." He closed the laboratory door and motioned for Harry and Natalie to follow him to the kitchen.

Stan Kooznetz was already there, his long face looking severe. "You've seen the setup?" he asked without preamble.

"It's not bad," Harry said quickly hoping to forestall any outbreak of temper.

"It's damn good, considering," Stan agreed. "But where are we going to work? Yes," he went on, with a wave of his hand, "I know we talked about the Van Dreyter house, but how the hell are we going to take it over? By military coup? What?"

Again Ernest interrupted them. "I thought you knew," he said. "But, of course, you wouldn't. The Van Dreyter house has been closed for three days because of the 'flu' epidemic. It's empty."

"Hallelujah," Natalie whispered as she sat down to wait for the rest to arrive.

*   *   *

It was a big house, built on lines that had gone out of fashion before the First World War. It had turrets and cupolas, attics and basements, a wine cellar, two kitchens, a formal drawing room and two informal salons, a tea nook, a formal dining room, an informal dining room, fifteen bedrooms (not counting servants' quarters), eight bathrooms, and three small apartments in the grooms' quarters in the old stable which had long since been turned into a garage. It also had its own water supply, pumped up from deep wells.

Breaking in wasn't as hard as they had thought it would be. One of the pantry windows was open, and Lisa Skye, being the smallest, was lifted through, and then she merely unlocked the back door.

"Will you look at this place?" Dave Lillijanthal breathed as his flashlight played over the cavernous kitchen. "You could cook for an army down here."

"They probably did." Amanda Divanello touched the central table, feeling the grooves left by decades of knives and cleavers.

"Do you think they still work?" Natalie asked, studying the eight-burner stove.

"Probably."

Harry cleared his throat. "We better get some exploring done," he said. "This might take some time."

"There are two wings to the house," Ernest Dagstern announced. "I took the tour last week. The west wing is the larger, and has the formal drawing and dining rooms. The north wing has more bedrooms and there's an artist's studio in the northmost attic bedroom. We can make our exploration in two groups." He gave Harry an apologetic look.

"I like the idea," Harry agreed. "I wish one of us had thought to come here."

"If we could have gotten out," Natalie put in, giving Dave Lillijanthal a pointed look. Dave shrugged.

Stan Kooznetz ran water into the sink. "I guess the wells are still good," he said, not wanting to indulge in too much optimism.

"Then, maybe I shouldn't have stolen that water truck," Harry suggested, but his words were cut short by Amanda Divanello. "No, you were right. We're going to hold that water in reserve. We may need it if the power breaks down and we can't use the pumps, or if the wells turn out to be contaminated."

"Let's get our bearings first," Harry said, and turned to look at the group. "Which of you want to take the cellars? We'll need notes."

Three hands were raised, reluctantly. Harry nodded. "Ted, you can be in charge," he told the gentle, methodical Edward Lincoln. "You, Dominic and Roger can take the cellars. Make sure you check out everything, including seepage, if there is any."

"Right." Ted nodded to the other two. In a few moments their footsteps echoed back from the long cellar stairs.

Kirsten Grant and Alexes Castor agreed to see to the garage, and Natalie volunteered to go with Radick and Maria Pantopolos to the attic. The rest divided the two main floors between them.

"I wonder if there are any alarms we're setting off?" Natalie said as she climbed the main staircase.

*   *   *

In the end they agreed that the formal dining room, with its three crystal chandeliers and rosewood table, which could seat thirty, would be their common room, their retreat, while the rest of the house, with the exception of the attic bedrooms and larger kitchen, would be converted to treatment areas.

"There's eight bedrooms in the attic, so we'll work out how to double up."

"We can take care of that in shifts. If we have to." Dominic Hertzog leaned back in the rosewood chair and went on, "I hope one of you has thought about shifts, because I've got a feeling this is going to be a twenty-four-hour place."

"What do you mean?" Amanda Divanello tapped the table angrily with her pencil, and watched Dominic as if he were a blue baby she had to operate on.

"I mean that I listened to the news. And tonight they've finally admitted that there is an outbreak of a 'smallpox-like' disease, which they are hard at work developing a vaccine for. Mark Howland was interviewed, and you wouldn't believe the way that bastard talked . . ." He stopped. "Sorry, Natalie."

"I've heard him, too. Don't apologize," she said, and saw approval in Harry's eyes. She felt pleased and confused.

"Go on, Dominic. What did he say?" Amanda insisted.

"The usual waffle. Assurances that the situation was surely temporary, that there was no need for panic, and of course a plea to the people not to travel so that this outbreak can be isolated. Then the City Patrol announced that all the roads out of this area would be closed so that this thing could be taken care of right here. So, no traffic from further away than Fresno or Sacramento, or Auburn on the east and Tracy on the west."

"You mean we're sealed off," Radick said gently. "I suppose it was to be expected, and yet, it is still a betrayal."

Amanda turned to Harry. "How soon can we be open for patients?"

Harry looked around the table. "If we work very hard, tomorrow. We can start on Saturday, around noon, I'd guess, to do examinations, and full treatment by Monday, if we're lucky. Figure Wednesday at the very latest."

Ernest broke in. "If you need any of my equipment, it's at your disposal. I can transport most of my lab over here, if that would simplify your work for you." He looked at them hopefully. "This epidemic frightens me. I can't sit back and ignore it, or wait to die."

"Your lab equipment would mean a lot to us," Harry said, and saw the others nod. "Thanks, Ernest."

Suddenly Carol Mendosa said, "I wish we had some nurses or paramedics. Without them, we'll have to do all the routine chores as well as the doctoring. Christ, I haven't changed an occupied bed since I was an intern. Where are we going to get the time to do it all? Why didn't they fire some nurses when they fired us?"

There was shocked silence. Then Natalie said, "Oh, great. We remembered blankets, we remembered food and water, but we forgot nurses."

Jim Varnay glanced up, his dark face revealing little of his thoughts. He bit his lip judiciously. "I can go back to Westbank tomorrow. I know some nurses," he said, ignoring Dave Lillijanthal's sly aside, "I'll bet you do," to say, "They'll listen to me. We've worked emergency room together for three years. Want to come with me, Ted?"

Ted Lincoln nodded. "Sure. We can do recruiting. We can phone the other hospitals. Inner City might have a few nurses to spare."

"No one has any nurses to spare, believe me." Carol Mendosa got up and paced the length of the rich oriental carpet. "We've got to get help somewhere. A couple of nurses won't be enough."

"They'll have to be. And if we don't get them, we'll have to manage on our own." Natalie had soken softly, but they all heard her. "Because if we don't, we're dead."

* * *

"Three nurses. I guess we can get by with them," Natalie said to Harry the next night as they sat in their room, which was the converted artist's studio at the far end of the north wing.

"We'll have to." Harry looked out the huge windows toward the skyscrapers of Sacramento. He felt awkward now that he and Natalie had time to themselves. He had agreed to share the room with her because it seemed to be expected, but now he wondered. He looked at the two narrow beds and the screen between them, and all the embarrassment he had never felt when Natalie shared his apartment came to him.

"What is it, Harry?" Natalie asked, studying him.

"Nothing."

"Would you rather have one of the men room with you?" Her question was so to the point that he felt angry. "It's not that," he lied. "I can't stop worrying about the diseases. Did you hear the news tonight? They have officially stopped issuing statements about the 'flu' epidemic."

But Natalie was not to be put off. "I'll talk to Radick, if you like, or ask Amanda if she minds letting me share her room."

Harry sighed. "Okay. It bothers me. I don't know why, but it does."

Natalie nodded, then rose and went to him. "Harry, if you want me to move, I'll move. But tell me, will you?"

He draped an arm around her shoulder. "Oh, never mind, Natalie. I'm being a fool. It'll pass. I'd probably be just as jumpy with Radick for a roommate. At least we're used to each other."

She gave him a dubious smile. "Okay. But if you change your mind, let me know. It isn't fair to either of us to drive each other nuts."

"That isn't likely to happen," he said, too glibly, and saw doubt in her eyes. He relented. "Okay. If things don't work out, I'll let you know."

* * *

"That makes how many patients today?" Harry asked Jim Varnay on Tuesday night as he closed the salon door behind an old woman. Converted now to an examination room, the fine flecked wallpaper seemed out of place next to the white cabinets donated by Ernest Dagstern.

"Thirty-three. And there's five more waiting." Jim touched the old-fashioned stethoscope which hung around his neck. "You know, I haven't used one of these things in years. Funny. I'd forgot how much you can find out by just listening with it."

"How do you mean?" Harry asked, looking up from his scribbled notes.

"Well, look, when you plug a patient into a diagnostic computer, it does all the thumping and listening and measuring, and sure, it can catch a lot of things people might overlook, because it can process information on a wide spectrum, and it isn't distracted by headaches or personal pressures or dislikes. I know that. But when you hear the sounds of the heart and the breath, there are so many . . . undefinable bits of information you get."

"Did you get any about that woman?" Harry gestured toward the door.

"Mrs. Saunders? Well, don't quote me, but I think her heart is catching up with her. There's a stress, and I don't mean blood pressure. Her heart sounds . . . tired."

Harry nodded. "What about her otherwise?"

Jim shrugged. "For the time being, all she needs is a vacation. Which she isn't going to get. And the first real exposure she gets to a bad disease, it's all over. She doesn't have anything left to fight back with."

Harry closed his folder. "Too bad. You ready for dinner?"

"Harry, I was ready for lunch, but it never seemed to happen. Damn right I'm ready. Lead the way." But as they were leaving the room, Jim paused for a moment. "Harry, has anyone said anything to you about a Tristam?"

Harry checked himself, memory flickering. "I thought . . . No. It's gone. I know I've heard that name before."

"Mrs. Saunders," he said. "She mentioned a Tristam. She seemed afraid of him. I was wondering if he were some kind of local hood, or just her own problem."

"I don't know," Harry said, and pulled the door closed.

* * *

"How many admits have we got?" Natalie asked Lisa Skye, who was sitting at the improvised admission desk in the foyer.

"Eight, so far. We've sent the borderline cases home." Lisa pushed her fine fair hair off her forehead. "I don't know, Nat. That kid with smallpox really upset me. I didn't realize what it could look like." She clenched her small-boned hands. "I'm going to have to talk to Radick, I guess," she said shakily.

"I know." Natalie unbuttoned the top of her smock. "I didn't appreciate what we're getting ourselves into. Really, I didn't. I thought it would be like Westbank but on a smaller scale. It frightens me, Lisa." She dropped a folder on the desk. "This one is going to have to be put on our house-call list. Severe asthma. As the stress gets worse, her asthma is going to get worse, too. She's got two brothers at home, one of whom she says is very sick, but she can't talk him into seeing a doctor. Apparently, some of the kids are catching onto the disease trouble, and they're mad. I can't blame them. I'm mad, too."

"Dave Lillijanthal's taking the house rounds this week. Do you have any special instructions for him?" Lisa held a pen, ready to add information.

"Yeah. He should take the case seriously. But he won't." Natalie leaned on the desk, feeling very tired. "Dinner should be about ready. Are you on night call?"

Lisa shook her head. "It's you and Stan and Radick." She consulted a page in front of her. "I'm on tomorrow night with Kirsten Grant and Howie Webbster." She put the schedule down. "It's going to get difficult."

Natalie nodded. "Did I hear right earlier? Did we get a typhus?"

"We did. He's on the second floor in the north wing. He's in very bad shape. And we don't have the drugs and equipment to pull him through, not now." She looked up at Natalie. "I wrote to my mother last week and the letter came back. And Amanda said that Laetitia wanted to make her usual trip to San Diego yesterday and was not allowed to go. Nat, we're sealed off. Not just trucks and food and flu scare, we're being kept here."

"I know." She thought of Mark and Peter Justin and was suddenly very angry. "This bright idea they had. I hope they're the ones who get the cancer and the diphtheria and the cholera and the tetanus and the polio. I want them to know what they've done. Not intellectually, but feel what disease does to the body, watch themselves die . . ." She stopped, feeling the horror, horror for herself.

"Nat," Lisa said softly after a moment, "I don't mean this the way it sounds, but maybe you better talk to Radick." She hurried on. "I don't mean it that way, Nat. But it's too hard to carry all that alone."

Slowly Natalie cooled her anger. She said to Lisa, "I know what you mean. And you're right."

* * *

Harry watched the patient, puzzled. The child couldn't have been more than eleven or twelve, a slight boy with delicate features. He shivered as Harry touched him. "Are you cold?" Harry asked.

"Some," the boy said.

Harry touched the boy again, and felt the skin hot and dry under his fingers. He could tell that the boy had a low-grade fever, but why? What was giving it to him? "How are you feeling generally?" Harry asked.

"Rotten. They's why I came here. I wouldn't've come here otherwise."

"Do you have an appetite?" Harry felt those familiar prickings that told him the boy was seriously ill. But the disease must be an elusive one, because he could not find a lead on it.

"Not much."

"How long have you felt badly?" Harry checked the pulse, which was a little fast, but not seriously so.

"Couple of days."

While he shook down a thermometer, Harry said, "You said you felt rotten: what do you mean? Is it because of your loss of appetite?"

"My gut's fine," the boy snapped, his sullen eyes on Harry's thermometer. "I get dizzy sometimes, and I have a headache." Harry put the thermometer in the boy's mouth, saying, "I'm glad you told me." He did not know what he had been told, but the persistent air of distrust worried him, and he wanted to break through the boy's hostility, and perhaps discover what was wrong with him. As he studied the boy covertly he toyed with the idea of having Ernest look him over. In the last few days Harry's respect for the chiropractor had grown. Headaches, dizziness, might respond to Ernest's expertise.

"Well?" the boy said when Harry took the thermometer from his mouth.

Harry finished recording it before he said, "Moderate. One hundred and three-fifths." Harry had been surprised. He had thought that the fever would be lower. He frowned. "Can we keep you here overnight?" he asked.

"No," the boy said, too quickly. "I got to get home, man."

"It would be better if we had some time to observe you. I don't like the thought of you walking around with a fever." Harry tapped the boy's shoulder. "What's your name, by the way?"

"None of your business. You fix me up. That's all I want from you." He pulled the examination gown around himself protectively. "I don't have to tell you nothing."

Harry nodded. "All right. Will you tell me where you live, so that one of the doctors can check on you tomorrow?" He saw the hostility in the boy's young eyes, and went on, "I know you don't like doctors, but I think you should let us see you again. What you have might be catching, and before you expose your friends to whatever you've got, I'd like the chance to try to cure you, or at least find out what's wrong."

The boy's gaze wavered. "Catching? What makes you think this is catching."

"Most diseases are. And we are in the middle of an epidemic."

"That's a bunch of bull!" The boy spat.

Harry stopped. "What is?"

"That epidemic. There ain't an epidemic. They're killing kids, that's what's going on. So don't talk epidemic to me, you bastard." The boy had flushed darkly, and when his outburst was over, he retreated into surliness.

"Who told you that, about killing kids?" Harry asked, deeply concerned.

"I heard it."

Harry tried again, leaning toward the boy, his face intent. "Can you tell me who? Look, I admit that kids are dying from diseases they shouldn't die from. We've seen too many of them to doubt that. But it doesn't mean that you're the only targets, or that you aren't really sick. Do you understand that? You have some kind of disease. If you don't let us treat you, you may get much worse, and you may give it to your friends. I don't think you want to do that. So please, tell me who thinks kids are being killed."

The boy gave him a poisonous look.

"It's very important," Harry said persuasively. "Don't you see, we can work together. And perhaps we can stop the worst of the outbreak before it happens."

"You doctors are all alike," the boy said, very worldly and tired. "You always think you can sling the bull and we'll go along with it because we're scared to die. Holy, holy, holy. I know what asses you are. I'm not gonna help you wipe us out." He swung off the examination table. "Can I get dressed now?"

Harry felt very helpless. "Certainly." He made one last try. "Will you at least promise me that you'll let us take blood and urine samples so that if there is anything seriously wrong with you, we'll have a chance to find out what? We need to know what you have if we're going to make this easier for you. And if you don't care about yourself, think about the others. Please." He did not know if he had made any headway with the boy. He waited, feeling fear.

The boy shrugged. "Can't hurt to leave you a little piss. You can put it on the flowers." He giggled. "You can take some blood out of my finger, but you aren't putting needles in me. That's how you're killing us. Tris . . ." He stopped. "We know about that way."

"Thank you." Harry schooled his face to show no surprise. Tris. He and Jim had been talking about Tristam. Was there really such a person? Was he the one they had to deal with? "Stop at the table at the end of the hall, and the nurse will tell you what to do."

The boy looked at him. "What if I *am* sick? What then?"

"We'll try to make you well, if you give us a chance. If you don't feel any better, come back in five days, okay? You'll know by then if you're going to get well on your own."

The boy gave him a measured stare. "Okay. Five days." He went behind the screen to dress.

* * *

"Well, what is it?" Harry asked Natalie as she bent over a microscope. It was very late, but the Van Dreyter house was still full of light, and the line of patients had not diminished.

Natalie shook her head and concentrated on the slide. "I don't know." She leaned back and passed one hand over her eyes. "Maybe I'm just too tired. I should be able to figure it out."

"Well, what does it look like, then?" Harry demanded, feeling anxious, and hating to admit he was frightened.

"A little like polio, but it isn't quite the same. I wish we had a real lab. Then we could find out very fast." She pinched the bridge of her nose. "I'm not thinking very clearly, Harry. You might want to get one of the others to take a look at this. Or do it yourself." She stood back from the table and let Harry peer into the microscope.

"I see what you mean," he said in a few minutes. "Maybe he's got a mild case because he's partially immune." He didn't believe that, but he could not find a better explanation.

"I don't know, Harry." She moved away from the table, and as she did, she noticed her hands were shaking. "I've got a bad feeling about that, Harry. Don't ask me what it is, or to explain it, because I can't. But I have that feeling. I wish I didn't."

Harry was too familiar with hunches to doubt hers. "Any idea what?"

"No." She breathed deeply. "I'm going to have to knock off, Harry. I've been doing lab work for the last ten hours, and I'm too tired. I'm not thinking clearly. I'd better quit now." She shook her head slowly as she studied the walls. "You know, I never thought that much about the color of walls, but I think I'd go crazy if I had to work in a red room all the time. It's too much."

Harry glanced at the walls, with their fine Chinese red finish. "I see what you mean. Are you going up to bed, then?"

"Yeah. I have to be on the floor by seven in the morning. And there's all that information to give Dave before he goes on house calls. I'm not sure he should do rounds by himself, Harry. What time is it?"

Harry glanced at his watch. "Eleven thirty-five, more or less. Make sure you take a hot bath; it'll get rid of the sore muscles."

She nodded. "I never used to think about this kind of work. All we had to do was plug in a support unit or run a test through a computer, and it was all done. But here, it's all our own doing. I miss that computer, Harry." She pulled her smock off. "When will you be up?"

"Not for quite a while. I'm on night call until Roger relieves me at three." He looked across the room at her. "You're doing fine, Natalie."

"Sure." She managed a wan smile. "Thanks."

* * *

Dave Lillijanthal was dressed at his most jaunty as he prepared to leave on morning house calls. He patted Natalie's shoulder, oblivious to the annoyed glare she gave him. "Don't worry, Nat. I'll do all the things I'm supposed to. I'll dispense pills and country wisdom and bedside charm like no one you ever saw."

"Dave, stop joking. We've got people out there dying and they need your help. This isn't like Westbank. You don't have the computers to back you up, or take over when you want your lunch. Show a little compassion, will you?"

He chortled. "Whatever you say, Nat. Anything your heart desires." He reached across the table and filled his cup a second time. "I'm really glad Carol brought along her coffee. It beats hell out of the substitutes."

Natalie opened her last folder. "Now, this woman . . ." She stopped, then went on in another tone. "Dave, are you listening?"

"Sure."

"This woman has a history of gastric ulcers, and if she shows any symptoms, any symptoms at all, you must call Peter Justin and get him to take her in. She's not in any condition to risk staying out of the hospital, no matter how many diseases are taking up beds. She's the sort who'll try not to upset you, so you'll have to be careful. Make sure she isn't in pain, and make sure she tells you the truth. Bring her back here if you have to."

"Worry, worry, worry." Dave made an airy gesture as she stood up. "You don't have to bother that pretty red head of yours over me," he said as he touched her hair. "Look, you know they aren't going to keep this disease thing up much longer. They can't. It's crazy. So we'll do our job marking time, and in form." He drank the last of the coffee. "Another couple of weeks and we'll be out of here, and we'll be home free. I've been thinking about teaching. I'd like to teach. It's not as much of a hassle."

Natalie frowned. "Dave, I wish you wouldn't talk that way." She handed him the folders and watched him tuck them under his arm. "We're in very serious trouble. We're dealing with too many dead people."

He laughed. "Right. But trouble never bothers me, Natalie, especially when it's someone else's." He strode over to the door. "See? I'm getting out of here before seven. I'll be back by teatime. Around four." He blew her a kiss and closed the door.

CHAPTER 7

The grandfather clock in the foyer had struck quarter after seven when the police arrived. Amanda opened the door for them, worried that perhaps their tenure at the Van Dreyter house was at an end. "Yes, gentlemen?" she said, none of her fear in her voice or her manner. "What is it?"

The older officer, a stocky man of about fifty, looked her over quite thoroughly. "You aren't supposed to be in this house, y'know."

"Nonetheless, I am here." Amanda met his eyes squarely, and waited.

"Yeah. My oldest kid came here a couple of days ago. You helped him. Well, one of you did. There wasn't room for him at the hospital."

"Is that what you came to tell me?" Amanda asked, wondering now if she should invite the men in.

"No. No, that's not what we're here for. Is one of your doctors a guy named Lillijanthal?" This was asked awkwardly, and Amanda knew there was trouble. "Yes," she said quietly. "Dave Lillijanthal is working here. He was out on house calls earlier. We expected him back before now."

The officer turned and called down. "This is the place. You better bring him on in." Then he said to Amanda, "I'm sorry, ma'am. He's been hurt."

"Hurt?" she echoed. "How?"

"Some kids got a hold of him. They did a good job on him." He stopped, as if realizing Amanda was shocked. "Why don't you call a couple of the other doctors to take care of him?" He gestured to the patrol wagon in the driveway. "We'll bring him on in and you can make room for him where you need to."

"Is it serious?" Amanda asked.

"Afraid so. We tried to get him in at Inner City, but they're filled up. The desk said that they were even putting beds in the operating rooms. We brought him back here. You people are the only ones left who can take care of cases like his."

There was a stretcher being lifted out of the patrol wagon now, and the men carrying it handled it gently. Amanda could see a shape on the stretcher under the blankets. And she saw that the blankets were bloody. She steadied herself against the door to stop her dizziness, then called into the house in a voice she hardly recognized as her own, "Somebody, help. Who's on call?"

In a moment she heard Harry's answering shout: "Be there in a minute, Amanda."

By this time the men with the stretcher were almost at the door, and she remembered. "No, wait. Don't bring him in this way. There are patients in the room. Take him there." She pointed to the french doors which opened from the formal dining room. "That's our room, over there. Please take him there."

The officer shrugged. "Okay. We'll take him there."

"I'll go and open the door for you." She closed the door and forced herself to breathe deeply. Then she started toward the dining room, calling once more to Harry on the way: "Harry, the dining room. Quickly."

Something of her panic must have been in her voice, for Harry was waiting for her at the dining-room door. "What is it, Amanda?" Then he saw her face, and his eyes narrowed.

"The police. They said they're bringing Dave Lillijanthal back. He's on a stretcher." She put her hand to her mouth. "You'd better let them in, Harry. I'll call Natalie, if you like."

"Amanda?"

She gave him half a smile. "It's silly, I know, but I'm not up to it. There's no way I can deal with this." She opened the door for him. "I'll send Natalie. She can handle this much better than I can."

"What is it, Amanda?" Harry insisted, holding the older woman's arm. "You've been doing fine."

She pulled her arm away. "Harry, I'm a pediatric surgeon. I've rarely worked on anyone over ten. I'm tired, my pulse is too fast, and if I faint on you, I'll be worse than useless."

Harry nodded. "Are you keeping up with your medicine?" he asked, thinking of her heart. "You said you'd be careful."

She made a fatalistic gesture. "I try to remember. Most of the time I do remember." She gave his arm an affectionate pat. "Thank goodness I don't have to explain myself to you. Who would you like me to send to you?"

Harry answered without hesitation, "Natalie, if she's available. She's been seeing patients most of the day."

"She's in the lab now." Amanda nodded. "I'll get her for you."

"Not if she's busy."

"Roger or Dominic can take over for her there." She regarded him steadily, then turned and walked down the hall.

Harry opened the door and switched on the light, so that the three great chandeliers glowed. He had already stopped being impressed by the grandeur of the house, and now walked to the french doors without noticing the lights and the steady shine of the fine crystal.

"Thank you for waiting," he said to the officers who stood outside the door carrying the stretcher between them. "You'd better bring him inside."

The older officer nodded. "Just as you say." He motioned to the other officer and they brought the stretcher inside. "He's been badly beaten," the first officer said, with a sympathetic but pessimistic nod toward the stretcher. "It's a good thing you doctors are here," he went on to Harry. "It's been getting pretty rough here, I can tell you. Well, sorry, but we have to be about our business." He pointed his partner to the door. Then he went out.

Harry murmured what might have been a thank you as he knelt beside the stretcher and reluctantly pulled back the light blanket covering Dave Lillijanthal.

He did not need an X-ray to see that Dave's skull had been fractured, for his head was lopsided, and a ragged bruise over his left eye was pulpy to the touch. Harry swallowed convulsively. Tightening his jaw, he continued his examination. Dave's right arm was badly broken; bone splinters pushed through the swollen elbow, contusions along his ribs showed where he had been mercilessly kicked after he had fallen. His groin was hideously bruised, and more than twice normal size.

"Dear God," Natalie said behind him, and Harry turned to her.

"I need your help," he said.

She nodded quickly and went to the other side of the stretcher. "What happened to him? Amanda only said he was hurt. She didn't say . . ."

"I know." Harry continued his examination. "We're going to need X-rays. We'll have to ask Ernest to bring his equipment over here.

Dave certainly can't be moved again, not until the swelling is down and we have the broken bones immobilized. I think we'll have to use casts, the old way. We don't have a bone-support unit here. I wish now we'd thought to bring one."

"Do you have any idea why?"

"No." Harry was busy gently exploring a shallow laceration along Dave's thigh. "His right kneecap is dislocated. We'll have to get that back into line, too. Ernest can do that better than we can. He's lucky, though. If the patella hadn't slipped out, he'd have a worse fracture here than the one at his elbow. I don't know if we're going to be able to restore mobility there. Look at it. The humerus and the ulna are both broken, and the joint's a mess. We need a replacement joint, but we don't have one. Of course." He stood up suddenly. "I'm going to call Westbank. It's one thing to kick us out, but it's another to refuse treatment to a man in this condition." He stalked to the door, tension in every movement.

"Harry," Natalie called after him. "See if you can get some pain suppressors while you're at it. We're running low already."

"They'll probably refuse."

"Get anything you can. I know there's still some morphine at the hospital, for the people who are reactive to analgizine. We're going to need it, and not only for Dave. We've got to have something to give that man we're bringing out of tetanus. He's been in terrible pain."

"That's Lucciani, isn't it?" Harry asked. "In the north wing?"

She nodded. "Make them understand, Harry. And if you can find Radick, ask him to come in here."

Harry stopped. "Why Radick?"

Natalie raised her pale brows. "He's a psychiatrist, remember? He's good with shock victims. He's also a licensed hypnotist, and as long as we can't drug the pain out of Dave, maybe Radick can talk it out of him. At least until we can treat him properly."

"I hadn't thought of that. You're right. I'll send him in." The door closed firmly behind him.

*   *   *

Radick's face was grave as he rose from beside the stretcher. "This is monstrous," he said quietly. "This will be very hard for Dave. He will not accept what has happened to him." He looked at Natalie, who waited a few feet away. "I have a few drugs in my case. I'll bring them down."

"What do you mean?" Natalie asked him suddenly. "He won't accept what?"

"This." Radick indicated the stretcher. "Dave is a Golden Child, Natalie. He has always been beautiful, and his life has been easy. He has never had to endure even so little a thing as disappointment for long. And now this. He is not very well prepared to deal with injuries of this sort. Or the recovery from them. Which you and I know will not be a total recovery." He looked at the ruined elbow again. "Even if we replace the joint, he will not recover wholly. This will be very bad for him."

Natalie hesitated. "What do we tell the others?"

Radick stared at her. "What do you mean, 'tell the others'?"

"Do we tell them that when they make house calls they might be beaten up?"

For a moment Radick said nothing, then, "I think perhaps it might be wise to wait until we learn what really happened to him. I don't like to say this of a colleague, but I have known instances when Dave was not as ethical as he should be, and not as discreet."

Natalie thought again of Mark, and hearing him with his mistress in the lab. It seemed a very long time ago now. And so Dave was such another. She nodded slowly, and realized she was not particularly surprised. As Radick had said, Dave was a Golden Child and everything was easy for him.

"Natalie?"

She shook off her thought. "Nothing, Radick. I suppose you're right. But I'm sure the others know that Dave had been hurt. We can't hide that, and I don't want to hide it." Her chin lifted defiantly.

"Of course. But we will hear from Dave what actually happened before we tell the others to be wary." He sat down on one of the elegant rosewood chairs and leaned his head back against the petit point headrest showing two wood ducks floating on a lake. He sighed. "I recall a time when my mother did petit point. Her work was beautiful. But it took so much time, and even then we were all very rushed."

"Is something wrong, Radick?" Natalie asked. "More than Dave?"

"I have been with a very troubled man this afternoon. He is intelligent but uneducated. He knows that there is something wrong happening here. He does not believe what has been told him, but he is terrified of what the lies might cover. So he becomes divided in his mind. He has much fear which he cannot admit to, and so he tries to close his eyes. He was once religious, and has returned to his faith. But there are no answers. He has been reading the Book of Revelation, and thinks now that we are living in the last times. But the Great Beast is not what stalks us. And the Horsemen of the Apocalypse . . ."

"Just the Fourth one," Natalie said, remembering a long-ago discussion in her first university psychology class. "Just the Rider on the Pale Horse."

"With the scythe." Radick nodded. "War, Slavery, Famine and Pestilence. The death figure is Plague, you know. There's plenty of death in the other three, so there was no reason to make a special category. But even War, Slavery and Famine avoid Pestilence, and you can't blame them." He thought for a moment. "The others do make the world ripe for disease. The Crimean War lost more men to disease than in battle." He turned to her. "I'm sorry. I realize this is no way to talk. I'm feeling discouraged and I'm taking it out on you."

She made a complicated gesture. "Did you see the follow-up on the kid who was in to see Harry? The one with the stuff that sort of looks like polio? I did the workup on him. I still don't know what he has." She studied Radick's worn face. "I'm frightened."

Radick nodded. "Of course you are. So am I."

On the stretcher Dave Lillijanthal moved slightly, then moaned. Natalie rose quickly and went to him. "Dave? Dave? It's Natalie, Dave."

Dave swung his left arm aimlessly, as if fending off some threat. His eyes were open but unseeing. He would have screamed if his voice were not already destroyed. His abraded side started to bleed once more.

Radick had joined Natalie, and gently moved her aside. "I think I had better handle this, Natalie." He went down on his knees and began to speak softly, reassuringly to Dave, and after a few minutes Dave lay still, his eyes open now, and knowing.

"Jesus," he croaked. "How'd . . ."

"Don't talk, my friend," Radick said. "We are trying to arrange for you to be admitted at Westbank. You are in need of their services and we haven't enough here to care for you adequately." He said, more gently still, "You have been badly hurt, Dave."

"Those kids . . ."

"Kids?" Natalie said, feeling very cold.

"Lots of them . . ."

The door slammed open and Harry came into the room, thunder in his face. "The ruddy bastards won't take him. I talked to Jim Braemoore and he said they didn't have enough room. Not even for Dave, and he worked there for eleven years!" He kicked savagely and sent one of the rosewood chairs end over end.

"Harry," Natalie said, and the tone of her voice stopped him. "Dave's awake, Harry."

There was a pause, and then Harry bent to pick up the chair. "Sorry." He came to the stretcher and looked down. "I won't ask how you are," he said to Dave. "I examined you."

Dave studied him, fighting panic.

"Ernest is bringing his X-ray equipment over, and we're going to get all the pictures we can. Then we'll do whatever we can for you. It might not be much. I'll see if I can get through to Inner City. They might take you over there."

"Thanks," Dave whispered.

Natalie pulled Harry aside. "Where are we going to put him?" she asked. "We've got so many infectious and contagious diseases, and the shape he's in, I wish we had an isolation floor."

Harry nodded, his head lowered. "What about the grooms' quarters over the garage? We can ask the nurses to let him have one of the rooms . . ."

"I don't know." Natalie frowned. "Besides, it's going to get awfully hot in there in a couple weeks. We aren't air conditioned here, remember."

Harry nodded. "We need some cool place where we can set up traction."

"The butler's pantry!" Natalie said, brightening. "It's between the kitchen and the reception office," which the informal dining room had become. "He won't be exposed to too much, and he'll be where we can all keep an eye on him."

"Good. We'll use it if"—his face darkened—"if we can't get him into Inner City. Or even County General. God!"

Natalie stretched out her hand tentatively. "Harry?"

"Ah, it's not you. But they make me so damn mad. This is their mess, and when we try to clean it up, this is all we get. Dave's beaten up, we're told there isn't room for him, they can't help us at all . . ." His face was desolate.

"Was there anything more?"

His tone was very dry. "Nothing worth mentioning. No, I take that back. Braemoor refused to contact the I.I.A., who, it appears, are running this show. He won't, and we can't."

"The I.I.A.?" Natalie asked, bewildered. "What does Internal Intelligence have to do with this?"

"According to Braemoore, it's their baby. Their bright idea." He rubbed his forehead. "It makes me sick, Natalie."

She nodded. "I know."

Radick had stood, and he walked toward them now, looking old. "He's under light hypnosis now. I don't know how long he will stay under. You'd better get him X-rayed while you can. I warn you now, Harry, that he's in worse emotional shape than physical."

"Meaning?"

"Meaning we may not be able to save him. At all."

Harry turned on his heels and started toward the door.

"What is it, Harry?" Natalie was alarmed.

"Eric Patman is going to help us. The hell with his ulcers. We have to have him. We have to have an immunologist, for Dave as well as the others." The door closed behind him, loud as a shout.

"He must do something," Radick said to Natalie. "And perhaps he is right."

"Did you mean what you said about Dave?" Natalie asked, as if she had not heard him.

"Yes."

"I see." She went back to the stretcher and looked down. Dave's face was composed, his eyes distant, and only a slight tightness in his brow showed pain. His skull fracture was not swelling now, but his head was very badly misshapen. His breath made a grating sound.

Natalie thought about the drugs they would need, and the surgical equipment if they were to help Dave. She knew they didn't have it, and admitted to herself that they were unlikely to get it. And Dave would be the one who would suffer. It was his skull, his arm, his body that was ruined. It was his pain. For the first time in many years she wished she believed enough in anything to pray.

* * *

Stan Kooznetz poked his head out of the makeshift lab. "Where are you going?"

Harry stopped pulling on his jacket. "Inner City. If I can't get through to Westbank. We need drugs, and a bed and surgery for Dave Lillijanthal. They've got to help us."

Stan considered him. "I'll go with you." Before Harry could object, he went on. "I worked at Inner City once. I know my way around. I know who we can talk to. Maybe we can find out who they fired, and bring them in with us." He saw the suppressed fury in Harry's face. "And maybe you could use some help. Wait a minute. I'll be right back."

"Haven't you got patients waiting?" Harry asked.

Stan stopped. "I have what looks like a couple of smallpoxes and an honest-to-god malignant tumor of the bladder. Nothing that Kirsten can't take care of. Don't leave without me."

Harry glared, but he waited for the three minutes it took Stan to be rid of his lab coat and arrange for Lisa to cover for him. "All right," he said when he came out the door at last. "Let's go."

Harry nodded, and they left through the side door.

"I heard that Dave is in very bad shape," Stan said as Harry started the smaller of their two vans. "Amanda mentioned it privately. It's upsetting her more than she shows."

Harry said nothing, concentrating on maneuvering in the tight space.

"Amanda said that this could be fatal." Stan said it conversationally, but his long face was somber.

"Amanda is right." Harry swung the wheel as they went down the driveway, and eased the van out into traffic, which he noticed was much lighter than it should have been at this time of day.

"Beaten?" Stan asked.

"Beaten. Kicked. Contusions, abrasions, fractures: you name it. They did a thorough job. And he has to have help. We can't handle this ourselves. We haven't got the equipment. We haven't got the supplies. And we certainly haven't got the facilities for the repair job he needs."

"As bad as that?"

Harry honked at a driver ahead of them blundering from lane to lane, then said, "You might want to look in on him later. We're putting him in the pantry for the time being. Natalie's idea. She's thinking clearly. I only wish I were."

Stan agreed that their work was much harder than any of them thought it would be. "It used to be like this all the time, Harry. I don't know how they managed."

"They didn't." Harry changed lanes and noticed that three cars had pulled off the road and were waiting on the shoulder, their drivers still in them. He guessed they were sick. "We could use a City Patrol radio in this thing."

"We could use a lot of things."

"Yeah," Harry said, and was silent the rest of the way to Westbank.

*   *   *

The lobby of the hospital was full and, to Harry's surprise, messy. He strode through it quickly, puzzled at the barely controlled chaos around him. At the elevators, he turned to Stan. "Where are you going?"

"To talk to Justin. If he'll talk to me. Where are you going?"

"Liz Martel. All the way up on seventeen. We've got to have pharmaceuticals, and right now. I know there's no way to get releases from the administration, so it'll have to be her. If I'm not there, I'll be at the diagnostic center on ten with Wyland or on seven."

"I'll try Liz first," Stan said.

The elevator doors opened and they entered. Harry pushed 16 for Stan and 17 for himself.

"Good luck," Harry said to Stan as the door opened on the sixteenth floor.

"And to you," Stan said as the doors closed between them.

Harry left the elevator at the top floor and walked down the littered hallway. As he passed the administration dining room he noticed that new and very limited hours were posted outside. He glanced in and saw that instead of the linen tablecloths and good service, the tables were set with the same plastic service that was used in the staff cafeteria on the first floor. Apparently the current emergency had even cut into the luxuries of the administration.

Three doors down, Harry turned and pushed through two sets of double doors into the pharmacy, and looked around him in dismay. "Christ!" he said.

In a moment a parapharmacist came from behind the disordered shelves, his face smudged with exhaustion. He looked up at Harry. "Yes?"

"Is Dr. Martel here?" Harry was almost afraid to ask.

"Yeah. She's taking a nap. D'you want her, or can I do it?"

Harry considered. "I'd better talk to Liz, thanks anyway."

The parapharmacist shrugged and went back between the shelves. In a few minutes Liz Martel walked toward him. She was still disheveled from sleep, and her usually crisp lab coat was crumpled. She hesitated when she saw him. "Harry?"

"It's me. What's happening around here, Liz?"

She turned tragic, Irish-blue eyes on him. "Everything. We can't keep up, and almost a third of the staff is out. It's been miserable." She shook her head. "What about you?"

"We're over at the Van Dreyter house."

Liz thought for a moment. "I heard something about that. I wondered if it was true or not."

"It's true, Liz." He studied her face. "Are you feeling all right?"

Her laugh was shaky. "I'm tired, Harry. Just tired. I got scared a couple of days back and ran a series on myself. Nothing." She leaned against her counter. "We've been so rushed."

"So I see."

"Oh, Harry, it's awful." She brushed her hand across her eyes. "I'm doing everything I can, but . . ." She gave a fatalistic shrug.

Harry made a sympathetic noise, then said, "Liz, I need your help."

Her look was filled with disbelief.

"Really. I need your help. You can help us."

"Us?"

"At the Van Dreyter house. We're taking in patients over there, Liz. We're offering treatment on a small scale. We're taking those people who can't or won't go to the hospitals. We've got beds, we've got skills and some of our tools. But we need medicines, Liz. We need drugs."

Liz Martel thought for a moment. "You're asking me to give you what you want without administrative authorization?"

"I'm asking you to help us."

"It comes to the same thing."

"Yes."

She shoved her hands into her pockets and looked away. "If I got caught . . ."

"Oh, come off it," Harry said, growing impatient. "You know as well as I do that there isn't going to be a chance of that. This pet epidemic of the I.I.A. is out of hand. In a week or two, there's no way they're going to be able to tell who did what to whom. But look, in the meantime, maybe we can save a few. Maybe. If you help me . . ."

The phone on the wall shrilled, and Liz went to answer it. She held out the receiver. "It's for you, Harry."

Frowning, Harry took the phone. "Yes?"

"It's Stan, Harry," said the tinny voice. "I've found out that Wexford and Justin have gone over to Inner City. So I'm going over there in one of the ambulances. They're transferring all the smallpox cases there. I'm leaving in a couple of minutes."

Harry felt a twinge of apprehension. "Do you want me to come with you?"

"It's more important you get the drugs and get home. I'll call you if I need to be picked up. Good luck."

"To you, too," Harry said, afraid to add good-bye as he hung up.

Liz was studying him. "Wexford won't give you any help, you know," she said. "Neither will Justin. They're in on this. They don't care what happens."

For a moment Harry wanted to make a cutting retort, but he held it back. He had to have Liz's help, not her anger. "We've gotta try, Liz. If we give up, we're dead."

"We're dead anyway," she said in another tone. "Tell me what you need."

"Antibiotics. Painkillers, all you can spare. Any vaccines that are still good. Trancs. Relaxants. We simply don't have anything."

"I can't, Harry. We're running short here."

"But Liz, look. I'll take anything. You've still got some penicillin and morphine, don't you? I don't have to have the new stuff. I'll use anything I can get. We have to have them, Liz. Don't make me take them from you. I will if I have to." Harry was startled to hear himself say this, and more startled to realize he meant it.

"But I told you, we're running low ourselves."

"Listen to me, Liz. We have smallpox cases and tetanus. Two diphtherias. Three cancers. A couple of polios. We need drugs for them. And then there's Dave," he said, and saw Liz turn white. "Liz?"

"Dave Lillijanthal?" she said softly.

"Yes."

"What's wrong with him?" There was so much anguish in the words that Harry found it difficult to answer her. "He's been beaten, Liz. Very badly beaten, I'm afraid."

"Dave?"

"I'm sorry." He remembered the occasional gossip about Dave, and had not paid much attention to it. Handsome men attracted such talk, just as they attracted women. Now he realized he was wrong to discount it.

"How badly?" But before she could hear his answer, she said, "Oh, Christ. Take anything you need, Harry. If it's for Dave, take it. Just don't take standard drugs. There's morphine and pentathol, if he has to have them. The cooler in the back has the penicillin." She put her hand over her mouth, then broke into racking sobs.

Harry touched her shoulder. "Liz?"

"Take your drugs and get out of here," she said in deadly quiet.

"Liz . . ."

"Get out get out get out get out!"

"Come with me."

"I can't. I can't." She turned away from him.

Harry stood beside her for a moment, feeling ineffectual. Then he walked back between the many rows of shelving and began looking for the large insulated boxes the drugs came packed in. He did not let himself hear Liz crying.

* * *

"We can keep them down in the wine cellar," Harry explained as he unloaded the boxes from the van. "It's cool enough down there for everything but the refrigerated stuff."

Kirsten Grant and Dominic Hertzog picked up boxes and carried them across to the kitchen entrance. Harry called after them, "Send some more help out here, will you?"

"Yeah," Dominic answered.

Harry went on stacking the boxes beside the van. In a moment Jim Varnay was out. "What a haul."

"It's going to have to last us as long as we stay here," Harry said. "It's not all that much."

Jim nodded. "I see what you mean. What was it like down there?"

"A mess. Is Stan back yet?"

"I thought he was with you." Jim hoisted one of the boxes to his shoulder with a grunt.

"No. He went to Inner City to see Wexford or Justin."

"Hell. There aren't any buses running downtown. He might have to walk to the beltway before he can get transportation."

Harry felt a flicker of worry, then dismissed it. "He said he'd call if he needed a lift." He waved to Natalie, who had come from the house, and held out a box to her. "In the wine cellar."

She took it. "Good. Did you get everything we need?"

"No, but I got what I could. Anything new turn up this afternoon?"

"A couple of cases of measles, not serious, and one hell of a tonsillitis." She hoisted the box, and followed Dominic and Kirsten into the house.

Jim Varnay picked up another box and started off. "I'll be back for more."

When Natalie came back, she said, "By the way, we've picked up four new nurses, thank goodness."

"Nurses?"

"From County General. They were kicked out for insubordination or some such idiocy. They'd heard about us and came over to help. Three women and a man. One of them's only done obstetrics, but she's willing to learn."

"We may need OBs before this is over."

"We've put them in the grooms' quarters with the others. Wallingham is the oldest. She was in charge of the intensive care floor at County General. I put her on duty right away."

"Good."

The last of the boxes were carried off, and Natalie walked back to the house with Harry. "Harry," she said as they neared the kitchen door, "I'm worried about Amanda. She's running out of energy."

"She's not a young woman," Harry said idly.

"She's got heart trouble," Natalie snapped at him.

"She told me she's taking care of it."

Natalie snorted. "Okay. But I think we ought to keep an eye on her. We can't afford to lose one more of us. Having Dave out of commission is bad enough."

"You're right," Harry agreed. "I'll keep an eye on her, then."

"Thanks."

*　*　*

There were over a dozen people waiting in the reception room, most of them sick. Harry scowled at the files handed to him, and nodded to Jane Fletcher. "Who's first in this lot?" he asked, giving a worried glance at the patients.

"Blairing and Santiago. I'd take Santiago first," said Fletcher with her nurse's firmness, and a knowing nod. "The boy, Jaime Santiago, he's very sick. I'm almost certain you'll want to admit him. Otherwise . . ."

"Okay." Harry tucked the files under his arm. "Send Santiago in."

* * *

"The Santiago kid has that stuff that looks like polio," Harry reported in the lab a little later. "Damn it, we need more information about it. Can you get a workup on it? And we'll need a complete series on Mrs. Blairing. Unless I miss my guess, she's diabetic, and might have something more on top of it. We'll have to use the old glucose-tolerance test. We aren't set up for computer diagnosis." He sighed in exasperation. "I'm beginning to realize how much we took for granted at Westbank."

Howard Webbster looked up. "I'll run her as soon as I can."

Fletcher looked in the door. "Phone for you, Harry. It's Stan."

"Okay," Harry said, and nodding his excuses to Howard, went into the hall. "Harry here," he said to the phone.

"Hi. I'm leaving Inner City."

"Any luck?" Harry asked without much hope.

"No. Both Wexford and Justin refused to discuss the matter. And Harry, Peter's got something." He paused to make sure Harry understood. "I spent almost an hour with him, and he looks sick."

"What does he have? Do you know?"

"I didn't have the chance to find out. But it might be important later on." Stan cleared his throat and went on. "No help from anyone down here. They're swamped with patients, and they really don't have enough staff to keep going. It's worse than Westbank. I don't see how they're managing at all."

"Wonderful," Harry said sarcastically. "If this keeps up much longer, they're going to need our help more than we need theirs."

Harry cursed mentally. He had hoped that there would be a way to stop the insanity now, but he no longer believed that. Now he feared what lay ahead, and the fear was ice in his vitals. "Do you need a ride back?"

"What's the patient load there right now?"

"Very heavy. We're all going to be working late."

There was a pause. "Okay. I'll get back on my own. Buses are running on the beltway, and that should get me there in about ninety minutes to two hours."

Harry said, "Are you sure? I can send one of the nurses to get you."

"This is their rest period. They need it. Don't worry about me."

"Whatever you say. I'll see you in a couple of hours."

* * *

Natalie knocked on the lab door later, and it was Amanda who admitted her. "Hi," she said. "Do you mind if I run these through very fast? I'll try not to get in your way."

"Be my guest," Amanda said without looking up from her microscope. "The extra slides are in the second drawer."

"That's handy." Natalie reached for the slides and set to work.

"What do you think you've got?"

"Leukemia. I saw one case in medical school. The patient was an older woman, a Christian Scientist who hadn't got the vaccine. It was very sad. It's a terrible disease."

"Is this patient old or young?" Amanda asked as she made a note on the chart at her side.

"Young. About seven. Very pretty little girl. I don't know what to tell her aunt. I hope it isn't, but if the cancer vaccines aren't given, and with the atmospheric carcinogen count the way it is . . ." She did not go on, filled with anger at the irresponsible decisions which had brought them to this dreadful time. "What have you got?"

"Another diphtheria, a typhus, which means that we're going to have to be very careful about sanitation from now on. And there're a couple of minor viral infections of no particular importance. And a couple cases of respiratory impairment, but I don't know what's causing it."

"There's a tuberculosis admit on Alexes' list. We've put him in a closed room, and we're taking all the precautions we can. I hope it isn't as serious as Alexes seems to think." Natalie put down her materials. "I used to think that the serious challenges had left medicine. I wish I could get that feeling back again."

Amanda sighed. "No. You've never taken this for granted. You think you have, but I've watched you." She paused, yawned, and said, "I must be more tired than I thought."

"Take a break," Natalie suggested.

"I've got to finish these things first. Then I'll sit down. No, about what I was saying: you're truly conscientious. That's rare. It's rare in doctors and everywhere else. I admire you for it." Amanda stopped. "And we should both get back to work."

Natalie gestured her agreement and set up her specimen for a blood count.

* * *

Radick nodded sympathetically. "You say the patient is young?" he asked Natalie, who told him the child's age. "Seven is very young to die." Radick was sadly thoughtful. "Do you want me to tell the parents, or shall you?"

"Guardian. An aunt. She's quite young herself, not more than twenty-five. I just don't know what to say to her, Radick. I've tried to think for the last half hour. How do you tell either of them that the girl has leukemia, and the disease is quite advanced?"

"I don't know. Oh, I can soften the blow, and perhaps help them avert the worst effects of the shock, but there is no way to alter the truth. If the child has this cancer, there is very little we can do other than lessen the worst of her suffering." He turned away, suddenly very angry. "I hope all those smug, anonymous men who made these decisions have to go through this. I hope they have to see stricken faces and the tortured eyes. I hope they have to watch impotently while their children die . . ." He broke off and looked chagrined. "I'm sorry, Natalie. I did not mean to burden you with my frustration or my rage."

She shrugged.

"That's part of the trouble. We can do so little, and then we start to hate ourselves because we can do nothing. I have often thought that physicians' arrogance—and it is a disease rampant among us—is an attempt to immunize ourselves against self-hate." He sat down on the bench at the breakfast table, which had become his office. "Very well. Send in the child and her aunt, and I will talk to them and do what I can, though it will be little enough."

"Radick," Natalie ventured.

"Go away," he said in gruff compassion. "Go into our common room and give yourself a few minutes to be calm again. We both need it." He showed her a gentle smile ravaged by grief. "Go away," he repeated softly.

"The girl's name is Melanie Lovat. The aunt's name is Sheila Wentworth."

Radick nodded. "Thank you."

* * *

The common room was almost deserted, and the litter of three days covered the formal dining table. Papers, coffee mugs, a crumpled lab smock, all lay on the fine-grained wood. By the tile-inlaid fireplace on the far side of the room several chairs were drawn up, and newssheets lay in piles on the low coffee table. Natalie made a half-hearted attempt to neaten the room, then dropped into one of the elegant chairs opposite Amanda.

"You look tired," Amanda said after a moment or two.

"So do you." She was more concerned than her voice showed. Amanda's face was clay-colored with fatigue, and her breathing was strained. "Have you kept up with your drugs?" Natalie asked, hating herself for asking.

"Of course," Amanda said. "But you know what it's like: it's hard to relax with this going on. So I don't sleep as well as I ought, I know it."

Natalie nodded.

"Have you seen the news today? They're admitting that the death rate is up sixteen per cent."

"Which probably means twice that," Natalie added.

"No doubt. Absenteeism is running at almost forty per cent, according to official releases. Undoubtedly some of this can be accounted for by those staying home to take care of sick family members, and some are staying home out of fear. But that's still too many." She sighed. "Is Stan back yet?"

"Not that I know of. He's planning to take a bus at the Great Beltway. Which means he'll probably be late. One of the patients, a Mr. Eastly, said he had to wait almost two hours for a bus yesterday." Fleetingly, Natalie wondered why she felt she had to have an explanation for Stan's absence. She told herself it was nerves. "Why don't you take a nap, Amanda? You aren't on duty for another four hours."

Amanda nodded. "Thank you. I believe I will." She rose unsteadily. "I might look in on Mr. Rice. He's going fast, and I think he's frightened." Amanda walked slowly to the door. "Will you call me when you go off duty? I don't want to set my alarm. It will waken Carol and Lisa on the other side of the screen."

"All right. If you're not up, I'll call you." Natalie watched the door close behind Amanda. Then, remembering Radick's instructions, she tried to rest and compose herself, which very quickly made her nervous. At last she reached for the screen and turned it on. Light, inane entertainment might be the counterirritant she needed.

A news broadcast was in progress, and she was about to try another network when she was caught by a name she thought she recognized. She turned the sound higher and waited.

". . . on the steps of Stockton's Central Administration Building. Dr. Patman, who was dismissed for cause from Westbank Hospital last month, claimed that the current outbreak of disease was a deliberate plot on the part of the government, an experiment in population control. Dr. Patman demanded that the administration answer his charges, and when asked to leave, he threatened to fill his own veins with certain toxins he said he was carrying on his person. The City Patrol was called to subdue Dr. Patman . . ."

Natalie watched, transfixed as Eric Patman's tiny figure struggled with the uniformed men on the screen. Then she saw him lift something, and whatever his words mouthed, the announcer's smooth voice covered.

"Dr. Patman had been suffering from depression, and had convinced himself that the current city health problem was engineered by certain nameless agencies of the federal government, according to Dr. Miles Wexford, chief administrator at Westbank Hospital."

"You clever bastards," Natalie said to the screen.

"On examination, Dr. Patman was found to have died from a self-administered injection of botulin."

Natalie was half out of her chair. "What?"

"A suicide note was found in his apartment, admitting his intention to kill himself in this manner if he could not convince the authorities to stop what he termed 'this unmitigated atrocity.' There will be a private hearing in the coroner's office tomorrow to determine Dr. Patman's state of mind at the time of his death." On the screen a bad picture of Eric showed him working with slides in his immunological laboratory, the very picture of a mad scientist.

"Liar!" Natalie shouted, getting out of her chair completely. The newscaster had gone blandly on to other topics.

Helpless rage washed over her as she watched the screen. Eric Patman was dead. He had killed himself to stop this horrible farce, and the news had made a slightly off-color joke of his sacrifice. Eric Patman was dead. Natalie found herself shaking, her hands held tightly together, her body tightened intolerably. Eric Patman was dead. Somehow she would have to tell the others.

* * *

Natalie was still awake, staring at the ceiling when Harry came into their room. She watched him without speaking while he pulled off his lab coat, his shirt, then his shoes. When he went to stare out the window, her eyes followed him. At last she asked, "What time is it?"

"About quarter after four." He did not turn around. "We lost Mr. Wanstern a little while ago. We couldn't keep him going any longer." He was silent for a moment. "I heard about Eric. God! Poor guy."

Natalie waited. She knew there was more.

"Stan's not back yet, either. Larsen, that new nurse? She called the City Patrol, but they haven't seen him. I guess that's something."

"He probably stopped to make a house call. If the case is bad, he could still be there."

"Yeah."

"If anything had happened to him, we'd have heard by now. They'd bring him here, the way they brought Dave."

Harry said nothing.

"Harry?" Natalie asked after a time.

"I'm here."

The desolation in his voice touched her. She got out of bed and silently, chastely, went into his arms.

CHAPTER 8

Dominic Hertzog studied the old-fashioned X-rays critically. "No, there's no doubt," he said with a sad shake of his head. "That's a malignancy, and there's not a damn thing we can do about it." He indicated an area of the X-ray. "You see this? That's where the trouble is." He took the X-ray off its lighted viewer and filed it away. "You could get more detail with a new machine, if we had one, but the report would still be the same."

The other doctors agreed uncomfortably. The formal dining room was bright with morning sunlight shining off the chandeliers and lovely walls, in contrast to the bleak fatigue of its occupants.

"What do you suggest?" Amanda asked.

"Drugs to stop the pain, if we can spare them. That's about all we can do now."

Harry nodded. "How long do you think he has left?"

"Stevensen?" Dominic asked, pointing to the file. "He could surprise us and last through the summer, maybe all the way through October, but I doubt he will. I'll give him six weeks to two months. He's not fighting back. If he'd had help before now, maybe a year ago, one of the hospitals might have been able to save him, or at least arrest the cancer. But now, with both the liver and the spleen involved, he's too far gone, even if we were set up to operate on him, which we're not."

"Do we have room to admit him?" Carol Mendosa asked with brutal practicality.

"Mr. Wanstern's room will be ready this afternoon. We can put him in there."

"Mrs. Kaylee died a couple of hours ago. There'll be space there, too."

"I'll put Larsen and Walsh to work on it," Lisa Skye said, since she had taken over the job of assigning nurses.

"Not Walsh you won't," Jim Varnay corrected her. "Walsh is sick. She's running a fever and has the beginning of a serious rash."

The others looked at him.

"It could be measles. It could also be smallpox. I don't know which, not yet. And I haven't had time to run her lab work through yet."

Carol Mendosa cleared her throat. "I see." She spoke for all of them when she said, "I was wondering when one of us would get sick. I guess it's happened. Tell her I'm sorry."

It was Alexes Castor who asked the tacitly forbidden question, "Has anyone heard from Stan yet?"

After a heavy silence Harry said, "No."

"I think he might have gone to Eric's autopsy hearing," Howard Webbster suggested. "He and Eric were pretty close."

"It could be," Alexes said, obviously clutching at straws.

"Perhaps he hasn't been able to phone. I remember that woman yesterday, Shipp? She said that a lot of phones are out of order." Kirsten Grant waited for the rest to agree with her.

"Where's Natalie?" Roger Nicholas asked, "and Radick?"

"Radick's with a patient. Natalie's on some kind of errand. She said she's going to try to get us some help if she can." Harry hoped that his irrational hope did not show.

"We could use it."

Ernest Dagstern spoke up suddenly. "I've talked to a few of my colleagues, and they're willing to extend lab space, X-ray equipment, beds, anything if you'll take on their patients."

Maria Pantopolos turned to Ernest. "How many patients are we talking about? There isn't room here."

"Oh," Ernest said quickly, "we wouldn't have to keep them here. My colleagues will put them up in their offices. You'd have to examine and give some treatment, but we'll do the routine care. We're excellent nurses, you know. We don't just fix whiplashes."

Harry looked at the others. "It might be a good idea. We can reach more people that way." He saw the others wavering. "At least, let's give it a try. If it turns out to be more than we can handle, we can back out. But we're already shorthanded, and if we can take some of the load . . ."

Dominic spoke up then. "I agree, Harry. We'll do a much better job if we can reduce the stress we work under. And I'm sure we can trust the chiropractors to know when to call for help if they need it."

Carol Mendosa shrugged elaborately. "I doubt there'd be any harm in it."

"Then, when do we start?" Harry leaned forward and pulled a new sheet of paper onto his clipboard.

* * *

In the hospital corridors trash eddied along the walls, building up to paper reefs by doors and obstacles. Natalie admitted her shock, but did not stop to pick up the refuse. She knew her way now, and at least on this floor there were no patients on the hall couches. At least, she corrected herself mentally, she had not seen any.

The lab doors loomed ahead, and she squared her shoulders. Now that she knew she must face Mark, her fright was less than it had been that morning. Then she still had a choice, she could still avoid seeing him. But now there was no question. A few steps more and she would be in his lab again. If he was there, she would speak to him. Calmly. Quietly. Reasonably. Her hands became fists at her side.

"I thought I told you . . ." said Mark's angry voice as she opened the door.

"It's Natalie, Mark." She let the door close behind her. Then she walked into the room.

Natalie was not surprised that the lab was neat, that the floors were clean and no litter collected in the corners. The shelves were in order, the equipment shiny and laid out just so. On the far side of the lab, his smock crisp, white, Board of Inspection proper, Mark glared up at her. After a moment, he said, "What are you doing here?"

She did not answer him directly. "I see your plan isn't going well."

"Too goddamn many of the staff are sick." He pushed the console beside him for a readout and swore again. "It's taking too long."

"Is it? It seems very fast to me. But over at the Van Dreyter house we don't have luxuries like that. We're relying on very old procedures, and it's working quite well." She hated herself for feeling defensive as she spoke. For what they had to contend with, they were doing well. She knew she did not have to justify herself to Mark, and yet she did.

"Feeling the good little martyr, are you? Don't expect me to be impressed. You had the chance to really help out and you threw it away. What are you doing here now? Did you change your mind?"

She thought him a beautiful man, his body of almost Greek perfection, a body like statuary. She realized now that he was truly stone: flawless, unmoved, unmoving. "I need your help, Mark. You have to call this . . . experiment . . . off. We're losing too many people; you know that, don't you?"

"Call it off? Before it's finished? We have to know what happens."

"So the I.I.A. can do it again somewhere else?" she asked quietly.

He looked at her sharply. "So you know about the I.I.A., do you? I wasn't sure you'd find out." He pulled the printout from the console and began to read it.

"Just like that, Mark? Just a little surprise that I found out that the federal internal security people are in charge of this atrocious farce? Don't you realize what's happening out there, Mark?"

"Of course I know what's happening." He offered the printout to her. "You might want to look at this."

"What is it?" She was determined not to let him sidetrack her.

"It's the current curve for the incidence of smallpox. We have others, for the other diseases. The disease rate is picking up now, Nat. From now through most of the summer it should climb steeply, then level off for a few weeks before going into a rapid decline. This is the most recent update, and making certain allowances for a slight increase in the death rate, we're more or less on schedule."

Natalie had put her hands over her eyes. "Oh, God," she said thickly, "you don't realize what you've done. Curves! Those curves are dead people, Mark. They're dying. You might as well be killing them yourself. That's just your hospital figures, isn't it, that report? Well, how about the people who aren't in hospitals and won't go to hospitals? Or hadn't you taken that into account? I have. I've seen more than a hundred of them at the Van Dreyter house. They're coming in with smallpox, with diphtheria, with typhus . . ."

He interrupted her. "Typhus?"

"Yes."

His brow raised. "We didn't anticipate having typhus so soon. It's not this early in our projected figures."

For one insane moment Natalie was afraid she was going to laugh. Hysteria bubbled in her, pushing to explode. With a terrible effort she mastered herself. "You mean that this disaster isn't going according to Peter Justin's choreography? How very inconsiderate."

"Now, Nat," he warned, his face growing ugly. He put down the printout.

"You cretinous ass! Look what your great idea has done to us.

Your priceless plan has one little flaw in it, and we're paying the price."

"Nat," he said patiently, "you don't know . . ."

"Shut up!" She was almost as surprised as he at this outburst. And she felt a deep satisfaction as she went on. "I've been listening to you for five years, and all you told me were lies. And now you're going to listen to me, and I'll tell you the truth. This great demonstration of population control you're so proud of has one or two things wrong with it. Don't interrupt," she snapped as he opened his mouth.

"Somewhere along the line you forgot that you aren't dealing with one, or even two, diseases, but many diseases. If you'd just wiped out one third of all smallpox vaccines, or cancer vaccines, or any of the others, that would be all we'd have to contend with: a moderate smallpox or cancer epidemic. An outbreak of polio, maybe. That would have made the job fairly simple. But no, you had to be greedy. You had to have the whole lot of them. So you put every major disease back in business. Which means that, statistically, each of us is probably going to catch *two different fatal diseases*. The hell with the four we statistically won't catch."

"Nat, you're being too emotional . . ."

"Have you been outside? Have you been outside this lab in the last week? Have you been outside the hospital? Do you have any idea of what's going on out there? Well?"

Mark hesitated. "I've had my hands full here," he said, then came toward her. "What do you want, Nat? You didn't come back for this futile gesture, did you?" The confidence was back in his smile, and he made his voice deep and melodic. "You little bitch. You want to blackmail me. That's it, isn't it?"

"No," she said, holding her ground.

He came closer. "You want me to call this off, don't you?"

"If you can," she said, and luckily stung his vanity.

"Of course I can. Me, Wexford, Justin and Cockburn, we're the only ones who can give the orders. No one else."

Natalie stared at him. "And you won't issue that order, because you like this life-and-death power. That's why you don't give a damn about how many people are dying, or how many diseases are let loose. You like this. *You like this.*" Her words were soft, but anguish burned in them. "Is there the slightest chance you'll help us? Let us use the labs, maybe, or at least have a little space to check out this new stuff we've been seeing more of?"

"What new stuff?"

She forced herself to speak calmly. "I'm surprised you aren't aware of it. Many of the patients we've seen have had a disease that looks like polio, but as far as we can tell, it isn't polio."

"Fatal?"

"Not that we know of. Not yet." She saw the fascination in his eyes, the gloating over the new disease. She closed her eyes and went on. "But there've been increasing amounts of it, and some of the cases look fairly severe. We wanted to run some tests, see what it responded to, what it is . . ."

"No."

"We'll work off hours, Mark. We'll bring in our own help, we'll supply our own slides . . ."

"No."

"I see. Not deadly enough for you, is that it?" How tired she was, now that she knew she had failed. "I only hope you live long enough to know what you've done. And not take pride in it." She turned away from him and walked resolutely to the door.

"Nat!" His voice was its most compelling. "Nat, let me explain to you." He started after her.

"You don't have to explain anything to me. I understand."

"But we know what's happening, Nat. We know where the outbreaks are the worst, and we're being careful. We're not monsters."

She had reached the door. "Aren't you?"

"Nat, we have to cut down the population. We must. Or we're all doomed. We're trying to find a way to handle the problem while there's still time."

Her face had hardened now, and she felt rage in her once more. "You had access to vaccines and you let your son die. You knew what was going on, you helped it, and you let your son die."

Natalie saw the blow coming and turned away from it, so that Mark's fist landed on her neck rather than her jaw. She staggered against the door, but took private satisfaction when she did not fall. She felt a surge of dizziness, then her head cleared. "You're not going to convince me that way."

"Philip was a mistake. You're talking as if I murdered him."

She read arrogance in his stance, and realized that he wanted an excuse to hit her again. "That's because I think you did." She was standing steadily once more, and knew she could walk out of the room without stumbling.

"Nat, he was only one child. You can have more." He moved toward her. "You were doing a good job with him. You're a good mother. There's still time for you to change your mind. When this is over, we can afford to have several children. You're at your best with children." He put out his hand persuasively, offering her so much.

"Generous!"

His face flushed. "At least consider this before you throw it all away for foolish heroics."

Quite suddenly she was nauseated. She knew that if she stayed near Mark much longer she would be sick. "Mark," she said as she pulled the door open, "you're obscene." Sensing that her contempt bothered him, she let the door close in his face.

*   *   *

Over two dozen people sat in the Van Dreyter house foyer-turned-waiting-room at noon, their faces carefully guarded so as not to show fear to their neighbors. Lisa Skye was busy with preliminary checks, going from one to another with patience and serenity. She saw Harry and motioned him to step aside with her.

"What is it?"

"Has Ernie brought that list of extra beds available?"

"No, not yet. Why?" Harry felt dread churn in him.

"We're going to need them. Today. I tried to call him at his office, but the phone wasn't working."

"*His* phone?"

"No, *our* phone." She steeled her pretty face, and her doll-like beauty changed to awesome resolution. "We have to get some other message service. We need information, Harry."

"Yes."

"We've got two smallpox for sure. We must get them into beds. And there's at least three, and possibly more, of that new polio. More and more of that stuff is showing up. I wish we had the time and equipment to study it."

"I wish we could do something to stop it," Harry said, and frowned as the knocker sounded. "More of them. That's all we need."

Lisa patted his arm. "No rest for the wicked."

"Good luck," he said as he went from her to open the door. He swung it open and stared.

"He's all yours, mister," said the larger of the two teen-agers who supported something between them that Harry recognized, after one horrified moment, as Stan Kooznetz.

Harry tried to speak, words coming disjointedly. "But . . . I don't . . . Why? . . . What did . . ." He reached toward one of the teen-agers.

"Tristam said to drop him off here. He's your problem now."

Harry clung to the name. "Tristam?" he said, then staggered under the weight as the boys let Stan fall into his arms.

In a few moments the two teen-age boys were gone, and Harry found, to his surprise and horror, that Stan was breathing. "Stan?" he whispered. "Stan? Can you hear me?"

The flesh in his arms quivered, and Stan made a dreadful guttural sound as Harry tried to comfort him. "No, Stan, you don't understand. This is Harry, Stan, Harry Smith. You're back at the Van Dreyter house . . ."

Behind him, Harry heard the door open wider, and then a sharp gasp. "What is this, Harry?" Amanda asked faintly. "I saw you come to the door, but what is this?"

"It's Stan," he said as calmly as he could. "I'll need some help getting him into the house. Call someone, will you, Amanda?"

"Nonsense," she said very matter-of-fact, "I'm quite capable of giving you a hand. Tell me what you want me to do." She was on the open porch now, and she was making a quick, dispassionate survey of the damage. "It will be best not to touch him more than we have to. What on earth do you think happened to him, Harry?"

Harry did not answer as he steadied Stan's weight against him. He braced himself to take more of the weight and then eased the door open. "Now, Amanda. We can get him inside. We'll need help after that."

"Maria can give us a hand. And Dominic."

"Fine. Just help me get him through the door, and then make sure there's a place for him." He hesitated as an idea struck him. "You remember on the second floor, that old-fashioned waterbed? See if it will still hold water, because Stan can use it. He'll need to be kept motionless as much as possible. The way those burns are . . ."

Amanda expertly lifted Stan's ankles over the threshold, sympathy showing in her lined face while he groaned.

"Yes, he's been burned, but those marks on his legs aren't burns, or the wounds on his hands," she said critically. "What is it, Harry?

Did they beat him? I haven't seen wounds like that before, except once, in Ian Parkenson's division. What did they do?"

Harry pulled Stan into the entry hall. "You're right, Amanda. He hasn't been beaten. He's been tortured."

* * *

"I don't care what you think," Carol Mendosa said as she turned on Harry. The others looked worried as she paced the length of the common room, showing in her tension the tension they all felt. "I say this has gone far enough and that we have to get out of here. Look out there in the lobby if you don't believe me. We have over forty people waiting, and there isn't a spare bed in this house. Where the hell are we going to put them? Well?"

"My colleagues will help," Ernest Dagstern promised.

"That isn't good enough. How long will it be before they're beaten, or killed, or die from one of the diseases we're treating? How long will it be before we all start dying?" She challenged the others with her eyes. "Natalie isn't back from Westbank, is she?" Carol asked, and saw the faces change. "That makes a difference, doesn't it, Harry?"

"It always makes a difference," Harry said, and realized with a start that there was as much anguish in Carol's face as he felt himself.

Amanda rose. "I have patients to look after. You must excuse me." She went slowly to the door, then turned back. "You're an excellent doctor, Carol. You must do what you think is right. I won't stop you from leaving, if that is what you must do. But I won't go with you." She opened the door and went out.

Radick nodded. "I cannot leave either, Harry. If the rest vote to go, I will help as much as I can, but I must stay here. There's still a little chance that something might prevent some of the worst diseases. And someone must look after Stan and Dave. We cannot move them and we cannot leave them."

"Look," Carol said, desperation changing the lines of her body from elegant curves to ridges. "You don't seem to understand, none of you. We're licked and we've got to admit it. If we stay here we're going to die. We're going to get sick or be killed. What happened to Dave wasn't an accident, just a random beating of a chance victim. They wanted a doctor. They proved that when they got Stan."

Jim Varnay shook his head. "Sorry, Carol. Maybe you're right, but I can't leave. Not yet, anyway. If there's worse and we get too shorthanded, that's another matter."

She turned her angry eyes on him. "You've got to be the big hero, don't you? You have to prove your bravery to your damn masculine pride." She turned away from them. "Men! You fools!"

"I'm with them, too," Lisa Skye reminded her gently. "I'm not saying you're wrong, Carol. But I have to fight. Otherwise I'll lose my self-respect, you see."

"Self-respect. What good is that when you're dead? If we don't get out of here, if we don't find out who's in charge and make them stop, then all this will have been in vain. Don't you see that? If they ever try this again, we'll have done it all for nothing."

Dominic Hertzog nodded. "I'm with you, Carol. But the rest can't see it yet. Give them a couple of more days of dead bodies and attacks on doctors, and they'll come around to your point of view. Believe me."

At that, Radick made a gesture. "We aren't going to solve any of this right now, and there are patients waiting for us. We must get back to them." He nodded to Harry as he rose. "I will talk to you later, Harry."

When the others had left, Harry turned to Carol. "You know I'm worried about Natalie. There's good reason to worry."

Carol would not meet his eyes. "You could have stopped her going."

Harry laughed. "Could I? If you think that, you've never had an argument with her. If she made up her mind to go to Westbank, neither you nor I could stop her. No matter what you or I said, she'd go."

"What if . . ." The words stopped. "We're losing ground here every day, Harry. We're in quicksand and it's sucking us down."

"Yes."

"Then, why don't you do something?"

"I *am* doing something," he said, and hoped with all his soul that this was true.

* * *

There were no lights in Stan's room off the laundry, because Tristam's gang had kept bright lights on his eyes for many hours, and now the sight of a lightbulb, even at a distance, made him scream.

The old waterbed was still sound and had been filled so that he could lie without moving and be spared pain.

Kirsten Grant checked his dressings and applied new pads where they were necessary. "We need the rain unit in Intensive Care," she said to Harry. "Changing dressings every hour isn't enough. He's got three infected wounds now, and I know that at least two of the other wounds are going to become infected. No matter how many times we change the pads."

"Do the best you can," Harry said slowly as he moved closer to Stan. "Has he said anything useful yet?"

"No."

"It's bad enough not having Dave and Stan working, but they're both taking up more time than any of us can spare." He saw the severity in Kirsten's face and went on in a different tone, "I'm tired, Kirsten. I've been up for almost eighteen hours on less than five hours' sleep. And I'm frustrated. It's true we can't take proper care of Stan and Dave because we don't have any intensive care units here. We're in no position to give either of them what they really need. But we do our best, which might not be good enough. Who's taking care of Dave right now, do you know?"

"Howard. He's given up part of his lab time."

Harry frowned. "We can't afford that." He stepped away from Stan and motioned to Kirsten to come with him to the door. "Kirsten, if he says anything at all that's the least bit sensible, will you be sure to write it down. Write it down if there's the remotest chance it might make sense. I have to know who Tristam is and why he's doing this. We can't let anyone else get trapped by him." Unbidden, the thought of Natalie rose in his mind, and he ruthlessly turned it away. "Do you have a notepad in there?"

"I think so. There's supposed to be one. Radick said he'd leave one."

"Well, make sure there is. And tell your relief to make sure to take notes. Sometime, Stan's got to tell us what happened." He attempted a smile. "I know it's hard. But Ernest is bringing us help, and you know he's reliable. If it weren't for him we wouldn't have our lab or the X-rays. If he knows other chiropractors, you know they're good doctors."

"Sure. But maybe they won't want to come when he tells them what's going on."

"If they saw Eric Patman die, they'll want to come," Harry said grimly.

"Do you think he really did that to himself? Injected himself with botulin?" She rubbed her arms, as if cold. "Botulin. Someone else could have done it, and then said *he* did."

Harry nodded. "I know. That's what I thought at first, but now I'm not so sure. Eric was that kind, you know. He had to make the gesture, no matter what. I think that's what he did. He made the gesture because he didn't know anything else to do. He thought the public had to be made aware of what's going on, I know that. He hated the lies. And you know what his ulcers had done to him. He wasn't getting any better, Kirsten."

"Oh, I know. But it still seems horrible."

Rubbing his eyes, he said, "Yeah. What time is it?"

"Going on five. Alexes will have dinner ready soon. There's an hour yet, if you have rounds to do. Alexes is doing patient trays first."

"Right." Harry had rounds to do—too many rounds, he thought. He had to look in on Mr. Catterndon, who was in the last stages of smallpox. Harry could not help him now, but perhaps he could take away some of the fear haunting the old man. And then there was that boy with what Harry was very much afraid was meningitis. He'd stop off at the lab and find out what the test results were before going to see him. Then, there was Miss Wiltshire, who had cancer and was in dreadful pain, and Mrs. Foss, who had pleurisy on top of pneumonia. Dinner seemed too remote, and Harry knew that at that moment he was given the chance to trade all his meals for the next week for one working respirator, he would take the respirator in a minute. He'd even welcome an ancient oxygen tent, if any still existed.

"Natalie didn't come in yet, did she?" Kirsten asked reluctantly.

"Not yet. And the phone's dead. I can't call the hospital to find out if she ever got there, or when she left."

Kirsten thought about this, then said, "Maybe Carol's right, Harry."

* * *

The common room was quiet, and even the light from the chandeliers was subdued, competing with the last of the sunset. Harry opened the door and was relieved to see that only Amanda was there, sitting in one of the high-backed chairs by the fireplace, dozing. A book lay open on her lap, lightly caught in her fingers. Harry almost spoke, but remembered the great fatigue Amanda had shown earlier in the day, and decided to let her rest.

A ship's clock chimed eight-thirty, and Harry sighed. He knew that he would lose Mrs. Foss sometime in the night, and that the boy definitely had meningitis. And there had been no word from Natalie. He picked up a paper from the table and glanced at it perfunctorily. The news was old, but there had been no newssheets for the last couple of days. He saw that someone else had done the crossword puzzle, and felt an irrational annoyance that he had not gotten to do it.

He was halfway through an article on an effort to save the vineyards when there was a sudden noise outside. Glass shattered as a rock hurtled into the room and thudded onto the carpet by Amanda's feet.

Harry was on his feet and across the room, looking out into the twilight before he realized that Amanda had not moved. One cursory glance told him that the attack would not be repeated, so he turned, with sudden unwillingness, back to Amanda.

He knew, long before he actually touched her, that her valiant heart had stopped.

* * *

Radick wiped his eyes again. "She knew this would happen, Harry. She knew her limits, and she decided to exceed them." His voice was thick with tears and grief. "Once we talked about when we were young. She said she graduated from high school just before Robert Kennedy was killed. She said she was sorry no one ever found out what really happened. She did special training in Geneva, in the early eighties. She liked to ski then. She told me how much she missed being able to ski." He stopped abruptly.

"I know," Harry said softly.

"Those faceless asses!" Radick slammed his hand down. "They are not worth her life, not any of them. What the I.I.A. is doing is criminal." Again he stopped, and then, mastering himself, said quite calmly, "I'll tell the others, Harry. But you know they will lose heart. Amanda is dear to all of us."

Harry looked across the room to where Amanda's body lay, covered with a long damask tablecloth. "I know."

* * *

The streets were dark and littered with refuse. Natalie walked slowly, keeping to the shadows. She had discarded her lab coat for an ill-fitting jacket of rough cotton, and her slacks were worn enough to pass anywhere in the city. Few people were out, and those that were moved furtively. Store windows were empty, standing open like toothless gums, and the litter attested to the raids that had emptied the stores many days ago.

Suddenly she tripped and looked down. A dead woman lay at an angle against the building, and Natalie knelt to check her. She rose again and found herself shaking. The woman had died of cholera. She had not seen that disease at Van Dreyter, and she feared now that the pandemic was further advanced than even she and Harry had feared.

But she was ten miles away from the Van Dreyter house, and it would take her a good part of the night to get back there. She knew now that it had been a mistake to come to Inner City, for neither Miles Wexford nor Peter Justin had been willing to see her. And there had been no way back to the Van Dreyter house but on foot, since there were no longer any buses, and private cars were open targets to vandals.

Down a side street she heard a scuffle. Something clattered, and there was a shout.

Natalie thought about it and knew that she would not let herself stop now. She began to walk faster and kept her mind on where she was going. There was too much to do at the Van Dreyter house for her to risk being waylaid here. As she lengthened her stride she found herself wishing that her shoes didn't make so much noise.

* * *

"No, we won't talk about it later," Carol Mendosa shot back at Harry. "You tell me right now how we're going to manage four hands short? Or is it five? Lisa said one of the nurses is sick, too. How much sleep can you get along without?" She braced her back on the kitchen wall and held her coffee mug almost like a weapon.

"I haven't got any answer for you, Carol. But I'm not leaving." He was glad that most of the others were on rounds, and that only Dominic and Alexes could hear their argument.

"How many of us have to die before you'll leave? Two more? Four more?"

"I don't want any of us to die," he said, and in spite of himself he had to stifle a yawn. He knew that he really ought to look in on Stan, and to spell Ernest, who was sitting with Dave.

"What about burial? Or haven't you heard that the coroner's

wagon hasn't been around since yesterday? Are you in any shape to dig Amanda's grave?"

Harry looked up sharply. "Stop it, Carol," he said softly. "Maybe you can handle this better than I can, but I can't bear to talk about Amanda yet."

"What about Natalie?"

"For Chrissake, Carol!" Dominic cut in. "I'm as antsy as you are. But leave it alone, can't you?" He filled his cup with more coffee. "I've got to get back to the lab."

"Any luck on the polio thing?"

Dominic turned to Harry. "It's a variant polio, all right. My guess is that it's mutant. That's the thing we have to stop. All the others we have the tools for already, but this stuff is brand new. And, now that we've got three deaths from it, it's safe to say that it can be fatal."

Harry slumped in his seat. "I see." His voice was as dull as his eyes.

Carol slammed her mug down and left the room.

* * *

None of the kids who surrounded Natalie were more than fifteen. They were dressed in standard, tattered clothes, and nothing but the feral light in their eyes revealed their intent. One of them, a little taller than the others, was the first to speak. "Where you going, lady?"

"Home," Natalie said, hoping her panic did not color her voice.

"Where's home, lady?" asked another.

"Six miles northwest, more or less," she said honestly.

"What do you do, lady?" This was the first kid again, and he was moving closer. He chuckled as he saw Natalie flinch. "You got nothing to be scared of. We aren't sick. We take care of ourselves."

Natalie said nothing, but saw with alarm that there were now three of the teen-agers in front of her, cutting off any escape.

"We got some questions to ask you," said another. "You answer them right and we'll leave you alone."

"You got any kids, lady?" said a new voice, one that cracked with adolescent change.

"My son died." Natalie had not meant to say it aloud.

"A lot of kids are dying, lady," the apparent leader said, without sympathy. When Natalie did not answer, he said it again. "Lots of kids are dying, lady." He started to clap slowly. *"Lots* of *kids* are *dy*ing, *la*dy. *Lots* of *kids* are *dy*ing, *la*dy. *Lots* of *kids* are *dy*ing, *la*dy."

The others took it up, clapping or snapping their fingers, their walks bouncing with the rhythm. Some of them laughed at Natalie's protesting, "No."

Again the leader spoke. "Tristam might be interested in you."

A few of the others broke off their chant to whistle suggestively.

"We haven't had a lady doctor yet. You a lady doctor? Most folks out this late, they're either robbers or doctors. Now, it don't look like you've stolen anything. But you don't have a bag. So what are you?"

"I'm a woman going home. I went to the hospital to try to see someone, and they wouldn't let me in, and there aren't any buses." She fought the rising pitch in her voice. "So I have to walk home."

"Don't you know they don't let you see anybody in hospitals, lady? Boy, you're dumb." The others agreed that Natalie was dumb.

"Maybe we'll take you along to Tristam, anyway." The leader pulled out a flashlight and shone it in Natalie's face. "I don't know. You aren't very pretty . . ."

One of the kids on the fringes, a girl, said, "Aw, Gordy, leave her alone. If she's got a dead kid, she knows what's happening."

In a moment of shock Natalie recognized Alison's voice. Was it gangs like this one that had kept the girl from helping her when she and Harry first went to the Van Dreyter house.

"Alison," Gordy said, "Come on, cut it out."

"No, honest, Gordy. I know who that lady is."

Natalie's heart sank. She started to speak to Alison.

"That's right about her kid dying. She used to live near where I do. She's nobody." The contempt in Alison's voice was very convincing, and Natalie was filled with gratitude.

But Gordy was disappointed. "If you say so, Alison."

"Come on, leave her alone. She's got enough troubles without you messing her up. Come on." Alison tugged at Gordy's arm. "Tristam told us to be back at midnight anyway, and it's almost that now."

"Okay." Gordy reluctantly allowed himself to be persuaded. He turned to Natalie. "But remember about the dying kids, lady."

"I will," Natalie said.

"Come *on,*" Alison insisted, and as the kids moved off down a cross street, she gave Natalie a one-finger salute, and Natalie knew she would not get help from that girl again.

* * *

Dominic leaned against the shovel and looked up at Harry. "Sorry, Harry, that's all I'm good for. Do you want me to ask someone else to come out? I know Howard's up and I think Roger is available."

"Never mind," Harry said as he looked at the sheeted bodies beside the incomplete graves. "I can dig a while, and then Ernest can give me a hand if he has some time. We've got to get them buried. It's going to be hot today, I think. The proper forms are in Lisa's desk. If you'll sign one of them, I'll sign the others." He gave Dominic a hand and pulled him out of the grave.

"I wish there were some kind of minister around here, someone who knew the words." Dominic rubbed his hands on his slacks and left long stains there.

"I didn't know you were religious," Harry said, as he jumped into the grave Dominic had just left.

"I'm not. But the words might help. It might help some of them in the house, some of those who aren't going to get well. I used to think it was silly, and maybe in a place like Westbank it is, but I don't know, around here it might help. My father was a very religious man, and when he died they did the whole routine—masses, prayers, all the pomp. My father said he liked the requiem mass because it was the same for everyone; no matter who they were or how they died, they were buried with the same words. It made his dying easier for him, I think."

Harry reached for the shovel and began to dig. The work was slow, he found, and not entirely because the ground was hard.

"I'll see if anyone can come out, Harry. Maybe only to keep you company."

Harry desperately wanted company, but the last hours of the night were the worst, and now they were too shorthanded to spare him the help. "Don't bother." He felt his breath coming hard already, and he leaned more heavily into his digging.

Dominic paused by the draped body of Amanda. "I liked her. I wish she hadn't died . . ."

For a moment Harry stopped digging. "Let's not talk about her now, Dom. This is rough enough without being reminded of Amanda."

"Yeah," Dominic said, reluctant to leave. "Do you think any of us are going to get out of this in one piece, Harry?"

"You saw a lot of deaths in radiology, Dom." He tossed another shovelful of earth over his shoulder. "You had a lot of machines to mask it, but it was the same thing." He wanted to believe it, he knew. If he didn't believe it his courage would fail him.

"No, this isn't the same thing," Dominic said softly, then went back to the house. Behind him the sky was fading from night to the first touch of morning.

* * *

On the third insistent ring, Harry went to the door. He was not ready to deal with emergency cases yet. A quick shower had taken the dirt off him, but the miasmic sense of death was still around him. Officially there were more than two hours until their nine o'clock opening of the Van Dreyter house to new patients, but where real need was concerned there was no limitation on office hours. "I'm coming," he called, disappointed to hear how harsh his own voice had become. He hoped that this time the trouble was not desperate, because he knew that grief was muddling his judgment, and that could be critical. He took a moment to steady himself while the bell pealed a fourth time. Then he opened the door.

"Harry!" Natalie cried out, the name assuaging her terror. She came through the door to cling to him. "God, Harry."

Now that he had his arms around her, Harry was almost giddy with relief. "Natalie. You're back." The words sounded inane, even to him, but her hold on him tightened. They stood together for many long minutes, and then Harry pulled back and demanded, "What happened to you? You were supposed to be back yesterday afternoon."

The anger in his eyes stung her. "Harry, I told Amanda I was going to Inner City if I didn't get any help at Westbank . . ." She stopped as she saw his face grow rigid. "Harry?"

"Amanda died yesterday. She didn't tell me." He reached out and closed the door as he spoke, to be doing something.

"Died?" Natalie looked puzzled, and knew that the realization would hit her later. "Her heart?"

"Yes." To change the subject, he said, "You look a fright. What are you wearing?"

"Just clothes. Harry, there's so much to tell you. There's a lot we didn't know. And we have to be ready. It's a lot worse than we guessed, and there isn't any help . . ." She put her hand to her mouth. "I'm sorry. I'm not making any sense." She took his hand in hers. "Is there any coffee? I could use a cup of coffee."

"Sure." He led the way toward the kitchen, saying nothing, anger with her still ripe in him.

Radick was in the kitchen, for it was his morning to fix the breakfasts. "Natalie," he said, and embraced her, "you must not frighten us that way again, little one."

"She left a message with Amanda," Harry explained reluctantly.

"Oh." Radick let her go. "I see."

"Harry told me about Amanda. I am so very sorry." She stopped. "No. I can't do this now. There's too much you have to know. It's too important." She made a strange gesture, as if pushing her sorrow away. "First, you have to know about this pandemic, and what's gone wrong. And you must know who Tristam is. Let me have some coffee, and I'll tell you."

Radick handed her a mug and filled it, saying nothing. He motioned her to a chair.

Before she started to tell them what she had learned, she asked, "Did Mr. Younts survive the night?"

Harry thought of the bodies he had just covered with earth. "No."

She nodded sadly. "I didn't think he would. He wasn't fighting back any more." She studied the mug for a moment and then began to speak.

Long before she was finished, both Harry and Radick were filled with worry.

* * *

The afternoon rounds were terribly slow, for there were fifteen new patients to be dispatched to Ernest Dagstern's few willing colleagues. There were no more beds to be had at the Van Dreyter house. But the patients kept coming, frightened, sick, aware that the hospitals had let them down.

Lisa Skye shook her head and remarked to Natalie that they had to get out of Stockton before August, or none of them would be alive.

"Why do you say that?"

Lisa patted a handkerchief over her damp forehead. "This heat. It makes everything worse. I'm glad my daughter is in Carmichael. You said that the central sanitation facilities aren't working any more, which means that we're going to have a big sewage problem soon, and that will make all the diseases more virulent. You remember what happened with the old epidemics, don't you? When the weather got hot, they got worse. It's in the high eighties today. A month from now we'll break a hundred during the day and be lucky if it cools to eighty at night." Her slender hands were unsteady. She grabbed the handkerchief more tightly. "I hate the heat."

Natalie nodded. "It's worse upstairs. I went up for a nap but it was stifling. So I came back. You said you've got a possible scarlet fever in this afternoon?"

"Yes. Howard's taking the case." She put her hand to her head again. "Do we have any aspirin? My head's killing me."

"I'll ask one of the nurses. Tony Michaelson brought some supplies with him when he came by. He must have taken them out of one of the pharmacy warehouses."

"Bless Tony," Lisa said with real feeling. The ambulance driver had been the one link they had not lost with the hospitals. Tony Michaelson was perennially on the side of the underdog, and was willing to take a great many risks.

"He said he was thinking of coming over here permanently to be an emergency paramedic for us. He's had the training, and we could use him."

"We could use a couple of dozen Tonys," Lisa said. She folded her handkerchief. "Will you mind running a test on Thornton?" she added after a swift glance at her notes. "She said she's afraid she might have picked up one of the bugs running around. We can't let our nurses get sick. We haven't enough of them to spare."

"Thornton's sick?" Natalie asked. "What with, do you know?"

"No. And all she says is that it's like flu. Loose bowels, sore joints, low fever and slight sore throat. I ordered her off the floor until you could see her. She's out in the nurses' quarters."

"I'll do it now," Natalie said with a nod. "And I'll see if Andrews will bring you an aspirin." She picked up a handful of files from the desk. "I'll bring these back to you after rounds."

Lisa nodded. "Okay. Thanks."

Natalie waved a dismissal, then walked through the house, her face now showing deep concern. She knew that once the nurses were ill, the load would be too much for the doctors. They had to find help somewhere, but she didn't know where. She went through the kitchen and noticed that Alexes had not yet started dinner. That would mean late meals again. She assured herself that late meals were better than none and went out the back door.

Away to the southwest stretched the city, dull in the late afternoon. Almost no traffic moved on the freeways, and the residential towers were not bright with life as they had been a month before. Natalie opened the first folder and studied it as she walked, glancing up once more as she turned toward the old stables.

The files slid from her hands as she heard the distant explosion and saw the dark oily cloud roll skyward. She knew that tall white building, its double-H profile making it distinctive even at eleven miles. She turned and ran back toward the house, shouting as she did, "Come quick! Get the cars! Everyone! *Inner City is on fire!*"

CHAPTER 9

By the time they pulled up, the fire had spread for almost two blocks. The buildings smoldered as people poured from them in a terrified rout. Only two fire trucks were on the north side of the hospital, and the water they pumped came in an inadequate stream.

Harry pulled the van alongside the nearest fire truck and rushed out, his emergency kit under his arm. "Who's in charge here?" he shouted at the first fireman he saw.

The fireman gestured with his thumb. "Captain Gottschalk. He's over there." The fireman frowned at Harry. "Who are you?"

Harry flashed the badge on his emergency kit. "Doctors," he said, and set off at a run for the car the fireman had indicated.

The man in the car was too old for this kind of job. His lined face and bristly white hair put his age over sixty. He was talking on the radio to another unit. "Then bring 'em around toward the river. There's got to be a way to get a firebreak."

Knocking perfunctorily on the window, Harry held his kit where the captain could see the medical badge, then he waited while the captain finished his conversation.

The air stank with smoke, and the noise from the fire, from frightened people, and from the equipment of the firemen was deafening. At this distance heat rolled out in waves from the buildings, and Harry felt sweat start to roll down his back. He knocked on the window once more.

"Yes," Captain Gottschalk said as he put his radio aside. "I'll talk with you now, Doctor." He pulled himself heavily to his feet. "I'm Theodore Gottschalk. And you?"

"Harry Smith. I've got four more doctors with me, and we have four vehicles to help evacuate burn and smoke patients. Or anyone else who might need help."

"What hospital are you from?" the captain asked, not really interested.

"We've got emergency headquarters at the Van Dreyter house, sir," Harry said, hoping the "sir" would do the trick.

"Oh, you're *that* lot. Good." Bemused, the old man turned back to the car. "We've been trying to get a helicopter assist from the Air Force base in Fairfield, but no one can raise them. It's the damn phones. I guess the exchange has another computer breakdown."

Harry was about to tell Captain Gottschalk that the I.I.A. was not allowing any calls out of the area, and that he would not get any help from the Air Force. But instead he asked, "Has any of the hospital staff got out? Can we get space for emergency treatment nearby?"

Captain Gottschalk looked confused. "The hospital staff? Oh, *that* hospital staff," he said with a meaningful nod at the fire. "Some of them got out. They're on the river side, to the east. Clinton tells me they have a kind of center going over there. That's Captain Clinton. You might want to talk to him."

Harry studied the old man and wondered what was wrong. He seemed to be making no sense, as if this emergency had no effect on him. "Are you all right, Captain Gottschalk?" he asked, and motioned Kirsten to his side.

"Me? Oh, I'm fine, fine. But fires take a lot out of you, you know." He sat down again and picked up his radio. "Damned inconsiderate of them to ignore an emergency call. I'll file a complaint, you can be sure." He tapped the radio again. "Well, Doctor, you do as you think best."

"What's wrong with him?" Kirsten whispered to Harry as he walked back toward the waiting vans.

"I don't know," Harry said, troubled. "He says that some of the hospital staff got out and have set up an emergency station to the east of the hospital, near the river. After we get set up here, I'm taking Ted Lincoln and we'll check it out. You and Roger and Jim can start a station over here, and let Dom and Alexes do the driving back and forth. I don't know what else we can do until we find out how much damage there is, and how many victims."

Kirsten agreed, saying, "I'll keep you posted. I wish we had more equipment."

"So do I. Maybe we can get some from the doctors on the other side." He looked at the burning hospital. "I wonder how it started."

"Natalie said she heard an explosion."

Three men ran by, heedless of trucks and people alike. One fell and cursed as he tried to get to his feet on the wet pavement.

"I know," Harry said, once the men were gone. "We'll have to be careful about that," he added.

"What?" Kirsten was at her van now, and about to open the door.

"Men like that. They had probably stolen what they had in their arms." He lifted his arm to shield his face as a portion of Inner City Hospital's outer wall collapsed. The heat was intense. His skin felt baked. "Kirsten, better move back a block or two, just in case they can't bring this under control inside this radius."

She nodded.

Behind them there was a squeal of brakes, and another ambulance pulled up. Harry turned, startled, and beginning to be frightened. If other hospitals sent help, he and his group might be in trouble.

The door to the ambulance opened and Tony Michaelson stepped out, his brown beard bristling, ready for the fight. "Harry!" he shouted to be heard, "I swiped some supplies from County General for you. Natalie told me to bring 'em along to you here."

Kirsten laughed. "I knew it couldn't be all bad." She nodded once to Harry, then went over to Tony, and they began to make plans.

*　*　*

Ted Lincoln drove with professional skill between the dark buildings. Three blocks away the fire raged, and the streets were filled with milling people and the strange refuse of their panicked flight.

"Almost there," Ted said with forced cheerfulness. "I figure we'll take a right at the next corner, and that will bring us to Riverside Park. If they've got a station anywhere on this side, it'll be there."

"We hope," Harry said, feeling withdrawn now, and fighting a growing anxiety as he watched the fire from the corner of his eye.

A young woman ran out of an empty building, shouting words that were lost in the other sounds. She reached the van and pulled at the handle, pounding on the side as she ran beside it.

"We'd better stop," Harry said as he saw the young woman's face, her wide eyes and distended mouth. "I think she's got trouble."

Ted obediently slowed, and had almost stopped when Harry saw eight or nine teen-agers waiting in the shadow of the next building, armed with long sticks. As the van slowed, they began to move from the shelter of the darkness.

"Get out of here!" Harry ordered Ted. "Fast!"

The tires screamed as the van lurched suddenly. There was a bounding noise as various missiles struck the sides, and then they were out of range and around the corner.

Ted held the van steadily, one arm over the horn so that the noise scattered the people who streamed away from the path of the fire.

"Tristam?" Ted asked when he thought it safe to slow the van.

"Could be. I didn't want to wait around and find out, not after what Natalie said." He let out his breath. "Is that Riverside Park?"

"On the left? Yep, that's it. And that looks like an emergency station, there, by the old merry-go-round."

Ted pulled the van up beside several other emergency vehicles, and waited while Harry got out. "I'll keep her on idle," he said. "If there's any emergency that should go immediately, I'm ready."

"Good." Harry slammed the door, then picked his way over the debris to the shelter by the merry-go-round. He walked into the shelter and was immediately assailed by the noise and smells contained within its corrugated walls. Long rows of inflatable cots lined each wall, each one bearing its human offering, like an altar to destruction. It was far worse than anything Harry had seen at the Van Dreyter house, and he hesitated.

"Yes?" said a haggard paramedic at his elbow. "Who're you?"

"Dr. Harry Smith," he said when he had recovered himself. "We're setting up an emergency shelter on the other side of the fire. We've got a van to evacuate any cases that might need more help than you can give them here." Though there was not that much more to offer at the Van Dreyter house, except quiet and more care.

"We've been trying to get help for the last hour, and it isn't doing any good." The paramedic nodded and introduced herself. "I'm Sheilah Braccia. And the doctor in charge is Katherine Ng."

Harry knew Dr. Ng slightly and had a very high opinion of her work. "If you tell me where I can find her, I'll tell her what we're doing."

Sheilah Braccia pointed toward the center of the shelter. "She's over there somewhere. There are some very bad burn cases. Mostly from those on the top floors who survived. Excuse me, Doctor. I can't stay." She pushed past him toward one of the cots where a young man moaned as the air touched the ruin of his skin.

Carefully Harry picked his way to the knot at the center of the shelter, stopping once to reset an IV which the patient had pulled out of her arm. He could see three figures in hospital whites bending over one of the inflated cots. The slight one in the center turned, and Harry called, "Kit! Kit!"

The doctor turned at her name, and then a confused expression entered her dark eyes. "Harry Smith," she said. "What are you doing here? I thought you'd been warned off . . ."

"I'm at the Van Dreyter house. Look, we've got some vans we've been using as ambulances, and we can take your most serious cases out of here, if you like. We can't supply intensive care units, but we're a lot better than this." He saw her consider this. "We're setting up another emergency station on the other side of the fire. Kirsten Grant's in charge over there."

She cut him off impatiently. "Good. We need more help. All right. I have one or two cases that have to get out of here immediately. Bring your van around and I'll let you take them." She looked at Harry, suddenly desolate. "Harry, we saved less than a quarter of them. Less than a quarter. Most of them were trapped in the building. They never had a chance. They burned. They burned." Her eyes were dry and her voice was flat, but Harry felt the horror of what she said to the core of him.

"Do you want me to stay? I can help."

She looked at him once more. "Would you? When the fire began I'd been on the floor over fifteen hours. I'm worn out. I can use your help." She made a helpless gesture with her hands. "You see what we have here. I've got one other doctor and three paramedics and a nurse." Her voice wavered toward the end, but she controlled it. "Thank you. You'd better get that van over here. The worst of the burns and one or two of the diseased patients must go."

Harry nodded. "We'll bring it up at the far end."

"Yes." Katherine Ng put her hand to her eyes. "Do you have stimulants? I need something to keep me going."

"I haven't on me, but I can get them."

"Thank you." She looked down at the patient on the cot. "You'll be taking him with you the first trip." Her short laughter was mirthless.

Harry looked at the tangle of charred clothes and the hideously melted features. "Christ. Who is it, do you know?"

"Oh, yes, I know. It's Miles Wexford."

* * *

Within twenty minutes Ted Lincoln had rushed off in the van, driving at the very edge of control, well past the speed of caution. Harry watched him go, then turned back into the shelter. Near him two children shared a cot, and their feeble hacking and mucus-covered lips were testaments to the smoke they had inhaled. Harry also noticed the rash on their bodies and wondered if it were measles or the early stages of smallpox.

"Not those," Katherine Ng said. "They're going to be okay now. But I need you for the borderline cases. That man there, the one with the lacerated thigh. Take care of him, and then the woman on number five cot."

"Okay," Harry said, and began work on the man with the lacerated thigh.

* * *

The kitchen had been pressed into use for surgery, and Alexes Castor had moved the meal-preparation equipment into the garage where there was a small workshop.

Carol Mendosa worked feverishly over a young woman whose legs were crusted, bleeding stumps. Ernest Dagstern was her assistant and nurse, and Carol was secretly surprised at his calm good sense.

Natalie, on the other side of the table, monitored the anesthesia. "Carol, you've got to make it fast. She's not doing well."

"I'm trying," Carol snapped. "I haven't done a lot of surgery, and never a double amputation. And never on a kitchen table." She stood still while Ernest patted the sweat from her face. "We should have nurses, we should have the laser equipment. This is close enough to butchery to make my stomach turn."

"Just get those things off her," Natalie said, with more feeling than she knew.

"Those things are feet," Carol snapped.

"Not any more," said Natalie.

* * *

Dave Lillijanthal lay in his makeshift traction, the elegance and beauty of his body now quite gone. He was half conscious, lost in that strange twilight where there was neither pain nor thought.

Beside him Celeste Larsen sat, her nurse's uniform crumpled and gray. Her hands were busy making bandage pads, moving almost independently from the stack of gauze, through the motions, and then to the completed pile. She looked up as Natalie came in. "You're through?" she asked, somewhat unnecessarily.

"We're through. For whatever good it did." She studied Dave, but her thoughts were obviously elsewhere.

"You lost her?"

"Yes. We'd almost got the left foot off. Without real equipment
. . ." Her voice trailed off. "How's Dave?"

Larsen stopped making the bandages. "I don't like the feel of him.
Radick was in earlier, and he was concerned."

Natalie gathered her hands into knots of frustration. "We don't
have the time or the staff for this. He can't be this way. Dave, Dave,
damn it, why did you have to let yourself get caught?"

Dave's eyes opened a little wider and he tried to turn toward her.
The slight movement, the helplessness of the man, were so pathetic
that it struck her to the heart. "Oh, Dave," she whispered.

"Natalie?" Larsen said, putting one hand on her arm. "Can't you
get some rest?"

"With two more vanloads coming in? I don't even know where
we're going to put them. I don't know how we're going to take care
of them. There isn't room enough for the patients we have now." She
brought her rising voice back under control. "I'm sorry, Larsen. It's
just that I'm tired and I'm scared."

Celeste Larsen regarded her with a thoughtful frown. "We were
talking, over in the nurses' quarters, about this. Thornton is sick, but
Tim Walsh and I are fine. We can take some of the less badly hurt
patients over there. Or, if you want to keep the patients all in one
place, we can make room there for a couple of you doctors. That can
free some of the attic rooms for patients."

"Larsen, I don't want to do that."

"I've already asked Lisa, and she thinks it's a good idea. You can
change your mind if you want, but I think it will work."

"Harry's bringing back a couple more nurses and three paramedics.
I don't even know where they'll sleep." Sternly Natalie told herself to
stop doing this. She had to make decisions, and they had to be made
now. She glanced at the pile of bandages. "Are those ready for the
sterilizer?"

"Yes."

"I'll take them in." Then she looked again at Larsen. "Larsen, do
whatever you think is best." She picked up the bandages. "You've all
done so well. We couldn't have done any of this without you." She
stopped again. "Do you know who's looking after Stan?"

"It's Alexes' turn."

Natalie frowned. "Alexes is with Kirsten, at the fire."

"But I thought . . ." Larsen hesitated.

"Lisa?"

Larsen looked more worried. "She's had her hands full in the lobby. We've had over fifty people here already."

Natalie felt suddenly cold. She put the bandages down again. "Larsen, stay here, will you? Unless I call you?"

"Certainly. But Natalie . . ."

"Not now." Natalie went back into the kitchen, and ignored Ernest's question as he looked up from his cleaning. The door to the laundry stood ajar. Natalie rushed through it, then stopped, one hand still on the knob.

Stan lay half on the waterbed and half on the floor. A drying track of blood ran from the drain set in the cement floor to Stan's wrists, which were still pushed against the jagged metal of the ancient broken laundry bucket.

Natalie's cry brought Ernest to her. "Natalie, what's the matter . . ." Then he saw Stan. "Dear Jesus," he whispered.

* * *

"How many patients today?" Harry asked as he climbed out of the van. It was midmorning and the night's work had left him exhausted and hoarse. He saw the dark circles under Natalie's eyes. "Did you get any sleep last night?"

"No, did you?" she countered as she closed the garage door. "I talked to Lisa half an hour ago and I'd guess we're past thirty so far. There are nine new cases of that polio mutation since yesterday. Which makes over fifty cases in the last four days. With thirteen fatalities. Carol did the house calls this morning and found a few more deaths from it."

Harry was helping Ted Lincoln open the rear of the van. "These are the last of them, except one or two Kirsten's bringing back from her side of the fire. They've got it out now."

"When will she be back?" Natalie asked.

"She estimated a couple of hours. She wants to be sure she sees all the firemen who got hurt."

"Were there very many?" she asked as she bent over the first cot. The man had a crushed arm where a stone pillar had fallen on him. His breathing was shallow but regular.

"Some," he answered vaguely. "Tony's helping her. He's also looking for anything he can salvage that we can use. There isn't much left, but he might find something. It's worth a try."

Natalie felt for the pulse in the man's neck. "Is this a fireman?"

"That's Captain Gottschalk. He's too old to be fighting fires. I talked to him a little last night. I got the feeling he didn't know what's going on."

"Poor old man," Natalie said.

"There's a lot of poor old men."

Ted Lincoln looked out from the van's interior. "Give me a hand with this, Harry."

Harry reached into the van and tugged at the last cot. Natalie watched the way he moved, seeing the soreness in each motion he made. She breathed deeply. "I have some other bad news, Harry," she said at last.

With Ted's help, Harry lowered the second cot to the floor. "What?" he snapped, preoccupied with the patient.

"It's Stan, Harry. He killed himself early this morning."

There was a stillness in Harry that went beyond his arrested movement, and beyond the shock on Ted Lincoln's face. "I see," he said in a moment. Then, in another tone that was almost hurtful for its coldbloodedness, he went on, "Well, that's one more bed free. And at least we've got Katherine Ng and her people to take up the slack." Quite suddenly he turned to her. "Oh, Natalie," he whispered as he saw her face, "I didn't mean that. Not the way it sounded." There was such pain in his eyes that Natalie held out her hands to him. "I know," she said. "It's too hard, Harry, that's all."

"We can close up now, Harry," Ted said. "That's all we've got."

Automatically Harry reached up and slammed the van doors closed. He looked at the two men on the inflated cots. "Those things are a godsend," he said.

Natalie nodded and made a perfunctory check on the second patient. "You don't have to share this one," she said bitterly. "The man's dead anyway." Without another word she turned and left the garage.

*   *   *

When Natalie woke, the sun was down and the northernmost attic room was beginning to cool. She put a hand to her forehead as she remembered the day. Her sleep had not refreshed her, and instead she felt slow-witted and heavy. There was a dull throb behind her eyes, and her skin felt two sizes too small for her skull. She swung her legs over the bed and sat, staring into the soft beauty of the early summer afterglow. She got up slowly, testing herself at each movement.

When she was dressed she went down the hall, feeling guilty now that she realized she was almost an hour late for duty.

"Natalie," Lisa Skye said when Natalie tapped her on the shoulder. "I didn't want to wake you. You looked so tired. And after this morning, with Stan, and so little sleep . . ." She stopped. "I'm glad you're up, though. I feel awful."

"Get some sleep," Natalie recommended, then asked, "What have we got this afternoon so far?"

Lisa handed her the file folders. "These aren't really complete. Kit Ng's paramedic's been helping me out. Her name's Sheilah something or other. Howard and Jim are seeing patients. Roger's in the lab and Maria's on the floor. If you need anyone else, send Larsen or one of the other nurses to wake them."

"Harry?" Natalie asked, since he hadn't been in his bed in their room.

"Asleep in the dining room. He stretched out in there a couple of hours ago. He didn't want to wake you accidentally." Lisa rose unsteadily. "You mind if I go now? I'm really feeling rotten."

Natalie took the file folders, then studied Lisa's face. "Lisa, do you have a fever?" she asked her.

"I don't know. I think it's just the heat . . ." She steadied herself against the desk. "Natalie?"

"I'm here." She put her arm around Lisa, and found with alarm that she was thinner than she had been even a few days ago. Doing her best to conceal her worry, she led Lisa away from the desk. "Lisa, stop off and have Roger run a couple of tests on you."

"I'm okay, Natalie. I'm too tired, that's all. Too tired."

Fright made Natalie speak sharply. "All right, you're just tired. But have the tests run anyway. We probably all should have tests, come to think of it. We've been exposed to trouble every day."

Lisa agreed wanly, then surprised Natalie by saying, "Oh, I don't think you were awake when Kirsten came back?" She didn't give Natalie a chance to reply. "She brought Peter Justin with her. He's in with Radick now."

"Peter Justin?" Natalie felt more startled than angry at this news. "What did she do that for? What else does he want of us?"

"He's sick, Natalie. He's got the new polio. He knows it. He's not like he was before. He knows that everything's gone wrong. He said he'd call it off if he could." She stumbled and Natalie reached to steady her. "I've got to get some sleep," she muttered.

"I'm ready to take over here," Natalie said and motioned Lisa away. But as she sat at the desk her thoughts were jumbled, divided between the news that they would now have to deal with Peter Justin, and concern for Lisa. A new, deep sense of foreboding possessed her, and she turned her attention to her patients. She told herself she must not think. There was too much work to do for her to stop and think.

*   *   *

Harry woke with a start and looked around uncertainly, not remembering where he was. Then he saw the faint shine of the chandeliers above him, lit by the dying fire, and he knew he was in the common room. Natalie had been asleep in their room and he had not wanted to wake her. But now he knew that a sound had awakened him. He got up slowly, then let out a shout as his bare feet were cut by broken glass.

The door opened, and in a moment the room was filled with light. "What is it?" Roger Nicholas demanded, his lab coat untidily fastened.

Harry looked up, then returned his attention to the sliver of glass still in the ball of his foot. The cut was bleeding freely, and this made it hard for Harry to pull the glass from the wound, for his fingers kept slipping.

"My God, Harry," Roger said as he rushed across the room. "How did you get that?"

Harry gritted his teeth. The cut was beginning to hurt badly now. "I think we've had another rock thrown at us. You better be sure that there's no one out there." He looked at the french doors. "Yep. A rock. There's another pane gone. I imagine we can expect more of this as time goes on."

Roger grunted and took charge of extracting the glass. "It would be nice to have some suture spray," he muttered. "I may have to take stitches."

"Not a chance," Harry said loudly. "I couldn't walk on it then."

Roger looked at Harry, annoyance and concern in his face. "What makes you think you can walk on it now?" he asked. "This glass"— he held the shard up to Harry—"that's what was in your foot. It went between the bones and could easily have cut your foot through if you had put a lot of weight on it. It's a very messy wound." He stood up. "Wait a minute. I'm going to get some bandages. Get that foot up in the air and keep it up until I get back." With these instructions over, he left.

The hard ache that comes with deep cuts had hit Harry, and he had to clamp his teeth together to keep them from chattering. The clammy chill of shock was on him, and he wished passionately for something hot to drink. He knew that Radick had some brandy with him. Maybe later he could have a glass . . .

Roger was back, bandages, tape and a small can of Cut-Seel in his hands. "Kit's coming with a basin. We'll clean that up in no time." He put his supplies on the table, then drew up a chair. "Let me see your other foot."

Harry lifted it without a word.

"All minor here," Roger said, relieved, when he had finished looking over the other sole. "You're lucky it's just one foot. Both feet cut and you'd be in a lot of trouble."

Harry felt the cold deepen as he considered what Roger said. "Yes," he whispered.

Katherine Ng opened the door. "Roger?" she called uncertainly. "I have the water here, but I thought you ought to know. There's something going on out by the garage. I heard footsteps out there."

"We'll check later."

Harry overrode this. "No. We'll check now. Whoever threw that rock might still be there."

"It's not that important." Roger took a firm hold of Harry's foot.

"Our nurses and our food are out there. It *is* that important." Harry lurched to his feet and swayed dizzily. "You go. Go!"

Roger hesitated, then went from the room.

"Kit, help me," Harry said. "I've got to get back there."

Katherine Ng put down her basin. "All right," she said, and went to Harry, taking his weight onto her slender shoulder.

The faint sound of shouting reached them, and Harry stiffened.

Wordlessly Katherine began to move, easing the pressure from his bleeding foot as he hobbled out of the room.

In the hall, Radick and Natalie gave him little more than a worried glance as they rushed toward the kitchen and the back door.

The sounds were louder now, and there was the unmistakable sound of a car motor revving up.

Jim Varnay rushed by, and in a moment Kirsten Grant ran past them, her bathrobe tied loosely over her underwear.

Harry swore, and Katherine said, "We'll be there in a moment. Don't worry, Harry."

The back kitchen door stood open, and in the uncertain light Harry could see milling bodies, and beyond, a produce truck. For a moment the figures struggled, an indistinct mass, then part of the group broke away and ran for the truck. There was a last scramble, then the truck roared away down the driveway, leaving a few of the doctors stumbling after it.

"I've got to get out there," Harry said to Katherine.

But she held him back. "Harry, there's nothing you can do. You're bleeding all over the floor as it is. Whatever has happened, they'll tell you about it. Here, I'll bring a chair for you and then see what I can do about that bleeding."

"It's not important," Harry said, but was already feeling water-boned as the rush of adrenalin left him.

Katherine had got him into a chair when Natalie appeared in the kitchen door. Her lab coat was torn and there was a red welt on her face that would be a bruise by morning. "Harry," she said in a voice torn with tears held back.

Harry tried to rise and was firmly pushed back into the chair. "What is it, Natalie?"

"Harry, they got half the food. Three of the cartons are gone. We don't have enough left to feed us all more than a week." Her hands started to shake and she pressed them to her sides. "Alexes tried to stop them."

Harry dreaded what she would say next.

"Oh, Christ, Harry. Alexes is dead."

* * *

For several minutes no one spoke. The common room was bright, the chandeliers showing with ruthless clarity the defeat on every face.

It was Peter Justin who broke the silence at last. "I think," he said in a thread of a voice, with none of his former meticulous arrogance, "I think that perhaps you could get through if I signed a report for you. The I.I.A. unit in control of this area is under the command of Aaron McChesney. He was in Auburn the last I knew."

Carol Mendosa rose. "How soon can we get there?" She challenged the others with her eyes. "Alexes is dead now, and Stan and

Amanda. Lisa's upstairs with a temperature of one hundred five. Dave's tied up in traction and his mind isn't working at all. Eric's filled up his veins with poison. How much more has to happen before you'll leave?"

Maria Pantopolos shielded her eyes. "She's right. We can't stay here."

Roger Nicholas nodded. "I was working lab tonight. We've got another dozen or so cases of that new polio. At this rate it's going to spread all over the state, no matter what the I.I.A. does about quarantine. They've got to stop it fast or there is going to be a real disaster on their hands."

"There already is," Natalie muttered.

Ernest Dagstern nodded. "We're out of beds. None of my colleagues will give us any more space, and you know we can't take anyone else here. With the burn patients from Inner City, and the others here already, we can't manage." He opened helpless hands. "I tried to find more space. But there was no way."

"How many people are waiting to get help right now?" Carol demanded. "It's almost two in the morning. How many people are out there?"

It was Natalie who answered. "When I turned the desk over to Ted Lincoln, there were twenty-seven people there."

"So you see." Carol sat down. "We should have left last week. We should have cleared out as soon as the new polio turned up."

Peter Justin cleared his throat, and said, "I have that polio." He waited while the alarm disappeared from the other faces. "I realized several days ago I was ill, and I was puzzled when I couldn't determine what my disease was. So I made a study and found pretty much what you have discovered, that there is a new variety of polio, and that it is very dangerous."

Dominic Hertzog glared at him. "You say that, knowing we're unprotected."

There was a strange calm in Peter Justin's eyes. "I say this because you have had the same exposure I have." He fumbled in his vest pocket, extracting at last a thick leather notebook. "This is my diary. It contains all the information I could gather about the new polio. When it first appeared I made notes on it of course, and then, later, when I realized that I had contracted it, I kept a record of the progress of the disease." He cleared his throat uneasily. "The incubation period, as far as I have determined, is four to five weeks. The disease usually begins with general malaise, loss of appetite, soreness and some swelling in the joints and a low fever. This turns, in the space of a week or so, into a higher fever, acute body aches and muscular debilitation, loss of weight"—he motioned to his shrunken body—"occasional vertigo, and the beginning of paralysis. The last stages, which have shown a slightly greater than fifty per cent fatality rate, last for anywhere from three to ten days. At the end of that time, if death has not occurred, the temperature drops to subnormal and the patient is lethargic for several days before a realistic assessment of the degree of debilitation can be made. Partial paralysis is quite common in those who survive." He put the notebook on the table. "If you want to take this with you, it will carry some weight with McChesney."

"And you?" Natalie asked, a residual horror in her voice. How like Peter Justin to make a graph of his own disease.

Peter Justin shrugged, and there was a ghost of his former elegance in the motion. "I know the course of the disease, Doctor. There is no earthly reason for me to leave with you. I would only take up valuable space. I will probably die no matter where I am. I can still do a little good if I remain here. I would like the chance to make up, even a little, for what I have done. You see," he added, trying to laugh, "Harry was right. I didn't understand what could happen. And I have a debt to pay."

Suddenly Harry spoke up, forcing his mind to clear away the cobwebs that morphine had brought. "What about our patients?"

Carol turned on him. "What about them, Harry?"

"We can't just leave them." His tongue was unwieldy, and he had to take more time to speak clearly. "There are forty-three people in this house who are our patients. We can't desert them. There are over one hundred house-call patients we see daily. What about them?"

"What *about* them?" Carol repeated. "You know we can't save them. Hell, with you out of commission and Lisa sick, we don't have enough of us left to manage the patients here and still make the house-call rounds. You know that, Harry. We all know it. But most of us don't want to face it."

For a moment Harry did not speak. His eyes were fixed on the floor, and he could feel his strength ebb as he sat there. "I guess you're right," he said at last. "But we need a couple of days here to make sure that our patients are taken care of. We can't walk out on them. Or maybe you can, Carol. But I can't."

Natalie nodded. "I'll start a schedule. We can be out of here by the day after tomorrow." She looked uncertainly at Peter Justin. "You will give us an authorization to get us through to this McChesney person?"

"I will." He held out the notebook. "One of you had better take this."

Natalie took it. "I'll make sure McChesney sees it. McChesney and everyone else. I promise you that, Peter."

* * *

The child was as young as Philip had been. Natalie tapped the scrawny chest and heard the air whistle. The child would not live. It was almost dead now. As she worked on the child, Natalie realized with a start she did not know what sex it was: she had not been told and had not looked. Under her hands the chest heaved spasmodically and then trembled. Natalie bent over to breathe into the mouth, noticing again the slightly sweet, slightly rotten smell of the child's flesh. She forced her own breath into the child's lungs.

"You can stop now, Natalie," Radick said behind her. "She's dead."

Natalie turned to him, unseeing. "Radick?" she said. She put her hand to her hair and then began to weep. "Radick, that's three I've lost tonight. Three."

Radick murmured a few words as he took her into his arms. "I know, Natalie, I know. None of us can bear much more of this. It is cruel to fight this way. We're destroying ourselves."

When Natalie had stopped crying, she looked back at the three-year-old girl on the table. "I don't know, Radick. There has to be some way to save them." Her eyes pleaded with him.

Radick touched her hand. "Now you must not lose courage, Natalie. You must realize that there is only so much you or any of us can do. Then we must find another way to fight." He pulled the sheet on the table over the little girl's face. "This is not the way. We must attack this pandemic at its roots, which means in the seat of power. We must make those men who created this atrocity realize what they have done. It will not be easy, Natalie. Men of power enjoy using it. Which is very bad when they use it for our destruction."

Natalie studied him for moment. "Radick, why did you stay to help us? You could have been on the other side."

He turned on her. "I could never have been on the other side. My position might have made some of them consider inviting me, but I would never have been on that side. I despise what they are. I have treated too many of them for whom power has become a disease of the soul. They are like lepers, eaten up with it." He stopped suddenly. "There are more patients waiting, Natalie. You'd best go to the front desk."

"And you?" she asked, sensing the torment he had tried to hide from her.

He waved his hand to turn her away. "Go, go, Natalie. You should not see this. I have done this to myself. Leave me, will you? Please?"

"If that's what you want." It was more a question than a statement. "I'll send Larsen in for the body. She's been taking care of that today." Natalie had almost closed the door behind her when Radick stopped her.

"No, wait. I must tell you. I must tell someone." He gripped the table, the tension in his body a pale echo of his inner conflict. "I did an unforgivable thing, Natalie. When I realized what I had done, I could not face it. But I cannot contain it much longer. It is too difficult, watching the deaths." He steadied himself. "You see, Natalie, I have treated those men. Miles Wexford was a patient of mine. Oh, I know it is not wise to treat one's superior officer or one's employer. I knew that then, but I was arrogant enough, foolish enough, to think that being a psychiatrist somehow protected me. It didn't."

Natalie said softly, "Yes?"

"Four or five years ago, back when this was starting, Wexford was my patient. He told me about this project. He felt a certain guilt about it and wanted to resolve those feelings. I suggested abandoning the project, and he agreed. I was naive enough to believe that he had. I am fifty-two; I have seen enough of this species to know better. When the deaths began, when the diseases came back . . ." He slammed his closed fist into the table, crying out as the knuckles broke. "I asked him about it, and he denied it. He denied it, and I accepted his word. I should have known—I *did* know—that it was a lie. But I turned away from it because I was afraid. Heaven forgive me, Natalie. I was a coward."

Natalie stood still, at once shocked and unsurprised. She wanted to say something to Radick, but found she did not have the words. "I'll send in Kit with something for your hand," she told him as she went out the door.

* * *

Harry had been dozing when the knocking brought him abruptly awake. He shook his head and forced himself to think clearly. A glance at the clock told him it was after three in the morning, and the dull headache and pain in his gut reminded him that he had not eaten that night.

The knocking grew louder and Harry got to his feet, wincing as he tried to walk on the cut.

At last he opened the door to find a boy, not more than twelve, his shirt wrapped around his arm, which Harry realized was badly burned. "You the doctor?" the boy asked as he stumbled into the foyer.

"Yes," Harry said. "I can see you're burned. Come into the light and let me look at it."

The boy held back. "I just want a painkiller and a bandage. It was hurting pretty bad a while back, until I put it in ice." Harry mentally thanked God for that. "But it's starting to hurt again, and I'm out of ice."

Harry pulled the boy toward the sitting room, which was now an occasional emergency room. "Let me see the arm," he said again, and winced with the boy as he took the shirt off.

The flesh was raw, vulnerable, and the burn had licked deeply into the tissues of his flesh.

"How did you get this?" Harry asked.

"It's not important."

An alarm sounded in Harry, making his neck prickle. "It's important if I'm going to treat it. I have to know what caused this."

The boy shot him a distrustful look, his unkempt hair falling over his dark eyes. "Okay. It was gasoline. I was messing with some gasoline and it caught fire."

Without being aware of it, Harry tightened his grip on the boy's shoulder. "What were you doing with the gasoline?" he demanded, his voice becoming harsh.

"Nothing."

This was a lie, and Harry knew it. "Tell me, or I won't do anything for you. I'll send you back where you came from, and you'll very likely die of infection, which will take a long time to kill you." Inwardly Harry was as horrified at himself, as he knew the boy was. He had never done anything like this, never used medicine as a threat. But he saw something in the boy's face beyond the terror, and he knew he had won.

"Okay," the boy said faintly. "But you gotta help me if I tell you."

"I will help you," Harry promised.

"Tristam had us make bombs again, that's what happened. One of them spilled before we got out of the hospital. We were in a big hurry, and I got gas all over my shirt. It caught fire when I got on Tristam's motorbike."

"What bombs? What hospital?"

"You're hurting me." The boy twisted away and would have run if the door had been open.

"What hospital? Tell me!"

Now at bay, the boy turned to Harry. "Westbank Hospital. We got bombs all over it, and they'll go off when the City Patrol sends the morgue wagon around." As soon as he said it, the boy collapsed unconscious his face ashen and his young body making a pitiful heap by the door.

CHAPTER 10

The first flames were licking the windows of Westbank Hospital when Ted Lincoln pulled the van up beside the park opposite the building. Natalie saw that there were only two fire trucks at the scene, and that they did not carry a full complement.

"Roger and Kirsten are setting up on the other side of the hospital. I think we'll get a good number of them out," Ted said, making the words encouraging.

"What do we do with them then?" Natalie asked. "We're out of room as it is." She opened the door. "Don't mind me, Ted."

Radick opened the side door and pulled out the folded shelter. "This won't take long to erect," he said as he wrestled with the material, spreading it out on the ground. Behind them the leaves of the park's elms quivered before the rush of wind and fire.

Ted Lincoln nodded. "I'll run the service on this side, and one of the others, Maria or Carol, will take the van on the other side."

Inside the hospital there was another explosion, and the shouts and screams of trapped patients were muted by the greedy sound of the fire.

"Christ," Ted whispered, turning pale.

"I wish Ernest were here," Natalie said, purposefully ignoring the inferno behind her. "He's strong. We could use a little more muscle."

Radick nodded and set up part of the framework. The assembly was easy and it took little time to put together the A-framed ribs of the structure. Radick nodded, breathing harder than he should have. "Good. The cover is ready. Ted, you get on that side, and Natalie and I will take care of the middle."

Natalie took up her spot, and when the durable, lightweight fabric sailed her way, she reached for the securing lines. For the next few minutes she busied herself with knots, looking up only when a few of the hospital staff ran forward, escaping the fire.

The first of the arrivals shouted, then dropped to his knees and pitched forward. As Natalie rose and walked toward him, she could see that most of the lab coat the man wore was burned away. Wearily she checked the man's pulse, and when she found it, called to Radick to bring her kit. This would be a long night, she knew, and she found an odd comfort in the routine of tending to stricken people. The pandemic, her worry—all this could be set aside while the fire raged over Westbank Hospital.

* * *

Katherine Ng steadied the last of the inflated cots which now filled the common room at the Van Dreyter house. The huge table had been pushed against the wall and its rosewood chairs were relegated to service in the foyer. The needlepoint upholstered lounge chairs were stacked in the corner by the fireplace, and the coffee table had been pressed into duty as a supply stand. The broken windowpanes were taped over.

Ernest Dagstern gave the room one critical check, then said, "Bedding. We'll need a lot of it." He turned abruptly and stalked out of the room.

"What's eating him?" Katherine asked Harry, who was laying out old IV units on the table.

"He's scared." Harry did not even look up. "Ted is due back with the first load in about twenty minutes. We'd better be ready." Sternly Harry told himself to stop fretting. The juveniles who burned down Inner City and Westbank would not go after such small fry as the Van Dreyter house. But he did not believe it. As he worked, so automatically, so precisely, he felt panic rise in him like bile. Already they had had windows broken and food stolen. It would be only a matter of time until this house, too, was burned. He tried to tell himself that the risk was not that great. And all the time flames danced at the back of his mind, mocking him.

* * *

Natalie slammed the van door, then tapped the side twice as a signal to Ted. She stood aside as the van made a tight turn and raced away down the dark streets. She glanced dispassionately toward the fire and saw that it had spread to two adjoining buildings. By now Westbank was a torch, its beams showing in the holocaust like the skeleton of some extinct giant. The sound was deafening, and Natalie wanted more than anything to be free of the sound.

"How many do we have in the shelter?" Radick asked as he came up to her.

"Fifteen, I think. I've dispatched four with Ted. The ones who can make it on their own are at this end of the shelter. I haven't even bothered with the ones who can't make it. We're running low on morphine. So don't waste it."

Radick sighed. "Triage. You're right, of course."

Across the road another building started to burn. Natalie frowned. "Did everyone get out of there?" she asked. "I saw a couple of firemen go in there to evacuate, but I didn't think . . ."

"Look," Radick whispered, pointing to a balcony on the second floor.

Natalie shielded her eyes against the heat and glare, and saw five women clinging to each other. From the balcony to the pavement was a drop of over twelve feet, and the women milled in terror, the fire behind them.

Radick moved forward and shouted, "The fire escape! *The fire escape!*" waving his arms as he tried to point out to them the outmoded ladders on the next balcony over.

"They can't make it. It's too far to reach," Natalie said, devoid of feeling.

Without hesitation, Radick ran for the building.

"Radick!" Natalie called to him. "You can't do anything."

He turned briefly and shouted, walking backward toward the burning building. "I'm going up the fire escape. I can help pull them across. I can reach them." He was running toward the women now, trying to catch their attention. He reached the fire escape and began to climb the extended steel ladder toward the second floor. At last the women saw him, and they pointed with almost hysterical relief.

The building collapsed at the far end, and the flames exulted, roaring like some demented monster as they got deeper into the building.

Natalie watched, fascinated, as Radick reached the balcony, climbed onto the rail, and securing himself to the next rise of the ladder, reached across to the women, holding out his one free hand to pull them to safety.

One woman was down the ladder and on the ground, and a second was just climbing over the balcony rail to Radick where he clung to the fire escape, when the wall gave way, and in a dreadful rush of heat and debris buried Radick and the women in burning rubble.

"Radick!" Natalie screamed. The sound was lost in the voracious thunder of the fire.

* * *

"What the hell . . . ?" Harry looked up, irritated, as the lights went out. Around him the inflatable cots were full, and three bodies lay on the formal dining table. The common room was not quite dark. In the east the sky had a band of silver-gray preceding dawn.

"Harry?" Katherine Ng said from the far side of the room.

"That's the lights." Harry limped toward the door, and heard Dominic shout in the hall beyond. He pulled open the door to find Peter Justin fumbling with a flashlight.

"These old buildings had fuses," Peter said absently. "Perhaps in the fuse box . . ."

"See if the street lights are working first. If they're out, then we're out. There's a generator in the garage, but it got damaged when the food was stolen. It probably won't work." Harry slammed the door in disgust and leaned against it. "Kit," he said after a moment, "are there any candles at your end?"

"I don't think so."

On the cots, the fire victims who were conscious stirred, frightened, and a few began to ask questions.

Harry cut them short. "I don't know what's happened. But I'll do my best to get us some light, at least until the sun is up." Glad for the activity, he once more started into the hall, and in the dark banged his shin against one of the rosewood chairs. Determined, he stumbled toward the kitchen.

He was rummaging for candles when Carol Mendosa appeared. "We've got a last vanload from Kirsten's station. She's closing down. The fire's too far out of hand." Carol drank deeply from her freshly filled mug of tea. "I don't think we can stop it now," she said dreamily. "It's out of hand and it'll burn until it stops of its own accord. There are no firemen to fight it. The last company retreated over an hour ago. All the people left are trying to get out, or they're too sick to care." She finished the coffee.

Jim Varnay wandered into the kitchen. "I need candles for the patients in my wing," he said gruffly. "They need light."

"I'm trying to find some." Harry heard the snap in his voice. "I don't remember where they are. How are things with the patients?"

Jim sank heavily onto a chair. "We've got four more dead. Hannah Cruz was one of them. She was pretty tough. I thought she'd make it. Two of polio, one cholera and one typhus. Not that it matters. They're dead."

Harry found a box of twelve candles. "Here. This is a start. When you get a chance, will you get those beds ready for burn patients?"

"Oh, for Chrissake, Harry," Carol said, disgusted. "They're going to die, anyway. Let them stay where they are."

Harry ignored her. "We can set up more beds in the nurses' quarters if we have to," he said, opening another set of drawers. "Here's some more." He set out five more boxes of candles on the table.

"We can use Dave's room, too," Carol said harshly. "He died in the night, or didn't you know? Maybe Howard should get that bed ready first, seeing as it's on the ground floor."

"Dave?" Harry said. "Dead?" For a moment he was still. "Poor bastard."

"Why feel that way? It's one more bed," Carol said, then threw her mug across the room so that it smashed into unrecognizable pieces.

*   *   *

Natalie shut the doors on the van and found a place to stand between two inflatable stretchers. Her eyes were gritty with smoke and fatigue, and she wished she could peel her exhausted, aching muscles from her bones and sleep.

"Are you all right?" Maria called from the front of the van. She raced along the deserted streets as fast as she dared.

"Sure," Natalie said listlessly. "What time is it?"

"It's after ten. We'll be through with this by noon." She cornered expertly and gunned the motor as she came to the main arterial.

A little later, Natalie said, "Someone told me that Dave Lillijanthal died."

"Yeah, it's true," Maria said, her mind on her driving.

"Too bad."

Up ahead was a group of stragglers, worn people carrying away their lives on their backs. They went without looking back as the fire pursued them.

"You heard about Radick?" Natalie asked when they were well past the stragglers. She was suspicious of people now, and looked with suspicion on any gathering.

"I heard."

A truck lumbered out of a side street and stalled halfway through the intersection. Maria leaned on the horn and swerved wildly to avoid it. As she pulled back around the truck, she shrieked as her bumper knocked against someone and sent the person flying.

"Should I stop?" Maria yelled to Natalie.

Natalie did not hesitate. "No. Keep going."

"But I might have hurt . . ."

"Keep going."

* * *

Natalie saw the look in Harry's eyes as she came into the kitchen, and the words of greeting died on her lips. "What is it?" she asked, and waited with a fear she thought she could no longer feel.

"Ernest came in with some burn victims about an hour ago. From Westbank."

She shook her head, not understanding.

"One of them is Mark," Harry said and saw her blanch.

* * *

They had put him in Dave's bed, because it would give him the least painful death. His beauty was gone, like a clay figure which had not satisfied the artist and been pinched and smeared in the sculptor's frustration. His disfigurement would have been hideous if there had been the slightest chance he would live.

"Mark?" Natalie said, not finding him in the tortured body that lay under wet sheets which smelled of medication.

The head turned its charred features toward her, and Natalie gasped, for not even Harry's warning had prepared her for the ruin there. "Nat?" said the cracked voice, as unlike Mark as the face was.

"Yes. I'm here," she managed to say. Her hands felt icy, and she doubted she could move.

"Sure." One eye was seared blind, but the other turned glitteringly on her. "Stupid interfering bitch!"

She cringed under the words, and her eyes were fever-shiny with tears.

"You had to interfere," the horrid voice went on, singsong, like a litany of vengeance. "You couldn't leave it alone. You had to mess. Stupid bitch! Stupid, stupid bitch!"

"Mark," she started to say, but he cut her short. "You did this! You did this to me! I could have made it, but you had to get in the way!" The voice cracked, and the breath came in strident whistles.

Under the sheets Mark's body convulsed with pain while the sheets clung to the scorched and ruptured skin, making the agony worse.

Natalie reached out to hold him down, to spare him some suffering.

"Screw yourself with a bowie knife," he hissed at her as she touched him. With a last effort he tried to pull himself erect. He made a strange sound in his throat, shuddered, and died.

* * *

By afternoon the fire had spread across the riverfront and was sending long snouts of flame into the heart of the city. At the Van Dreyter house, both power and water had failed, and the generator could not be repaired to run the pump of the well or the lights in the house. A stillness hung over the house with the afternoon heat.

"Then who do we take with us?" Carol asked, speaking for the few doctors at the breakfast table. "Burn victims or disease patients? Five of the vans are working, which means we can take twenty people at the most."

Harry nodded. "We take the ones who need the most help but who have a good chance for survival."

"Triage," Natalie murmured, thinking of Radick.

"With any luck we'll make Auburn by morning, and that means help by tomorrow evening at the latest. Peter can pass out the morphine until then, can't you?" he asked Peter.

The deterioration of Peter's condition made speaking difficult. "I think so. But I doubt I'll last much more than twenty-four hours. My temperature was one hundred three this morning, and I am sure it is higher now."

Natalie marveled at his coolness, at his detachment. She felt a curious compassion for the epidemiologist, who saw his own death with so little feeling. "Lisa might be able to help," she said.

"Lisa has typhus. She can't do anything," Harry snapped, then said in quick contrition, "Never mind me, Natalie. I didn't mean that."

Roger Nicholas rubbed his eyes before speaking. "Well, we'd better make our selection quickly and get moving. We have to be out of here before sunset. If there's going to be trouble here it will be after dark."

"We'll put up barricades," Peter Justin said calmly. "I am sure we will be able to protect ourselves. Particularly if the place looks deserted." He raised his hand to forestall objections. "You may think that we will be more vulnerable, and in a sense you're right. But the house will be sealed, and I am certain we can hold out until tomorrow night."

Reluctantly Harry nodded. "You're right."

"Who goes where, then?" Carol asked. "Who drives, who rides, who has charge of the patients?"

"Jim and Maria and you will drive. I guess Roger and Ernest . . ." Harry said.

Ernest Dagstern surprised them all. "I'm not going."

They all turned to the stocky little chiropractor. He met their inquiring eyes evenly. "I won't leave until these patients are safe. Dr. Justin can't do it himself, and you know it. And Dr. Skye is in no condition to. They need my help. I won't leave as long as they do."

The room was hushed. Then Harry cleared his throat. "That's your decision, Ernest. I promise you we'll be back as soon as possible." He felt badly as he said it, because it was a trivial promise, compared to what Ernest would do.

Carol pushed away from the breakfast table. "We'd better get moving, then. We don't have a lot of time."

"Who is going to make the decisions about which patients go?" Harry stopped her, and the others hesitated.

"I will," Peter Justin said calmly. "It's my specialty."

*　　*　　*

The rear doors of the van slammed shut, and Harry tried to make himself comfortable on the narrow bench that crossed the door when it was closed. Ahead of him the inflatable stretchers filled the van to the driver's seat, with only a slim aisle between them.

In the front, Natalie rode beside Jim Varnay, who was second in line in the five-van cavalcade. Ahead Ted Lincoln rode with Dominic and two of the nurses, and behind Carol Mendosa drove Kirsten and Katherine, with Maria and Roger behind them and Howard Webbster bringing up the rear. They had decided to travel together as far as the fire, and then they would split into two groups, in case of trouble. Jim and Ted would take the northern route through the city, and the others would go around by the southern.

Harry glanced out the small rear window as they pulled away from the Van Dreyter house, standing forlorn against the bright afternoon.

He hated to leave it. For leaving was defeat, and defeat rankled. He turned his attention to the human cargo they carried.

In less than twenty minutes they had reached the edge of the fire. There, with the agreed exchange of signals, the vans parted company, and Harry saw the three in Carol's group moving southward, lit by the glow of the fire.

They were almost to the Old Capitol Bridge when Jim suddenly braked to a halt. Ahead, Ted slowed, waiting.

"What is it?" Harry asked, afraid that the fire had beaten them to their crossing.

Natalie opened the door and, to Harry's surprise, got out.

"What is it?" Harry said again, louder.

Jim Varnay shook his head. "I don't know. A kid just ran in front of the van, so I stopped. He's alone. Natalie said she'd talk to him."

*   *   *

The kid was a scrawny fifteen, and his bright-blue eyes were red-rimmed from lack of sleep. He stood in the street, his caution gone as Natalie came toward him. "Yes?" she said, when he did not speak.

"You're a doctor, right?" he demanded, and ran one bony hand through his tangled taffy-colored hair.

"I am," Natalie said, ignoring the word of warning Jim called to her. The kid intrigued her. She studied him, saw his desperation, his recent hunger, his restless worry disguised as bravado. "Do you need a doctor?"

"No, not me. I'm okay. It's my . . . friends. Some of them are sick. I don't know what's wrong. You got to help them." He planted his feet apart. "I saw you coming from the house earlier. You're running out."

"We're going for help," Natalie said, in spite of the twinge his words gave her. "How many friends do you have? What's wrong with them?"

"They're sick." He shouted this, then tried to calm himself. "I promised them I'd take care of them. I promised them I wouldn't let them die." Suddenly he crossed his arms over his chest. "I'm Tristam," he said, as a challenge.

Natalie heard Jim Varnay start to open the door. She called to him. "Stay where you are, Jim. I'm in no danger. Tristam didn't come to hurt anyone." She nodded, as if making up her mind. "If you'll wait a minute," she told the red-headed boy, "I'll get my kit from the van."

"You'll come?" He was amazed.

"Of course." She turned back, and reached into the cab, and found that Jim had grabbed her arm. "You're not going back out there," he said softly. "You know what that kid did to Dave and Stan."

"I know that his gang left me alone once. I know that he needs help." She pulled her arm free.

"Tell him we'll be back tomorrow."

She looked into Jim's dark face. "They might not have a chance tomorrow. We might not find them again."

Suddenly Harry leaned over the partition. "Natalie."

Her eyes went to his, and for the first time in her life she felt the loss of intimacy that went far beyond the intimacy of lovers. "Don't ask me to come with you, Harry," she pleaded. "I couldn't tell you no and I must stay here."

For Harry the world rolled back as he read the emotion in her face. He did not feel the throb in his foot or the headache which had bothered him all that day. Now he wanted to hold her, to keep her with him. Involuntarily he stretched out his hand to her and lightly, lightly touched her face. He heard himself say, "You do what you think is right, Natalie."

Through strain and fatigue her smile was radiant. "Thanks for your love, Harry," she said as she took her kit from the van. She moved quickly, easily, a burden taken from her. "I'll see you in a day or so." With a wave to Jim she slammed the door and knocked on the side of the van as a signal to drive on.

When the van had picked up speed, she turned to Tristam. "All right. We can go now."

* * *

It was shortly after midnight when Jim Varnay pulled the van in behind Ted Lincoln's at the cordon around the town of Auburn. Below them in the valley the fire still waved, a bright flag in the night.

There were shouts up ahead, and Harry listened without hearing while Ted dealt with the National Guard troops manning the cordon.

"They're letting us through," Jim said after a while. It was the first words he had spoken to Harry since they left Natalie with Tristam.

"Good." Harry tried to stretch his stiff legs in the van, but the cramps only got tighter. He sighed.

Jim put the van into gear and followed Ted's van into the town. He pointed out the window and said, "Look. We've got an escort."

Harry turned disinterested eyes on the line of National Guardsmen that flanked the vans. He turned to look at the patients on the inflatable cots, not really seeing them. It was almost over. It was going to end. He put a hand to his eyes, wishing he could feel something in response. But there was only the ache in his head and the dull hurt of exhaustion. In his soul he did not think he could be at rest until he saw Natalie again.

There was a sharp rap on the door and a young Guardsman shouted to Jim to park and get out.

Harry rolled down the larger window on his side. "We have sick people in this van. They need immediate medical help," he said, and found that his sore throat turned his words to croaks.

The Guardsman nodded and yelled at someone else.

Harry opened the door and fought off a moment's dizziness before he got out. "We're from Stockton," he said to no one in particular.

"This way, sir," the Guardsman said, pulling Harry's arm.

Harry looked at him, puzzled, and was about to ask a question when his legs at last gave way and he sank to the pavement, asleep.

* * *

Aaron McChesney was precisely neat from the line of his mustache to the set of his clothes. His eyes were metallically cold and he looked as if he could stab you to death with the old-fashioned crease in his trousers. He closed Peter Justin's notebook as Harry came into the room, still groggy from sleep.

"Good afternoon, Dr. Smith," he said with a cordiality that went no farther than good form required.

"Good afternoon," Harry said automatically. "What time is it, anyway?"

McChesney narrowed his eyes critically, but answered the question. "It's three forty-seven."

Harry looked at the clock, alarmed. "That late? I didn't know I'd slept so long." He did not feel rested: the aches in his joints were worse and his headache made it a penance to look around quickly. He supposed a meal would help, but he did not have an appetite.

"Yes. Your other two vans came in early this morning."

"Two?" Harry said. He did not want to ask what had happened to the third.

"You've certainly caused some excitement back in Washington," McChesney said as if Harry should be pleased. "We've been in conference all morning about you."

Harry cut through the man's effusiveness. "When do we start back to Stockton?" he demanded. He thought of Natalie. She was expecting him. He had to get back. And the Van Dreyter house would have to be evacuated. He tried to organize his thoughts in order to talk to McChesney. In the clean pullover he still felt stuffy and hot.

"Oh, that will be taken care of," McChesney assured him. "That's all behind you." He shuffled the stack of printouts by his left hand. "We've been running some of Dr. Justin's information through the computers here. It seems you people really came up with something. We're trying to work out a new policy for the treatment of this polio varietal that's developed here."

"Polio varietal," Harry snapped. "You make it sound like a new kind of wine. "It's a disease, mister, a deadly, ugly disease." He fingered the collar of the pullover.

"It certainly sounds like it is," McChesney agreed smoothly. "And your group certainly deserves recognition for your work on it."

Harry's mind drifted back to the terrible days at the Van Dreyter house. "You could say that."

Aaron McChesney seemed somewhat put off by Harry's manner. "Um. Yes. Well, you can see then, why we've decided to send you back to Washington to speak to the special closed session of the Cabinet."

"What?" Harry winced as he pushed himself to his feet. He steadied himself against McChesney's desk. "Do they have to have me? In person?"

"Yes. It's all arranged. You leave at five. The Cabinet meeting is the day after tomorrow. That should give you sufficient time to organize your report, and we will send verification for your discoveries."

"No," Harry objected. "Look, Justin's back there, and Ernest. There are patients in the house. And Natalie's with Tristam. If we don't get back to them. I told her I'd be back. We can leave now, and I'll still get to that damned meeting day after tomorrow." He leaned forward and blinked to clear his swimming vision.

McChesney rose and put a hand on Harry's shoulder. "Dr. Smith, you're exhausted. You've been through a harrowing experience. Certainly we'll have to do our best for the poor people left behind. And just as soon as we have a full evaluation, you can be certain we'll go and get them."

Harry shook the hand off. "We go now!" he said. "They'll die, don't you understand? Natalie will die." He turned away from McChesney. "Tell them I won't come to Washington until I know Natalie's safe."

"Dr. Smith," McChesney said, his exasperation making his tone less smooth.

Harry reeled, his eyes blinded with pain.

"Here, here," McChesney said, becoming concerned. "Let me get you something. Apparently you aren't over the effects of your ordeal. I'll be back in a moment . . ." He left by a side door.

Harry let himself sag against the wall, feeling bitter laughter rise in his throat. The ache in his swelling joints racked him, but he found now he could smile. He knew now that what he felt was not the effects of fatigue or hunger or stress. "I've got it," he said to the neat, colorless walls. He had the polio, the new polio. He rubbed his forehead and accepted the ache there for the token it was. By now, he realized, even his handshake would be deadly.

He could not go back. He thought he had got out of the plague, but there was no escape, not now, not for him. He forced himself to breathe slowly, and felt the strain beginning.

"Here, Dr. Smith," McChesney said as he came back into the office. He held a glass of water and a medicine packet. "This should help. I'm sorry. I certainly should have realized that you aren't quite yourself."

Harry took the glass. "I'll be all right now," he said. He drank the water and swallowed half of the medicine packet. Then he put the glass down and turned to Aaron McChesney. "I think you said something about a Cabinet meeting? Will you go over that again?"

* * *

The small jet lunged down the short runway, then pointed into the sky. Harry shut his teeth against the nausea as the plane rose. In a few minutes the pilot began to level off, and Harry let himself relax. He thought over the talk he had had with the others before he left, and he knew that Ted Lincoln and Maria Pantopolos would make every effort to see that the patients at the Van Dreyter house were evacuated. He had done as much as they would let him do there.

The Cabinet meeting was less than forty-eight hours away. He knew that he could hold out that long, long enough to tell those powerful men what they had created, what they had done, and then to tell them what he had done.

The incubation period for the new polio was about five weeks. They would have that long to find a cure, or they would face paralysis or death, as Harry was doing now. He would give them the choice they were unwilling to give others.

Now the plane banked, and Harry could see the land below, lit by the long golden fingers of afternoon. Far away the fire in Stockton shone like a torch, and as Harry watched it, he thought of the brightness he had seen in Natalie's eyes, and he felt himself grow cold.

And then the mountains rose between them as the plane sped eastward into the night.

DAY BOOK